The Case of the Damaged Detective

5-Minute Sherlock: Case #1

by Drew Hayes

Copyright © 2019 by Andrew Hayes

All Rights Reserved.
Cover used with permission from Audible.com

No part of this publication may be reproduced, stored in a retrieval system, or transmitted in any form or by any means electronic, mechanical, photocopying, recording or otherwise without the prior permission of the author.

This is a work of fiction. Names, characters, places, and incidents either are products of the author's imagination or are used fictitiously. Any resemblance to actual events, locales, or persons, living or dead, is entirely coincidental.

Prologue

The bass thundered through the warehouse, a relentless storm against the eardrums as the team made its way inside. Complaints had been coming in all morning about the noise. It wasn't too uncommon for tourists and locals to end up in this industrial area holding secret events—hidden parties for those looking to have fun off the beaten path. Usually, they were cleared out by sunrise, long gone before other businesses started opening up.

This time, the party had apparently run long.

Pushing into the main room, the police were nearly blinded by the flashing lights. A huge screen with a hastily-fastened projector was showing a video that matched up with the music, in theme if not beat-for-beat accompaniment. Mist filled the air, the last gasps of a sprinkler system that had largely burned out after soaking the entire room. A huge shadow was cast across the screen, one of a single person dancing and flailing wildly to the noise. The lead officer started forward, only to be grabbed by the man behind him, who pointed down. Flashlights clicked on to get a better view than the strobes could offer.

Corpses. Hundreds of corpses lay along the floor.

All of them had trails of blood running from their ears, eyes, and noses, which was strange enough. More bizarre was the fact that they were also wearing identical expressions: a pinched face like they'd been trying to concentrate so hard that something in their heads just gave out.

The police exchanged cautious glances. This had just gone from a routine noise complaint and some trespassing to a deadly, serious situation. Guns came out, and they approached the dancing shadow. As a unit, they moved, quiet and steady, until they were nearly on top of him. The lead officer stepped out, weapon at the ready.

"Stand down!"

At his words, several flashlights trained on the dancing man. They could now see that he was youngish, probably in his mid-to-late twenties, uncommonly tall, and fully nude save only for a curious hat perched atop his skull. While the words didn't seem to reach him through the unceasing bass, the flashlights did catch his eye. He whirled on them, scowling.

"About time you lot showed up! How do your superiors think I am going to solve a case like this without attendants for support? Now, someone fetch me a pair of trousers. I can hardly expect any of you to concentrate with my glory hanging in the wind for all to see."

1.

Agent 221 waited patiently in the secure room. Aside from him, the only things in it were a metal table and two matching chairs, none of which he'd touched beyond taking a seat. There was a time to raise hell, and a time to play it cool. Given how his last week had gone, this was definitely the "play it cool" scenario. There had been some minor issues in the last few years, since The Incident, but nothing this bad. Right now, he needed to swallow his pride and say he was sorry. Heads were going to roll over this one, and he'd burned up too much goodwill to be sure his was safe from the chopping block.

When the door flew open, it revealed Gwendolyn walking through. Gwendolyn was a hard woman to pin down. Some days she looked sixty, other times no one would guess she was a day past thirty. Weight went up and down, as did hairstyle, and occasionally even height—small changes, here and there, that totally altered the way she appeared. Even when they didn't always see eye to eye, Agent 221 had respect for the skills of his handler.

"You have really screwed up this time."

That was the other nice thing about Gwendolyn. In a system where obfuscation and nuance were second nature, she was one of the few who told it like it was. Well, that was how she treated Agent 221, anyway. The others probably got a tactic that best suited them.

"Do you have any idea how lucky we are that those codes were scooped up by another team at the sell point? It's the only reason you aren't in shackles right now."

Gwendolyn let out a heavy sigh before taking the seat across the table, setting her briefcase on the ground. "You changed the plan at the last minute and let them get away. Give me a good reason. Please. Anything justified with intel, something I can sell upstream."

She wasn't going to like what came next, but Agent 221 had to deliver the news anyway. Calling an audible over concerns of a plan's chances for success was one thing; hiding facts in a situation like this would skirt the line of treason.

"Based on my assigned asset's behavior, I had reason to suspect he was going to double-cross us, so I made the decision to shift small details of the plan which would the undermine his capacity to sabotage the operation."

"I see. Obviously, you have some sort of proof. A text, a photo, a conversation, anything to suggest that the man who had been a loyal resource for ten years would suddenly flip on you. Because if you don't, if this is more of that same shit from what happened with Poole—you're running out of favors."

Pain rippled through Agent 221's right leg at the mention of the name Poole. He managed to keep the snarl off his face, although it required more effort than should have been needed for a man of his training. Some wounds, literal as well as metaphorical, simply never healed right.

"I can share with you the many reasonable foundations for my concern; however, they were based on my observations and interactions. There would be no tangible record to present."

The words sat heavily between Agent 221 and Gwendolyn. Finally, the handler pulled her briefcase from the floor and dropped it onto the table with a substantial clatter. Digging through, she produced a single-page document, sliding it across the table's shiny surface. Agent 221 accepted the sheet, reading as Gwendolyn explained.

"That is your discharge paperwork. You might notice it's fairly slim, but given the kind of work you've done, I think you'll understand why we don't want to write down any more details than we have to. Besides, given the circumstances of your dismissal, it's not like we'll have to worry about things like pay and benefits."

Everything Gwendolyn said lined up. They were dumping him on the street, not even so much as a recommendation. It was a solid threat, one they would certainly follow through with if needed… but were this their true intention, then no one would have bothered bringing in Gwendolyn. Anyone could give bad news; they needed the handler to make an offer.

"It's a good stick," Agent 221 said. "Now show me the carrot."

No reaction, not so much as a tremor of surprise on her face that he knew there was more. "I'll share with you what I can. Even with your clearances, there's not too much I can give you right now." To her credit, Gwendolyn didn't put on a show or make him work for the information.

They both knew what this was, and that it would go faster by being upfront. "There's a job that needs doing. One with very specific, odd circumstances. We've recently come in to something special, something that we want guarded."

More pages from Gwendolyn's briefcase, this one with a picture or two in the mix.

"Three months ago, a Pennsylvania town's officers responded to a noise complaint only to find an entire warehouse full of dead people. They didn't know it, but it was the fourth scene like that we've discovered in the last two years. Different countries, different types of venues, same trail of corpses. Someone out there has been testing a new drug, dosing a bunch of underground partiers who wouldn't look as out of place if they OD'd. This drug messes with the brain, and I mean serious, jackhammer-renovation kind of messes with. At the previous three scenes, every single person was also dead. Autopsies revealed brains that looked like they'd suffered multiple bleeds, strokes, and aneurysms simultaneously. Their minds were annihilated, and the perpetrators left nothing behind. No clues, no leads, no witnesses. Until three months ago."

The photos were blurry, likely by intent. Agent 221 could make out a man standing among the sea of bodies, his face obscured by the shadow of the camera's flash and the brim of a deerstalker hat.

"Someone survived, I take it."

"In a manner of speaking, but we can get to that later," Gwendolyn confirmed. "Yes, that man in the photos managed to live through exposure to the drug. Since taking him into our custody, we've discovered quite a bit, most of it troubling. Based on what we can discern, this isn't some string of meth dealers looking to whip up the next hot ticket. This drug appears to augment the processing power of the human brain."

Agent 221 hid a grimace behind more paper shuffling. "Please don't give me that 'we only use 10% of our brains' crap."

"That's obvious bunk, but it doesn't mean someone couldn't find a way to push our minds beyond their normal limits. Think of it like hyper-powered steroids for the brain instead of the body, with side effects even more disastrous."

Gwendolyn paused, taking a moment to punch in a few words on her cell phone. From anyone else, it might have seemed rude, but Agent

221 knew how important speedy replies to those sorts of messages could be.

"Anyway, the point is someone out there is trying to overclock people's brains. That's scary enough in theory. Add in that we now have a survivor, meaning that they're getting closer, and it becomes downright terrifying. If there's going to be a drug like that out there, we're damn sure going to have the formula as well. Which is why we've been studying the survivor. We are testing blood, DNA... just assume every fluid actually. We're also scanning him every which way to Sunday. Unfortunately, we haven't been able to reverse engineer anything yet."

"If he's on this super brain drug, can't he help out? Or does it not work that way?" Agent 221 didn't want to seem overeager, but it was hard not to be a little curious.

At that suggestion, Gwendolyn pressed the heel of her hand against her forehead. It was a technique for suppressing headaches, one that Agent 221 had previously only seen in response to his own antics.

"While the man survived, we can hardly call him a success story. Even alive, he was still affected. The drug seems to have made him—erratic, might be the best way to say it. Impulsive, direct, overly self-assured, and with little capacity for understanding the rules of polite society. Focusing is a big problem for him, even when he's activated."

"I'm sorry. *Activated?*" This potential assignment was getting stranger by the minute.

"Through trial and error, we've found that he can sustain elevated brain function for short periods of time—roughly five minutes. It takes a lot out of him, and he usually needs a nap afterward, but in those moments his whole brain lights up like a Christmas tree. You should watch the medical geeks freak out when they see the scans. Outside of activating that talent, he's not going to be much help to anyone. Still, he's the only known survivor of these experiments, so—quirks and all—we're going to make sure and keep him in our possession."

New pages came out from the briefcase, these more familiar to Agent 221. Supply lists, potential routes, vehicle options—this was an operation briefing packet. Agent 221 had seen enough of them to recognize a transportation mission when it was set before him. The details were light, and probably would be until he committed to taking the job, but there was enough to get started.

"Which brings us to you, Agent 221. Our subject's condition requires special accommodations, as it turns out. Normally we'd just throw him in a comfortable, secured area and be done with it. However, that won't work for this one. His brain is in a delicate condition; it requires constant stimulation to stay functional. The man has no issues entertaining himself, don't worry about that, but locking him down too much results in boredom. Boredom slows mental function. Although he won't die from a dull afternoon or boring movie, without stimulation he decays. Our top science people, whatever field this falls under, tell us that if it drops below a certain threshold, he'll most likely die the same as the others. Since he is our one and only test subject, we've determined that to be unacceptable."

Now it all made sense. They couldn't let someone like that run free, and locking him down would just be another way to lose him. Covering him from a distance with teams was viable, but someone had to run point: a man on the ground, at the subject's side at all times. Personal, constant security.

"Bodyguard is a little below my pay grade," Agent 221 pointed out.

"Your pay grade is currently zero, if you turn this down," Gwendolyn reminded him. The handler's tone softened, albeit only slightly. "Look, I'll tell it like it is. You're out of leash. Ever since Poole, you've been compromised, seeing traitors where there weren't any. After this last one... that could have gone bad. *Real* bad. And you know it. Losing you would be a shame, but as things stand, most of the higher-ups think we already have. This is your comeback chance. You don't have to trust anyone: just keep the asset safe. Once he's delivered, we'll have ample protections in place, so just keep him alive until then. Do a good job, maybe we can look at putting your skills to better use."

A contrition mission. Show he was sorry rather than saying it by babysitting this science project until things settled down. Agent 221 didn't consider himself an especially prideful man—some cover-identities didn't permit it—so he didn't mind the job itself. The bigger issue was whether or not they'd really be willing to trust him again after this was over. It could be a ruse, some trick to squeeze a little more work out of him. At least it *was* work, though. He could contemplate his next move while on this cushy assignment, a paid vacation to consider his options.

"Tell me about this guy that I'm protecting. He have a name?"

"He does, and it's classified," Gwendolyn shot back. "As is his hometown, former dwelling, blood type, genetic makeup, and any other tidbit that could be used by our enemies to determine hereditary or environmental factors in his survival. The subject can't remember them anyway; we only found out via fingerprints, research, and testing. Don't worry; he has a new name he uses. Goes by Sherman. Sherman Holmes. Seems to have decided he's a great-great-great-grand-nephew of Sherlock Holmes."

Agent 221 had heard of stranger delusions, though rarely in people the government wanted to protect. "Has anyone tried explaining to him that those are fictional stories, and there is no actual Sherlock Holmes?"

Another pinched expression on Gwendolyn's face. "Sherman can be difficult to talk out of something. Remember, you're dealing with someone whose brain was chemically deep-fried. He's trying to cling onto reality with any handhold he can find. It works out for us, thankfully. Offers an easy way to bring you in. He's been asking for someone almost since he arrived."

One last folder emerged from the briefcase and hit the table. Agent 221 gave it a quick scan, familiarizing himself with his new identity. For the most part, it was standard stuff, a nondescript background and a vague job that would bore people out of asking follow-up questions. When his eyes hit the name, however, Agent 221 did glance over the top of the page, back to Gwendolyn.

"Really?"

Some of the pain in Gwendolyn's expression faded as she smiled back. "The man wanted a Watson, so that's what we're giving him. Congratulations on the new name and identity. Try not to wear it out too fast; we're not sure how Sherman will react if you change your name."

With a sigh of annoyance, Joel Watson, a man who until moments ago had been Agent 221, went back to familiarizing himself with the file. If there was a delusion he needed to play into, best he learn the part well.

2.

Everyone in the lab looked a touch off. Not in a dangerous way or a manner that suggested they were planning to pull a gun and rob the place. More like they were on edge, nerves turned brittle. Given that they were in a secure facility, surrounded by cutting-edge equipment as well as armed guards, Watson could make an easy wager on what the cause was. It didn't bode well for his impending meeting, but he tried to keep a positive frame of mind.

It had taken five days to get everything in order. Sherman was to be moved to a new location, something more private and specialized. So, a new location, with a new lab, and most likely the same poor scientists, since relocation still beat training a new staff, especially on something this specialized and confidential. Besides, those were the rules of secret projects: never bring in more people than needed.

"You're the Watson, yes?"

Watson had heard the approach before the man spoke. He turned to find a solid man with a strikingly bushy mustache and a lab coat waiting for a reply. Unlike most of the others, there was nothing nervous about him. The fellow was collected in a way that made Watson immediately wonder if he'd ever been in the field.

"I am. And you are?"

"Sherman took to calling me Gregson, and since none of us are using real names on this project anyway, it stuck. I did a little reading and I think he means it as a compliment. As much as he can." Gregson motioned for Watson to follow, which he did. "They've brought you up to speed on his condition, I trust. Sherman is partially connected to reality. He interprets everything through his own delusion, but he can carry on a somewhat coherent conversation if he feels like it. The 'if he feels like it' is going to be a caveat on most of this. Based on our observations, he is driven almost entirely by simple desire and curiosity. If something interests him, he'll play along. If it doesn't, we've stopped wasting time trying to convince him."

"You said he is driven *almost* entirely by those impulses," Watson noted. "If there's an exception, I should probably know about it." They were strolling through an area with several large machines, only about half of which Watson recognized. He'd spent a fair share of time in the hospital after his leg was shot and looking too long at the machines stirred up memories best left in the past.

Gregson nodded, shaking that huge mustache as he did. "Despite his issues, Sherman consistently falls back on his Holmes delusion. Some of our staff speculate that it is the foundation upon which he's managed to build this form of sanity. Anything that he can be convinced is expected of a detective, he'll do. Presenting his own condition as a mystery to solve is how we've gotten him to play along this well."

The duo arrived at a serious door. Watson considered himself something of a specialist on doors; he'd had to slip past many of them on various assignments and could often discern how valuable the prize was based on the door used to guard it. This was a door for people who did *not* want to be robbed: metal, thick, with a dozen visible sensors and even more that would be hidden. Armed guards on either side checked both Gregson's and Watson's credentials before finally permitting Gregson to swipe a card.

A hissing sound of a lock releasing filled the air. Then the door swung open, revealing what looked like an oversized bachelor's apartment. Seriously oversized, in fact; this one room was larger than Watson's entire first apartment. Since reading that Sherman had shown panic issues with tight, confined spaces, Watson had wondered how they were getting around that down here. Three large televisions were mounted on the back wall, one playing cartoons, another showing MMA bouts, and a final one rolling through some kind of documentary about rising housing costs in cities. A huge desk took up the majority of one wall, covered in books, bobbles, powders, and various other tidbits. Old magazines covered half of a large couch, and a few more were piled up near the edge of a barely touched bed.

In the center of the chaos stood the man who could only be Sherman Holmes. Tall, lean, and modestly handsome, Sherman would have been any other generic face on the street: that is, until he whipped around and stared Watson in the face. The eyes gave him away – too wide, twitching slightly, like he was trying to see everything in the room at once. "Intense" was the word Watson would use to describe them. A sort of mad intensity that would pierce the mind of anyone who gazed into them for too long.

"At last!" Sherman bounded over, clapping Watson on the shoulders and examining him carefully. Aside from the deerstalker hat atop his head, Sherman wore jeans, a t-shirt, and a cumbersomely large brown coat that hung past his knees and was positively covered in pockets. From one such pocket, Sherman produced a magnifying glass, giving careful inspection to Watson's forehead.

"Nice to meet you, I'm—"

"Hush, Watson! Of course I know who you are; I am the world's greatest detective, after all. Beyond something as innocuous as your name, I have successfully deduced that you are a resident of Oregon, a frequent patron of the ballet, and one of the few men who can claim to have defeated a full-grown gorilla in hand-to-hand combat."

Eyeing Gregson, Watson received a quick shake of the head. Playing along had its limits, then. "I'm afraid none of that is true, Sherman."

"Hmm, must be ahead of the curve then. Give it time; I will be right in the end." Sherman was unbothered by being corrected; he continued to examine Watson for several seconds more before finally taking a step back. "You are, and I say this with true sincerity, a terrible fit for this job. Truly, the worst Watson they could have sent me. But as you *are* now my Watson, that makes you assistant to the world's greatest detective. Do try to improve yourself before you drag down my shining reputation."

Perhaps Watson possessed a bit more pride than he'd realized. He'd been dressed down for many issues through his life, far more often since The Incident, but competence had never been among them. Watson was only a year or so older than Sherman looked, still fit and in almost-perfect health, save for one leg injury. He wasn't strikingly good-looking; however, in this job that was an asset. Stand out too much, and people remembered you for the wrong reasons. Above else, Watson was a professional, which was how he managed to slap on a grin as he replied to Sherman. "I will do all I can to live up to such a title."

"Let us hope you put more effort into that than you have your acting." With a swirl of his coat, Sherman spun around, heading back over to his desk. "Begin making arrangements for our departure, Watson. Gregson will fill you in on the new details I have added. Make haste, for time is short, and we cannot leave the world absent my genius for any longer than strictly needed."

Scooping up a book, Sherman began to read. If the fact that the tome was upside down bothered him in the slightest, there was no sign of it on his face. No sign of anything hidden, actually. Based on their brief interaction, it seemed as though Sherman wore everything on the surface. His words certainly hadn't been those of a man with tact, or the capacity to conceal things. If it was true, that could make for a nice—if temporary—change of pace, a break from all the double-talk and trickery of his old job. If it was an act, on the other hand, then Sherman was an incredible deceiver. Men with Watson's training weren't fooled too easily.

Gregson tapped his shoulder, motioning for Watson to follow. They left the room, which resealed behind them, before heading down a different hallway than they'd entered through. Once they were farther from the guard, Gregson spoke.

"As you can see, Sherman's condition is hard to classify. He doesn't conform to the exact specifics of any existing mental disorder since no one else has ever lived through what he has. If this ever becomes public, we'll likely name the condition after him, because there is nothing quite like it. Despite the fact that he is endlessly sure of his own genius—well, you just saw how he did at a round of deduction. It's essentially the same for other activities too. Sometimes, if he's deeply invested, we'll see some upswings in mental activity, but for the most part he's going to be like that."

"And you're sure it's *his* brain we want to learn about?" Watson asked, just to make certain they were on the same page.

Gregson lit up at the question, which shouldn't have been a shock. No one rose this high in a specialized science unless they carried a deep love for the subject matter. "Oh, very much so. The side effects are something to be dealt with, absolutely, but the benefits are incredible. When Sherman activates his enhanced cognition state, you can't imagine the sort of neural activity we're seeing. The first time I looked at the scans, I nearly peed myself."

"Right. So he's a genius for short bursts at a time." That could be useful, even if the subjects did end up like Sherman. A few minutes of brilliance could make a lot of difference when used strategically.

This time, Gregson's face fell slightly, giving Watson the answer before he replied. "In theory. Sherman has had difficulty in focusing through the torrent of information he accesses, even while activated. With practice, we believe he'll be capable of mastering his five-minute enhancement window. As things stand, he has yet to reach that point."

The more Watson learned about this assignment, the better he understood why Gwendolyn had foisted it off on him. Sherman was a long shot, that much was evident already, but worse, he was the kind of long shot they couldn't afford to ignore. Someone was making mental amplification drugs, and one test subject living pointed toward them getting better at it. If an enemy, even the wrong ally, got their hands on that kind of power, then there was no telling how the world could change. Useless though Sherman was, the mysteries locked away in his mind were potentially priceless. Or, it had just been luck or dosing that saved him, and this whole thing was a giant waste of time and money.

"Let's go over plans for transport." Watson opted to focus on the aspects he could control. Everything else was above his pay grade. "I know we can't fly because he doesn't like small spaces, so I assume there will be a convoy to escort us."

Another sour look from Gregson. "They didn't update you, did they?"

Suppressing a drawn-out groan, Watson shook his head. "Of course not; that would make far too much sense. Let's take it a step back. Tell me what changed about the transportation plans."

3.

The answer, as it turned out, was quite a bit.

Officially speaking, it had been determined that the most effective way to conceal Sherman's value as an asset was to make it seem as though he were any other person. Throw a ton of security around a car and watching eyes will know there's something valuable inside. Toss your prize out with the trash and most people could look right at it and not know what they were seeing.

All of that led to Watson being stuck outside a big box store, standing next to a blue convertible. The car, picked for its open roof to keep Sherman happy, was the other reason Watson wasn't inclined to kick up a fuss. It was a beauty, built to look like a classic with a few modern, custom touches woven in by their tech department. Oil slicks and rear-rockets might be movie fodder, but there was something to be said for satellite radio and an extra NOS tank, two of the features Watson had pushed for. As the only one not suffering from drug-induced brain issues, he would be the default driver for the trip, and even with poor company, days of driving this car were a nice perk for an otherwise lousy job.

From the highway, a van sporting a ride-sharing logo on the front pulled into the parking lot. The driver was actually one of theirs, but the foundations of great lies were the details. Want to seem like a normal guy? Then probably best not to show up to a meeting place in a car with government plates. Paranoia was an art form in the world of deception, and Watson was practically the Picasso of it. He hadn't always been like that. His leg throbbed at the thought, and Watson pushed it down it as usual. No rubbing an old wound or showing weakness. He was on the job now and, apparently, Sherman hadn't been wowed by their first meeting. Time to make a better impression.

The van pulled up, and from it emerged Sherman, dressed precisely the way he had been earlier. Here, in the parking lot of a Virginia store, he stood out like a sore thumb that was also screaming at the top of its thumb-lungs about alien invaders. Once they reached the new lab facilities, however, Sherman would practically blend in to the background.

Dragging a single gigantic bag from the van, Sherman dropped it at Watson's feet before making his way around to the passenger side. "You are punctual, at least. Perhaps you shall make a proper assistant one day."

Watson exchanged a look with the driver of the van, who gave him a look that unmistakably read like "He's your problem now" before she pressed the gas and drove out of the parking lot at an unnecessarily brisk rate. The look wasn't wrong; Sherman was indeed his problem for now. Once the transportation was done and tempers from the latest issues died down, Watson had faith he'd end up back in the field. Even if they didn't like him, he was a man who got results, and eventually that would matter more than any personal animosities.

A blaring horn shook Watson from his reverie. Sherman had leaned across the seat and jammed a palm into the steering wheel. "Perhaps your time is limitless, but as the world's greatest detective, you can hardly expect that sitting in this car waiting for my bag to be loaded is the best use of my day."

Reminding himself that they had a long ride and he shouldn't start things off badly, Watson swallowed a retort and tossed the bag in the trunk with a tad more force than was strictly needed. Making his way to the driver's seat, he was pleased to see Sherman was back in his proper place. Watson buckled up before bringing the engine to life.

The lovely roar it elicited was music to Watson's ears. Brief music, though, before Sherman grabbed the volume knob on the radio and turned it almost to the maximum. From the car, smooth jazz blasted forth, as Watson's previous radio selection was still queued up. Sherman gave him a look that was downright contemptuous before clicking a button to scan the stations. Watson countered by lowering the volume, and Sherman didn't fight back. Whether he was okay with quieter music or simply hadn't found something he wanted to listen to remained to be seen.

"Since we've got a few days ahead of us, I thought we should try to get to know each other," Watson said. They needed to broach normal conversation eventually, and he'd finally figured out a basic-enough topic to apply to anyone. "Practically speaking, how about we start with what foods you like? That should help me better plan out our stops."

"A fine idea, Watson. Nourishment does demand priority; a brain needs to eat at least nine thousand calories a day. Of course, that is in its raw, wild form, without a body to command." Sherman tapped a long finger against his chin for several seconds. "As to the query itself, I am afraid I have no answer to give. Food at the facility was nutrition-oriented, which is to say it tasted like the fetid rotting corpse of a long-forgotten pig. At present, I have yet to encounter any food which I would describe as enjoyable."

Watson pulled them onto the highway, not needing to check the direction. West was going to be the answer, save for the rarer occasions it was north. His mind tried to stay on navigation tasks rather than dwelling too much on what Sherman had just said. He knew the man couldn't recall many details about his life before, but he really couldn't even remember something as everyday as eating things he enjoyed?

"I suppose that makes you an open canvas. Lucky for you, a road trip is the perfect opportunity to stop and sample a variety of cuisine from across the nation. By the time we arrive, I bet you have a few new favorites."

"I am certain your lies are delightfully received by others; perhaps save them for that appreciative audience." Sherman clapped his hands together and stopped the radio's scanning. He settled on a public radio channel, one currently airing a documentary about the history of cheese. The volume went up a few degrees, though not quite to the blare it had been the first time. "Excellent, something of value." From one of the many pockets on his jacket, Sherman produced a new book and cracked it open. "Constant stimulation, Watson, endless education, that is how one keeps a mind from growing lax. As one would expect from someone of my brilliance, I possess perfect recollection, which means each tidbit I absorb only makes me more dangerous of an adversary."

That was an interesting claim. Curious, Watson waited a few moments, then tapped Sherman on the shoulder and pointed upward. They were passing by a large billboard advertising an erection enhancement pill with a dense chunk of legal disclaimer at the bottom. After making certain Sherman had seen it, Watson posed his challenge. "Can you recite that billboard from memory?"

His reward for the question was Sherman rolling those insane eyes in a way that felt genuinely unnerving. "When I need to, Watson. When the thrill of a mystery piques my mind to its true form. If you need me to spell out every obvious implication, I fear you shall be even less suited to this job than I initially suspected."

Silently reminding himself that it was bad form for a bodyguard to wring the neck of an asset, Watson put on his best appeasing grin. "Then I'll just have to work harder to show you how right for the job I am."

"Start by remembering what I just told you about your lies." Sherman plucked the deerstalker hat from his head and tucked it under the seat as the car picked up speed. Beneath it was a crop of dark, messy hair that looked as though it hadn't seen the outside in a good while. The hat stowed, he nestled into the corner of the seat with his book, adopting a half-leaning position that could not possibly be comfortable given his height. "Keep an eye out for highwaymen and brigands, Watson. Can hardly have a duel on the open roads without proper supplies."

Watson had no idea what that meant, so he just turned up the radio a few more degrees to kill any need for idle conversation. Maybe getting to know each other wasn't such a hot idea after all.

* * *

"Doctor Dunaway? We just heard back from the tracking team. Target is officially out in the open."

The woman reporting was stiff and formal, as were most of the personnel assigned to him. They never knew how to treat him; Dr. Donovan Dunaway was a man who fell outside the system their kind was comfortable with. He wasn't technically part of their organization, yet the superiors knew he was important enough to demand respect. On a personal level, Dr. Dunaway didn't mind any of it. They were a means, nothing more, human-shaped tools to aid him in the pursuit of perfection.

"Took them long enough."

From his worktable, Dr. Dunaway rose and stretched his back. Laid out before him were what looked like, to the untrained eye, a massive assortment of machines, lab equipment, and strewn-out notes. The impression would have been largely correct, save for the fact that the notes were placed deliberately. When dealing with information this sensitive, Dr. Dunaway had found it best to use data systems only he understood, lest others decide to part the doctor from his research.

"I still can't believe your people let another survivor slip through our fingers. Be thankful the government doesn't know what to do with treasure even when they hold it in the palm of their hand. Your people do remember that you're supposed to observe for the moment, yes? Can't have you all blundering in and messing things up before we properly understand their security measures. Once we make a move, they'll *know* there's information worth plumbing out of his skull. That uncertainty is all that's kept him from being properly guarded."

"I would say that some of our connections and resources also aided in getting him out in the open," the woman added.

Dr. Dunaway looked at her, almost as if for the first time. "I suppose that's a fair point. You have a good head on your shoulders." His disinterested expression twisted, eyes filling with new possibilities. "Ever wanted to see what you'd be like as a genius? Our new version of the serum is more stable than the previous ones; I'd give you a full two percent chance of survival."

"I will respectfully decline." Her response was automatic, just like all the other good little drones he asked. Honestly, what were clandestine evil organizations coming to if they weren't employing power-hungry back-stabbers ready to clutch any advantage they could get? Well, it wasn't his organization, so Dr. Dunaway had no room to complain as long as they kept doing their jobs.

"Then make yourself useful and hunt my target." Dr. Dunaway finished his stretching and turned back to the table. "And tell the others not to disturb me unless it is necessary. I'm working hard to make sure that we have everything in order for when our guest arrives."

Facing the equipment, he allowed the anticipation to live naked on his face for a few indulgent seconds.

"That man's brain is going to give us so much information. He might even be the last piece we need to make the serum functional. I'll have a proper welcome awaiting him. For a man giving his life to the cause of science, it is the very least I should do."

4.

After two hours, the history of cheese had given over to an oral history about aglets, the plastic tip on shoestrings. Every time Watson reached the point of wondering if he'd rather just drive the car into a pole than keep listening, he imagined having to talk to Sherman if they survived, and suddenly the aglet's tale grew interesting again.

Eventually, a break became unavoidable. Modern touches or not, the weight of some of their car's concealed features put a strain on the gas, forcing them off for a refueling. They could have gotten a vehicle with better mileage, but Watson preferred more frequent stops to using a less-effective tool. He was of the opinion that things would always go wrong, so it was best to be properly equipped.

Gassing up was easy; it was what followed that put Watson at a crossroads. Leaving Sherman alone in the car was out. Even if he weren't... Sherman... the man was still a valuable government asset. Unfortunately, the more Watson brought him into public places, the greater they risked someone remembering him. Anonymity was their best defense; the less memorable and remarkable they were, the better Sherman would be able to disappear from anyone hunting him.

"Let's go take a pit stop." Watson put the cap back on the gas tank and sealed it, turning a key in the lock to make sure no one added anything extra while he was out of sight. "Bathrooms, stretch our legs, we can even pick up some snacks. Give that food thing a try."

There was a moment where he thought Sherman might be ignoring him, but after a few seconds the book closed and his charge stepped out of the car. "A fine idea, Watson. Even you can have a bolt of inspiration, it seems. Nothing like a good stretch to drive the conspiring demons from our knees. Yes, let us partake in some nourishment; I have much mulling to do in our journey, and energy is an essential part of the equation. Voiding my bladder also holds a certain amount of appeal."

It was the closest thing to true agreement Watson had received from Sherman, so he didn't make a fuss over the "even you" crack. He just led the man into the gas station, Sherman's messy hair getting caught in a rogue gust of wind. Seeing Sherman without the deerstalker hat was a tad odd, although it *was* just a hat. Watson had somehow expected him to be more bonded with the accessory. The hat wasn't the source of the delusion, however; that was all coming from Sherman himself.

As they approached the door, Watson scanned the area automatically. He'd picked this station for the vast expanse of land around it—no clean vantage points to spy or snipe from—and enough open space to spot anyone coming before they arrived. Three cars were present besides theirs: a van, a sedan, and a sports car with the license plate "IM GASY" parked in a handicapped spot without a placard. While none of that was likely to be pertinent in their brief stop, Watson clocked it all the same. He had a lot of failings—more in recent years—but being bad at the mechanics of his job wasn't among them. No matter how annoying Sherman was, Watson would keep him safe until they arrived. After that, the real question was whether or not Watson would be able to resist strangling him.

Stepping through the sliding glass, they were blasted by a bolt of cold air, to which Sherman bared his teeth and growled like a dog. Watson's eyes went wide and he scanned the room to see if anyone noticed. Luckily, the only two workers—a middle-aged man and a high school boy—were both involved in a quiet, whispered conversation and paying their new customers minimal attention.

Without wasting a single step, Watson marched Sherman over to the restrooms. After a quick round at the urinals and the sinks, they were both feeling more refreshed.

"Go check on the snack aisle and see what looks like it might be good," Watson instructed. "I'll happily answer questions you have about different flavors and ingredients. We'll get a whole grab bag of stuff to try."

Sherman's laughter was uproarious and wholly unwarranted. "Oh dear, Watson, I say, that did clean out the old lungs. Good joke indeed, the idea that I could need *you* to answer questions for *me*. Keep that up, and you might prove to be incrementally useful."

Given that he was already in trouble, Watson found himself wondering how much worse things could get if his charge turned up with a few minor bruises. Then, reminding himself that Sherman wasn't in full control of himself, Watson forced a grin as Sherman headed toward the candy and snack aisle. They had to at least make it through the first day without injury.

With Sherman distracted, Watson went about his own tasks. He cataloged the gas station's roadside assistance inventory at a glance, assessing which parts of it could be useful. Before the trip, he'd been permitted to put a shopping list together, one filled with items stowed covertly in a secret compartment in the trunk. As a rule, since The Incident, Watson never liked any one person to know everything he had. That was why he'd planned on picking up a few supplies along the road: nothing truly essential, just some options in case things got interesting.

He was checking the expiration date on a can of Flat-Fixer when a loud voice caught Watson's attention.

"Hey! You can't eat those!"

In his heart, Watson knew before he turned his head. Sure enough, there was Sherman, half of a chocolate bar hanging out of his mouth. Before their eyes, he let it tumble to the floor, where it shattered into pieces. "You are quite right about that. No wonder almonds are naturally poisonous. Clearly humans were never supposed to place such a foul taste upon their tongue. I much prefer the soothing tingle of these mint-based confections."

Sherman reached into a box of dark circular candies and popped three into his mouth, followed by a bite of what appeared to be bubblegum tape. In the time Watson was shopping, Sherman had managed to accrue quite a collection of sweets in his arms, most of them halfway opened at the least.

"That's not what I meant! You have to pay before you can eat them." The older man at the counter, evidently the one in charge, was gaping at Sherman in shock, as though he couldn't fathom the fact that he was explaining basic commerce to someone.

"What a tremendously flawed system. I'm supposed to purchase food without knowing its taste? Your lie is both hollow and idiotic, and I refuse to entertain the idea of ethical guidance from a man who has been trying to covertly coerce an underaged employee into working off-books hours. Silence yourself, you uncouth imbecile, before bringing further shame to this establishment."

That had been a *lot* to process, and Watson had been ready for Sherman to say something crazy. The most interesting part, to him at least, was the expression of shock and fear that ran across the old guy's face. Had Sherman been right? Initially, Watson would have dismissed that as the usual flow of crazy, however that was a definite reaction to Sherman's accusation.

In fact, the man was still having his reaction, mouth opening and closing as he glanced from his young employee to Sherman and back. "How dare you come into my business and make those kinds of accusations. I should call the police!"

"You should lower that simpering mouth of yours onto my glorious organ, so that I might spit an ounce of intelligence into your body." Sherman popped a few more of the mint-chocolate circles and headed toward the door. "I tire of your wasted words and pointless existence. Watson, deal with this. Try to hurry, before a toddler wanders past the window and this man forces it to stock the cigarettes."

He was gone in whoosh of sliding glass, leaving Watson behind with a man turning a brighter red with every passing second. How to play this? Too soft wouldn't work on a guy like that, and too firm would make him dig in. A mix then: back and forth, keep him off-guard. They weren't getting out of here without being remembered, so Watson would settle for no authorities being called.

Watson walked up to the front, pulled a piece of paper from his pocket and a pen from the counter, then proceeded to write a phone number down. When it was finished, he handed it to the kid, a subdued-looking boy with the name "Ed" on his nametag. "Ed, hang on to this, we'll need it later. Now then, sir, as for you, please allow me to pay for the food my friend took. He's going through some stuff and meant no harm."

"No harm? No *harm*? He starts stealing my merchandise right in front of me, then when he's caught, has the nerve to insinuate that I would illegally manage my workers. That's libel!"

"Slander," Ed mumbled. "Libel is written."

There was a second where Watson thought the older man was about to unload on the kid with both barrels. It was there in his eyes, unmistakable. The rage didn't come, however. Ed was spared, probably for however long it took Watson to leave. Sherman might not have been exactly right about the situation, but he'd definitely nailed this guy's character.

"Look, my friend took probably ten dollars' worth of candy. Add in my Flat-Fixer, and I think we can both agree this is more than fair." From his wallet, Watson produced a crisp fifty-dollar bill and set it on the counter. "The extra is an apology for his disrespect."

Something flickered in the older man's eyes, an uncurling of greed Watson had seen in countless amateur tyrants. He thought he had prey in his teeth and wanted to press it for all he could. "Only fifty? What about clean-up? Restocking? I'd say it's at least three hundred if you don't want the authorities involved."

"Sounds good." Initially, Watson planned on going up to a hundred if it meant walking out of here, yet he suddenly found himself unwilling to pay a single dime more. Screw this jerk. "But just so we're clear, if you do, we're calling *all* of the authorities. Ed, go ahead and dial that number I gave you. On speaker."

Ed did as he was told, a malicious gleam in his eye as he watched his boss suddenly look confused. The owner clearly thought he'd been the one with all the cards. Time to dissuade him of that notion.

From the phone came a voice almost boring enough to be robotic. *You've reached the Department of Labor. If you know the extension you wish to reach, please dial it now. Otherwise, your call will be answered by the first available associate.* Hold music began to play, a dull background annoyance Watson quickly put out of his mind.

"Here is where we play a new game. If everything about this business, from the hours your people work, to the licenses, to the food storage, to the lightbulbs in use is legitimate, then call the cops. If so, then I punch in my buddy's extension and we have him come on down as well. Then we can make a call to the IRS. Now, I know what you're thinking—this is a bluff, right? It's just a number, that doesn't prove anything. And you're right. Could be a bluff. So you have to ask yourself this: would you rather take the fifty bucks, or roll the dice on someone who knows the Department of Labor phone number by memory?"

There was very real hatred in the owner's eyes as he accepted the money, pulling it across the counter and into the till. "Thank you for your patronage."

"Thanks for the service. And Ed, what's your full name, if you don't mind?"

"Mullins, sir. Edward Mullins." Too late, Ed seemed to realize that might not be great information to give a stranger.

"Good to know. I'll give my friend a heads up that if anyone from this town with that name calls in, anything they report is to be treated as highly credible." Watson glanced to the owner, who was fuming. "Since your boss runs such an up-and-up business, though, I'm sure you won't need to use that connection. Also, just some advice, maybe look for a new gig."

Watson strolled out, not wanting to press his luck anymore. He'd already taken it further than it needed to go, but he never liked watching people with power shove others around. Nice to see Sherman catch a guy like that in the splash zone of his lunacy – the same Sherman who was currently sprawled out in the convertible, eyes fluttering.

"Hey, you okay? Sherman?" Watson darted over, checking the man's pulse.

"Fine, Watson, perfectly fine, just a bit drained. I decided that I had not yet fully made use of the restroom facilities here; however, I presumed I was no longer welcome inside, so I was forced to use my enhancement window to find another alternative."

"You used your window… to find a place to pee?" Even being intentionally wasteful, that was something. Especially since Sherman had just voided his bladder minutes prior.

That earned him a snicker from Sherman. "Ludicrous idea, Watson. No, obviously I needed my augmented mental functions in order to pick the lock on the car door. With urine voided, I had only the remaining waste to deal with, and as a culture we agree that such is a private display. As I was no longer allowed in the station, I made use of an alternative rest room."

It took him a moment to sort through the needlessly complicated language, but Watson gradually put it all together as he turned on the engine, realizing they needed to leave faster than he'd expected. "Just so we're clear, you're saying you used your abilities to break into that guy's car and poop inside of it?"

"Really, Watson, must everything be spelled out for you?" Those were the last words Sherman managed to get out before his head flopped against the glass and loud snores tore from his throat. Gregson had said activating the enhancement took a lot out of him. That was about all Watson knew regarding the ability; everything else was too classified for his eyes, apparently.

As Watson put them back on the road, he was tempted to blast the radio once more before deciding against it. They might not agree on much, but Watson couldn't say the owner hadn't deserved something extra. So far as he was concerned, Sherman had earned this nap.

5.

Although Sherman came to after roughly an hour, he remained largely silent for the rest of the day's drive, instead burying himself in books and the radio. Watson kept half an eye on him as they rode, noting the pace at which Sherman was tearing through his assortment of paperbacks. The man couldn't actually be reading them, not at that speed, yet he kept at it.

Then again, Watson found himself wondering just what Sherman *was* capable of doing. He'd seemed to pull a lot of details about the gas station owner from one whispered conversation, and based on the jerk's reactions, Sherman was right on the money. Had it been pure luck? Highly unlikely, all things considered.

Ultimately, Watson opted not to risk accidentally starting up a conversation while they were stuck in the car. He waited until that night, when they pulled into a modest motel, The Charming Inn, and paid cash for a room. The security here was adequate, and the neighborhood low-crime, which was why this had been selected as a waystation. Watson already had the layout and exits memorized, in case they needed to flee.

Arriving in the room, he wondered if perhaps his research shouldn't start including décor as well. It looked like they'd stepped into a museum run for and by grandmothers: doilies ran across the tables, thick quilts on the beds, and a bowl of butterscotch candies sat on the nightstand. Adding to the effect were the walls, which had been slathered in a paint colored medicine-pink. It was not the worst room Watson had been forced to hunker down in, but it was probably going to make the top ten list.

"Excellent work, Watson. No criminal would expect to find the world's greatest detective in the midst of a geriatric nightmare. If we can avoid the twin dangers of heart failure and dementia, we may just survive the night. Well, I suppose only you need to worry about the latter. Bit too late for me."

Watson absorbed the words as he watched Sherman pull more shirts, jeans, and underwear from his bag. Did he know about his condition? It was hard to imagine what the world must seem like to someone in his state, so if he'd caught on that he was altered, what did that mean? Probably nothing; if Sherman even recalled the fact in ten minutes, it would be a surprising amount of mental consistency. Still, it was something he'd mention to Gregson during the day's debrief. It was time to get on that, in fact.

"You're up first for the shower," Watson told Sherman. "There might be a tub in there as well, but use that at your own risk."

"I am well acquainted with the risks of kickboxing a bathtub," Sherman shot back, easing the worry in Watson's gut slightly. Although the words didn't necessarily mean anything, most of what Sherman said seemed random.

Except that he'd been right in the gas station...

"Before you dive in, I've got a question. How did you know what the owner and that kid were talking about today? I work hard to pay attention, and I couldn't catch that much, so I'm curious what tipped you off."

Sherman's left eye twitched a fraction of a second before his matching hand pressed against the side of his temple. "Auditory cues of the conversation telltale body language lip movements sweat release skin mottling—" He finally managed to stop the flow of words, giving his skull a firm shake. "A bevy of reasons, Watson, I am sure. As the world's greatest detective, I trust my intuition most of all, and it told me from the start that the man was a nefarious sort."

"Pretty sure detectives are supposed to trust facts over intuition," Watson pointed out, still trying to make sense of what he'd just seen.

"Thank you, Watson. Now, when I need a woefully underqualified opinion on my profession, I have an asset I know I can turn to." Sherman grabbed a handful of clothes, definitely not a full outfit, and strolled into the bathroom. "Fascinating. I have yet to use a carpeted lavatory before." Those were the last words before Sherman shut the door.

Watson waited until he heard the water going, then pulled out his cell phone. Even with Sherman out of the room, he kept his voice low as he gave the string of code words signifying his identity. After several clicks and pauses, Gregson's voice greeted him.

"You two are making good progress. I wasn't expecting you for a half-hour yet."

"There's a lot of ground to cover, didn't want to waste time." Also, Watson wasn't especially inclined to draw this assignment out longer than needed. "Not sure how long we have before Sherman is done. The day went relatively smoothly, just a small incident that might need dealing with."

As quickly and quietly as he could, Watson recounted the gas station incident to Gregson, who was notably unsurprised by any of it. "Try to understand: Sherman doesn't process the world the same way as us. He is being constantly bombarded by information. Sometimes, he can make a little sense of it. More commonly, it gets jumbled and warped, leading to his more… *interesting* observations. The rule of thumb is to assume Sherman notices everything, even if he can rarely understand it."

"Oh yeah, I think he used his enhanced cognition window as well. He mentioned that after we were done. Said he used it to crap in the guy's car, then took an hour-long nap."

"Fascinating," Gregson noted. "I'll have to check my notes, but I believe that may be the first time he's used the ability outside of testing. Usually, he needs coaxing. Letting him out into the world may not be an entirely bad thing; we're already getting some useful data from the experience."

In the bathroom, Watson heard the water die. "Time to go. I'll be in contact tomorrow. As things stand, no changes to the plan or route." The phone was off a full minute before Sherman strolled out wearing jeans and socks. At least he'd grabbed some form of pants in the crapshoot of clothing.

"My timing is perfect as always, I see. Did my handlers have anything worth passing along while you were squealing about the day's exploits?"

Watson ignored the barb. "Nothing of note to report on their end. And touching base with the other people coordinating your security is not what 'squealing' means." Perhaps Watson didn't ignore the barb quite so well as he thought he had.

"Spare me your semantics, Watson, we both know whom you serve." From in his bag, Sherman produced a pair of earbuds and an MP3 player. For many obvious reasons, no one had given Sherman a phone, but Watson was surprised to see even a device like that. If he had music he liked, why not use it on the drive? "Gregson was kind enough to give me this as a departure gift. I sleep better with sound, we have discovered."

With a flick of the dial, Sherman tapped play, letting loose screaming nonsense from the speakers. Watson had hunkered down through bombings that were less grating to the ears than what had to be the absolute thrashiest of metal music. Yet, his charge looked oddly serene, finally clicking it off.

"I am given to understand most people don't consider that soothing, thus Gregson also included the tiny headphones."

Silently, Watson made a note to be nicer to his contact. The man could just as easily have only given Sherman the music, forcing him to sleep through it as well.

"How can that possibly be relaxing?"

It was rhetorical, but Sherman actually considered the question sincerely. "To you, silence is relaxing, I presume?"

"Maybe a little white noise like a stream or something, but in general, yes," Watson confirmed.

"That is because your mind, most minds, are naturally silent places. Peace is defined as stillness, a lack of thought. Quiet is the natural state of being, so immersing yourself in it puts you at ease. The same principle applies for me, with a key difference. My brain is *not* a quiet place."

Right. Gregson had spelled it out: Sherman was constantly under siege from information. Something to drown it all out, that might very well be his best way to unwind. In fact, now that Watson thought about it, it could explain the books and the radio in the car as well. It wasn't about any individual show or novel, it was about distraction.

But if Sherman was really absorbing so much information all the time, just how dangerous would he become if he was fully capable of using it? Watson had a feeling he would need to see this cognitive enhancement for himself.

* * *

In a parking lot three buildings over from The Charming Inn sat an unremarkable sedan with two people in nondescript clothes. One, a man wearing cargo shorts who kept shooting his own pants dirty looks, was on the phone while his partner, a woman in a romper, kept watch.

"Uh huh. Yeah. They're in the motel for the evening. We're playing it aloof tonight, parked a ways off. Checking for anyone doing sweeps and scanning for remote communication. So far, just them, but it's too early to be sure. Yes. Yes. I know. Good. Now can we re-open the discussion about our disguises? I don't care what 'the kids' are wearing! And I don't think it's this! Yes. I—yes. Okay. I'll pass it along."

He ended the call, letting out a heavy sigh. "No go."

"For heaven's sake, Tom, you said you could talk them into a change." Lowering her binoculars, Jenny shot him a dirty look. "Do you know how hard it is to use a gas station bathroom in one of these things? I have to take it all the way off."

"Oh, and I'm in love with looking like I stepped out of the Dad Parade." Tom took a breath to calm himself down. "Look, they aren't going to do us any favors when we keep coming back without news. We'll wait until we have something juicy, then see about getting a wardrobe change authorized."

"I don't like this job. These people are sketchy, and they insisted on way too much control over the operation. We should have said no." Jenny picked the binoculars back up as she spoke. What they should have done was irrelevant; they'd taken the job and had to see it through. This wasn't a business where "never mind" was a thing.

Tom nodded. "We might have bit off too much, but the pay is worth it. Not to mention who is going to owe us a favor if we succeed. At least all parties involved want this done cleanly. No one killed, especially the target. Non-violent jobs with this level of pay are hard to come by, even rarer that we can double-dip."

"When you put it like that, maybe the romper isn't so bad." She glanced down once more, taking in the design. "Who am I kidding? Yes, it is. But I'll deal with it. Hopefully, it won't be too long. If these two don't have more backup, then we can do the job soon without much trouble."

"At least another day of watching," Tom replied. "We're supposed to be waiting for the go order. Besides, I know it looks smooth, I just don't trust it. This much money, for one unguarded target with a single bodyguard? There's something we aren't seeing. On a job like this, we stay safe, agreed?"

Jenny nodded, causing the binoculars to wobble. "I think you're being a tad overly-cautious, but since that's your job, no sense in being mad at you for it. Yes, we take it slow and safe. Something is definitely off here, just wish I knew what it was."

Silently, Tom wasn't so sure he agreed. A job like this, they might be better off cloaked in ignorance. When the dust settled, an employer might not want anyone left alive who knew too much. Not necessarily a likely scenario, yet also not one to dismiss when dealing with people this dangerous. They'd have to keep that in mind when it was time to settle up. Those concerns were for later, though.

For tonight, they had a motel to watch.

6.

As a rule, Watson was not a heavy sleeper: such was always the case, from his humble origins to his time as an agent. The Incident had only made things worse. Now, Watson needed pills to have a full night's sleep that didn't come packaged with nightmares from *that day* – pills he naturally skipped taking when he was sharing a room with a mentally-unstable man he barely knew. So it was a surprise to him that in one bout of Watson's brief unconsciousness, Sherman went from being passed out in the other bed to sitting at the doily-covered desk going over an old tourist map. The fellow could sure move quietly, when he wanted.

Rather than rise immediately, Watson took a moment to observe Sherman silently. Seeing someone when they thought they were alone was often revealing; plenty of useful tidbits could be gleaned from such moments of vulnerability. Not surprisingly, Sherman proved to be a unique case. He was hunched over the map, pen scratching as he scrawled unknown thoughts onto the crisp pages. If Watson walked over and found a bomb recipe or a manifesto about mint-chocolate candies, neither would shock him. And, if Watson was starting to get the swing of things, Sherman might not remember writing anything after five minutes had passed.

"Whenever you're done lying about, the day is ready, Watson."

Should have seen that coming after yesterday. Even if Sherman couldn't fully process or use all the information he was experiencing, someone waking up probably tripped those amped up observational senses. "I was playing a game with myself where I tried to imagine what the hell you were doing to that map. My best guess is that you're redrawing the county lines into something more fun."

"An unexpectedly competent idea," Sherman replied. "But as usual, well short of my true genius. Fear not, Watson, after yesterday's tedious and dull journey, I have improved upon our itinerary. We will no longer be passing through these places. We shall mount a great expedition of their nooks and crannies, an exploration of all the road has to offer."

This was getting less funny by the word, so Watson swung out of bed and walked over to Sherman, clad only in his basketball shorts and sweat-wicking shirt. Even when sleeping, Watson dressed for action. Plus, the workout shirts didn't bunch up as much when he tossed and turned. Peering down at the map, he could see an entire tapestry of new routes, winding throughout the entire state inefficiently, looping back and forth several times. It looked more like the path of a drunken cartoon character than a comprehensive route.

"Just at a glance, this would take us a week or so to get through, and we've got plenty of states after this one. If we were that late, I'd be branded a traitor and they'd assume you were trying to escape."

It wasn't Watson's place to say no, necessarily. Even aside from their bodyguard/asset dynamic, Sherman was a valuable resource, one whose mental happiness was part of taking care of him. Pointing out potential flaws felt like a safer stance. Should Sherman opt to really push the issue, Watson would have to call Gregson and see what the bosses said. Ideally, he'd like to not let it get that far. Managing his burden on his own was part of being a good agent.

A recollection of his conversation with Gregson gave Watson a new idea, one he hastily implemented. "And of course, the longer we're on this trip, the more the world is denied having access to its greatest detective."

The first round of words barely seemed to reach Sherman, but that last addition brought him up short. "Quite right, Watson; we cannot afford to spend all our days meandering about. There are cases to be solved, culprits to be uncovered." Sherman took the pen and made a massive "X" through his current plan. On top of that, he started sketching a new path, one that still took them off-route, but only slightly.

"For the good of the world, I will limit our explorations to the bare necessities: spots of interest worth learning from or necessary mental stimulation to break up the monotony of the road and mislead the spider-stalkers trailing the car."

Ignoring the weirder parts, Watson realized this put them at a crossroads. He could push more, try to get Sherman to give up the side trips entirely, but that might not be for the best. Sherman did need stimulation, and if he kept the tourist traps limited to stuff on the way, that could be an easy way to keep him happy. They could at least try it for today and see how things went. If it was a disaster – more than Watson already braced for – then they'd skip the next ones.

"How about we keep it to one spot per day? That should give us time to explore and keep us on pace to have you doing detective work as soon as possible." Watson had told many lies in his life – dictionaries full, in some operations. This one came as easily as the others before it, even if Watson might not have cared for the taste. Whatever they did with Sherman, it certainly wouldn't involve working as a detective. Sherman didn't really deserve that. Oddball or not, he was just a man caught in circumstances beyond his control. Those decisions happened over Watson's pay grade, though. He was just here to make sure that unique brain arrived safely.

"That does seem to be the best option," Sherman agreed. "Quick enough to keep your masters from pulling on your leash, but at a pace where actual exploration can take occur. Not to mention, limiting it to one spot a day will deny the spider-stalkers a chance to catch up. Busy yourself with readying for the day, Watson. I have a route to calculate."

Two times he'd mentioned the spiders now. Probably nothing, more of the usual oddness, but Watson had no qualms with being overly cautious. Not anymore.

*   *   *

"What are they doing?" Tom was clutching the wheel tightly, taking note of the convertible's blinker as it moved toward an exit. They'd just stopped for gas an hour ago, and there were no nearby stations, so unless one of them was having a bowel emergency, this move made no sense. "The itinerary should have them heading straight to the next motel."

"Clearly, they decided to take a different route," Jenny replied. "Moment of truth. Do we follow or not?"

"Let's see where this is going, at least. If we have to lose them, better we get an idea of where they're headed." Tom changed lanes, following as far back as he could risk. It was still extremely noticeable as both cars took a minor exit leading only to farm roads, even worse as the convertible slowed down hurriedly once it was off the highway. The target was trying to force them into passing by going below the speed limit—a simple precaution to see if someone had reason to stay in the rear.

There was no way around it: Tom couldn't hold this position. He stayed behind for less a minute more, then took the second dirt road on the left that they passed. First was too coincidental; second looked like they were driving somewhere specific.

Tom could see the convertible head past, off toward a destination they had no idea about. At his side, Jenny was already on the phone. "We're going to need some new wheels – can't risk them recognizing this one. Uh huh. If they're on a detour, we'll catch up at the motel tonight. If they're going rogue, we need to renegotiate the job."

Tom grit his teeth as he listened to the conversation. Not an auspicious start to their second day on the assignment.

* * *

Had Watson been the one to select their destination, he might have picked a spot that seemed up Sherman's alley, narrow though that was: a museum, a piece of local history, something with facts and details for a "detective" to sink his teeth into. A haunted orchard wouldn't have even cracked the top ten, let alone been his choice. Yet that was where Sherman directed him after a few hours on the road. To his credit, he'd picked one that only cost them half an hour in driving time, total, so Watson could hardly object on a practical level.

Ghosts were one of the many things Watson put no stock in. As a man who'd worked around death long enough, his presumption was that if such beings existed, one would have started haunting him by now. The lack of poltergeists in his vicinity felt like solid confirmation that if there was an afterlife, the door only swung one way. Sherman, on the other hand, appeared deeply intrigued.

The place was largely empty, as few people wanted to tour a haunted orchard in the early afternoon. Long rows of trees stretched up and down the property, dotted with a few lodging and processing areas, each with a suspiciously bloody history. It was even harder to swallow the idea that the place was infested with ghosts once Watson learned they still ran it as an apple orchard when the season was right. Essentially, they'd stumbled into somebody's idea for how to make a seasonal location profitable all year round. Pretty ingenious, when Watson considered it.

"Over in the cider press, I can show you where a pair of sisters crushed their final apples before turning on one another in a jealous rage. Each, you see, had been sleeping with the other's husband." Their tour guide – a pleasant woman who told the tales like she really believed them, which she very well could, for all he knew – was leading them along the path to their next destination. Personally, Watson would have condensed the tale a little; both of them happening to be cheating was a little much. Then again, it did add an air of authenticity to the story. Reality had a habit of pulling coincidences no one would accept in fiction.

"Close," Sherman interrupted. "The man was, in fact, a doppelganger who could change his shape. In reality, they were both with the same man, the orchard's overseer, and never knew it thanks to their staggered shifts." Sherman had been correcting her like this as they went, receiving only a polite smile every time he attempted to add his own spin. They were in a haunted orchard with the sun overhead; clearly their guide knew the only customers she'd be dealing with would fall on the eccentric side.

As they talked, Watson kept scanning the area. There had been a car that exited the highway at the same time as he and Sherman. It pulled off on a different road shortly after, but the memory stayed with him. Was it possible that someone else happened to need the same exit? Absolutely. Was Watson the kind of person who could accept that? Not even close. If they were being trailed by something other than imaginary spiders, Gregson needed to know… assuming everyone in that chain of command could be trusted. This tail, if that's what it was, sure found them fast for it to be mere happenstance.

Watson decided that, for now, he and Sherman alone would determine the side trips. No need to give potential enemies a heads up on where they'd be going, and so long as they kept to the general schedule, then the people in charge would deal with it. If someone was on their tail, he'd find out soon. And they would have the chance to discover why, despite all of his recent issues, Watson was still a highly capable asset.

7.

In spite of the name, Watson preferred The Meandering Muskox to The Charming Inn. Initially, the moniker had put him off. But a slew of positive reviews paired with above-average security features won him over. It didn't especially matter since the locations were all pre-set, but Watson took comfort in knowing their lodging assignments showed some signs of competent vetting.

As it turned out, he rather liked the atmosphere of the place. Wood and the outdoors were heavy themes. Every building looked like some manner of cottage, even the giant one housing dozens of rooms. It reminded Watson of his youth: days spent hunting in the woods, honing skills he'd never imagine needing so frequently when he grew up.

The lobby was enormous, huge beams running along the ceiling over a vast lobby centering on an indoor propane fire pit. Toward the back of the building, noise was coming from the restaurant and bar; Watson snuck a few peeks at the plaid-covered bodies inside. Tempting. He needed a place where anyone who didn't belong would stick out, and that would fit the bill. Plus, they were hungry; their detour had led to arriving late. Watson's initial plan was to hunker down and have something delivered, but on-site dining might work as well. Assuming Sherman could handle a crowd.

On that point, Watson wasn't sure what to expect. Sherman had issues with confined spaces, that much had been discovered early on. However, the scientists had never had enough reason to risk putting him around a bunch of strangers. Without any data of his own, Watson was forced to ask the closest expert on Sherman's condition he had available.

"Want to go grab something in there, or if that's too crowded, would you rather I got us some food to go?" Watson got the question out just before accepting the key from the pleasant fellow working the front desk. They needed to get their luggage out of the trunk, but given how reinforced that car was, no two-bit hoodlum was going to break in before they were done eating.

To his shock, Sherman actually considered the question, rather than snapping off a quick barb. "Hmm, an unexpectedly reasonable query,

Watson. I must say, I cannot recall being around such a group, therefore I have no solid information on how I will react. We must investigate!"

Sherman was halfway to the bar before Watson even realized he was moving; the guy could be fast when he wanted to, using those long legs to skulk across the lobby. Watson raced ahead, greeting the cheerful hostess who immediately led them to a wooden table with two chairs, away from the bar but not by as much as Watson might have preferred. Still, for a busy night, he couldn't complain about the seating, and it had the bonus of offering Watson a good view of both the bar and part of the lobby. Anyone who strolled in looking out of place would be noted instantly.

"Watson, tell me, if one sandwich is labeled 'Maid-Rite,' am I to assume all the others are made wrong, or is this some manner of dated colloquialism? Or is it fashioned from the flesh of one who actually worked as a maid?"

More than a few stares turned their way, as Watson realized with a start that he'd been so focused on how useful this place was to spot people who stood out, he'd neglected to factor in that they would stand out as well. Had he been alone, there would be no issue: Watson knew how to look like a tired traveler who wanted only a hot meal and no trouble. Sherman, on the other hand, was hardly renowned for his ability to avoid attention.

Well, Watson had been wondering how Sherman would hold up in a crowd. If he could survive this, lower-stakes situations should be easy.

Of course, Watson knew the importance of that "if."

"Local delicacy, no human parts used," Watson shot back. "I'm going with the breaded pork tenderloin sandwich and a side of potatoes. You can't go wrong with anything potato around here."

Several of the starers backed off, their concerns and pride placated. Nobody liked having their home trash-talked: drunks in bars located on the edges of hunting territory even less so. Two ignorant tourists were a problem; one being shown the local flavor by someone who was already a fan—they still weren't going to be welcomed, but it bumped them down to "inoffensive" overall. That was Watson's favorite place in someone's mind. Leave no memory, make no impression, pass through the world unknown.

"Hey there, hun, what can I get you two?" The woman who arrived at their table was young, yet she held her pad and body with the confidence of someone intimately familiar with her job. Even as she paid them attention, her eyes were scanning the rest of the bar, checking for untended customers or brewing trouble.

"Breaded pork loin sandwich, side of the mashed potatoes, and a salad," Watson told her. "Iced tea to drink, unsweetened."

"I shall do the same as my assistant, only forgo the tea. Not a fan in any incarnation. Instead, let me try one of these craft drinks. It's all gibberish to me, so I shall lean upon your expertise. I have few tastes to use as metrics, so simply choose your favorite and I will accept the recommendation."

To her credit, their server barely even batted an eye at Sherman. "Got it. Drinks will be over in a jiffy, food will take a bit longer; kitchen is pretty busy at the moment. I'll see if I can't rustle up some cornbread for you to snack on while you wait."

She was gone just like that, without ever making so much as a single scratch on that notepad of hers. Even so, Watson had complete faith their order would be correct. As a rule, he had a knack for telling when someone was competent in their role. And thanks to her interruption, their environment was no longer the sole focus of Watson's curiosity. "You don't like tea?"

"Tried the stuff at the lab, truly ghastly. How anyone forced that down is beyond me." Sherman had pulled out one of his books and set it on the table, giving it a light read. Interestingly, he seemed to be more at ease amidst all the noise surrounding them than he had in the car. Chaos soothed him, so at least that was consistent.

"There's more kinds than just the hot stuff," Watson told him. "I just thought it was kind of funny because, you know, the whole Holmes thing. Didn't he love tea?"

"Probably, but that has no bearing on me. Your ancestors likely boiled frogs for sustenance and prayed to the moon to fix a cut; it doesn't mean you are compelled to do the same." Sherman sat a little straighter, meeting Watson's eyes for a rare change. "I am merely a descendant of the most famous Holmes. Beyond our mutual love of one profession, I have no desire to be a carbon copy. My life and my tastes are my own, or will be as I discover them."

It took more self-control than normal for Watson to resist pointing out that, no, Sherman wasn't descended from Sherlock Holmes—that was a delusion his chemically-burned brain had latched onto. Really, though, who would that be for? Sherman had at least picked a fantasy that centered around contributing to society; there were plenty of worse people he could have decided to be. If he'd imprinted on Jack the Ripper, Watson could be in charge of guarding a very different man.

Noise from the lobby drew Watson's eye. A trio of large men clad in camo were stomping up to the front desk. Either they belonged here, or the people trailing him and Sherman were extremely dedicated to their cover. Watson ruled out neither.

"We appear to have dressed poorly for this establishment, Watson." Sherman had taken the time to look around too, apparently noticing the plaid and camo ensembles surround them. "Next time, give me proper notice, and there will be time for disguises!"

The enthusiasm came unexpectedly, at the end of the sentence, seeming to catch even Sherman off-guard. "Seems I might be partial to costuming. Fascinating."

Not necessarily the word Watson would have used, especially considering the outburst had earned them some fresh stares. "We don't need disguises, Sherman. We aren't trying to blend in, we're just having a meal before bed."

"And a drink." Their server returned, setting down an iced tea and a glass of dark liquid. "Went with a local hard cider for your drink, one of my favorites. Not too sweet, not too tart, but if you don't like it, give me a holler and we'll get you something else." She was gone again in a blink, off to take orders from another table.

Before Watson had time to offer any input, Sherman grabbed the glass and took a heavy sip, draining a quarter of the drink. "Knowing full well that it is a low bar, I must still say, this is *substantially* better than tea."

"Yeah, just go easy on…" Watson trailed off as he watched Sherman put the glass back to his lips and chugged the entire thing in a single go. No one had said Sherman couldn't have alcohol, or any other type of food for that matter, so Watson hadn't objected to the order. Only now, however, was it occurring to him that if alcohol worked by affecting brain chemistry, and Sherman's mind was already unnatural, there was really no telling exactly what impact it might have.

With a satisfied sigh, Sherman slammed the glass back down onto the table, inadvertently catching a corner and shattering it. "Oh my, that was refreshing. I shall require several more of these before the evening is done."

Watson could already see the man moving. He was a big one, broad shoulders and a gut that only accounted for part of the fellow's mass, with muscles contributing to the rest. A thick scraggly beard meshed into his unkempt hair, leaving only small breaks for the eyes and nose. Worst of all was the twinkling bits of glass visible in that beard, shards from Sherman's very visible mistake.

The hand fell on Sherman's shoulder smoothly, no trembles or uncertainty. Had he acted a tad more aggressively, Watson wouldn't have allowed him to get that close, but he had more the bearing of a man looking to yell than fight. Yelling was fine; he could do that all day. No one damaged a package in Watson's care, however.

"You got glass in my drink." Looming over Sherman, the local leaned down closer. "And in my food." Even closer. "And in my face."

"By devil, it seems you're right. Quite impressive, if I do say so myself. The trajectory on the glass to have made it from my position into your facial hair must have been truly exceptional. I wonder, perhaps I clipped a dimensional vortex and warped the velocity. Too simple a notion for one like you to comprehend, yet the variable nature of the universe opens up tremendous possibilities."

Mostly rambling, with only one pseudo-insult. For Sherman, it was downright diplomatic. Sadly, the man glaring at him wasn't quite so dumb that he missed the implication of the word "simple" during the spiel.

"You come into our bar, break the dishware, shower me in glass, then call me stupid? Time for you two to get out of here. Cash on the table for your order, along with a tip, and we let you both walk."

Given the way Sherman had acted, it was a fair offer. Plenty of people in here would have swung first without offering a chance for peaceful resolution. Were he in charge, Watson would take the deal without a second thought. The problem was, that question had gone to Sherman, who was impossible to predict.

"As a counter-offer, may I suggest you move your microbe-infested face away from mine, before the stink attaches permanently?" Sherman was smiling, not a single ounce of fear on his face, no matter how warranted it would have been.

Killing off the rest of his tea, Watson only wished they'd gotten served before this happened. He loathed working on an empty stomach.

8.

In so far as silver linings went, getting to a motel ahead of one's target wasn't much of one, yet Tom and Jenny were both very grateful for it as they watched the show play out. After losing Watson and Sherman, they'd headed for the evening's lodging, planning to let them catch up. In doing so, Tom and Jenny had not only taken note of the particular crowd, they'd been provided with enough time for a shopping trip as well.

Both were clad in faded, used camo they'd picked up from a nearby thrift store. New stuff would have stood out among this many real hunters. Their line of sight on the target wasn't spectacular; part of taking an out-of-the-way booth meant they were harder to spot, and it was harder to see out as a result. Thankfully, they had enough view to see the glass breaking incident, as well as the huge hairy man lumbering over to Sherman's table.

"This is trouble," Jenny whispered, inaudible to anyone else over the constant roar of the bar. "We need him alive, brain as undamaged as possible. That guy looks like he's going to paint the table with that golden skull."

Tom silently agreed. It was both a problem and an opportunity, though. If this bruiser could separate Sherman and Watson, probably by knocking out the latter as soon as he intervened, it would be the best chance they might get to snag their prize. "Let's play it cool. His bodyguard should at least be able to distract the guy. We're still early in the process, but if an opportunity presents itself, we strike, orders or not. Otherwise, we hang back unless the danger gets real. Can't let our target get beaten to death in a bar fight."

Neither of them could hear the conversation going on at the table. To them, it seemed to escalate with no warning. One moment they were worried about Sherman's brain, the next they were watching, wide-eyed, as Watson sprang into action.

Silently, Tom said a prayer of thanks that they hadn't been dumb enough to try taking the target by force.

*   *   *

Had the man been more aggressive, Watson would have led with the now-empty iced tea glass. Cuts could be tricky, however, and the man didn't deserve anything permanent for what was a fairly measured response to a rude intruder. Unfortunately, the moment that big fellow lifted a fist, Watson lost the option of a completely peaceful resolution. He hoped the patrons here would learn a lesson about being so quick to turn to violence.

In a single movement, Watson burst up from the table, using the momentum of his half-leap in the punch he drilled directly into the side of the bearded man's neck. At the last moment, Watson pulled back a touch and angled his strike toward the spine; his goal was to take the guy out of the fight, not collapse his windpipe. Sure enough, seconds later the burly beast was laying on the ground, clutching his neck as he worked to breathe. The initial threat was minimal, had been all along. Watson wasn't worried about fighting one person; he was concerned about the bar as a whole.

Already, casual, drunken, fun looks were morphing into something angry as they took note of their friend on the ground. If anyone paused to consider the fact that he easily had a size advantage on both men, possibly even combined, they would be hard-pressed to call it an unfair fight. Such was not the strength of those far into the drink, unfortunately.

"Sherman, come with me, right now." Watson spat the words over his shoulder before addressing the rising number of people before him. He had a gun holstered if needed, but drawing in a place like this was crazy. Beyond the amount of hell he'd take for firing on civilians in a restaurant, this was a hunting bar. The moment Watson drew, he'd be outgunned on every side. No, he either talked or fought his way out of here.

"Everyone, I want to apologize for what just happened. My friend here has a… condition… that causes inappropriate behavior. We hoped there wouldn't be problems, but obviously we caused some. Let me just pay for what we ordered, and a drink for your friend, and we'll get out of here without making more of a mess."

Maybe if they'd gotten here a little bit sooner, before the beer flowed quite so freely, Watson's words could have reached them. It was pointless speculation in the end. They'd arrived when they'd arrived, and now Watson was staring down a slowly growing crowd of patrons glaring angrily at him.

"No matter what happens next, you stay close to me, understand?" Watson reached over and gripped Sherman's shoulder, yanking him nearer.

"Are you planning to sucker punch the entire bar?" Sherman asked. He, at least, seemed unconcerned about their precarious situation.

"It wouldn't be my first choice."

First choice or not, it was becoming more likely as the crowd drew closer. Big distractions like setting off a fire alarm wouldn't work; they were tipsy enough not to care about conventions like alarms. He'd knocked out their friend, they wanted drunken payback: that was as far as the equation they were capable of processing went.

"Everyone, sincerely, I really wish you'd let this one go."

The response Watson received was a red-headed man in dark tank top swinging for his head. Big, clumsy, easy-to-read – that hooch in their systems cut both ways. Watson avoided the blow and repaid it with a quick jab to the ribs. That bought him some space as the copper-top backed up, coughing and rubbing his side.

Watson gauged the others as his first attacker retreated, carefully looking over their stances. Brawlers, the lot of them, focused more on power than precision. A fine tactic, against the right opponents, and with the numbers advantage in a bar fight, it was the preferable strategy. Targeted strikes were harder to throw the more hectic a scuffle grew. Drunken restaurant slug-fests weren't known for their order.

Two came at him next, a pair of guys who looked nothing alike yet moved oddly in sync. Watson backpedaled, guiding Sherman closer to the exit in the process. As he avoided their swings, Watson also helped himself to a few items from the tables he passed. One of the pair came too close, only to have a candle's worth of hot wax dumped on top of his head. It wouldn't kill or seriously wound the guy, but the feeling was distracting, and when it dried, he'd have a herculean effort to get it out of his hair.

The second of the pair slunk in, managing to score a hit on Watson's stomach. For an instant, red flashed in Watson's eyes. It was hard to fight these people without leaving lasting damage; holding himself back was also leaving him vulnerable. But he'd been at this for far too long to lose self-control over a single gut-punch.

When the attacker came for a second helping, Watson caught his arm and flipped him, slamming the gentleman down heavily on the floor. Technically, he could have cushioned the blow more, but there *was* still a tickle of pain in Watson's stomach.

Beating three people in such a short span should have bought them some room, but already more were closing in. Worse, they were getting closer to Sherman as well. Although Watson truly hoped he could avoid going down this road, it seemed he was going to have to start scaring them away. No more careful fighting; he'd have to leave the kinds of injuries that made people seriously reconsider if this was a battle they really wanted.

Before he could break the first nearby knee, a new sound came from far back. Watson couldn't make out the exact words, but it seemed to be a couple having a yelling match. Based on a few salacious details he could make out – *babysitter*; *pounding*; and *frigid* – it was probably quite the spectacle. In fact, it was drawing so much attention that Watson and Sherman were momentarily less interesting.

An opportunity was an opportunity, and Watson was especially fond of an option that didn't require him leaving half the patrons here in casts. Grabbing Sherman, he plowed ahead, easily breaking through the smattering of distracted bodies guarding their rear. Without slowing, he and Sherman bolted through the lobby and out the front door.

Checking behind to see if they were followed, Watson rushed them both to the convertible, firing up the engine as soon as he was behind the wheel. At his side, Sherman glanced back at the motel, confused. "Aren't we staying the night here?"

"That was the plan, until you showered Bubba the Hairiest Redneck with glass and then insulted him. Now we get to drive around, because there are no suitable alternative lodging spots within a two-hour radius. Once everything cools off, we'll circle back and break into a room for the night."

"Quite right, Watson. Can't have the spiders slithering into our location."

Tempted as he was to point out that spiders didn't slither, Watson instead focused on the more salient points. "Or angry bar patrons who might bribe or threaten the front desk to get our room number."

Slamming on the gas, Watson pulled out of the parking lot, pointing them toward the highway. If they had to drive anyway, he might as well get a jump on refueling and save them some time in the morning. Watson had a talent for making the most of unexpected developments – quite possibly why he'd been put on this job in the first place.

"You know, you could have apologized." Watson watched The Meandering Muskox fade in the background, trying not to think about how hungry he still was. Gas station food would be another meal, apparently. "You're the one who broke the glass."

"Am I expected to know the inherent tensile strength of an untested container, or calculate the precise trajectory of a stray shard? Ridiculous! You should know by now that my brain's considerable capabilities are dedicate to far more essential tasks. What happened there was a clear accident, and assigning blame to it makes as much sense as urinating on an earthworm to stop a rainstorm."

No shame, not even a sense he'd done something wrong. Watson took a deep breath to calm his very active nerves. He had to remember that it wasn't intentional. Sherman didn't act like a jerk because he was cruel or thought it was funny. The man was processing a different kind of reality, doing his best to make it mesh with this one. Or maybe he'd been like this before. Without any way to tell, Watson gave Sherman the benefit of the doubt, largely because it made coping with him more tolerable.

"In the future, situations like that can be easily resolved by simply saying 'I am sorry' and nothing else. If you want to be the world's greatest detective, you'll need to learn *some* people skills. Getting witnesses to cooperate, cultivating alliances with police, all of that revolves around not immediately spitting out whatever thought pops into you head."

Sherman snickered, low and dark. "Watson, what another spectacularly wrong assessment. Truly, you outdo yourself day after day. To start with, I do not wish to *be* the world's greatest detective, I *am* the world's greatest detective. Granted, the world does not know that, but general awareness does not denote the level of one's skill. Secondly, mastery of social technique is not a topic I need to waste space in my prodigious mind on. There have always been those who prefer coddling to simple truth, and I have already made a concession to them by employing a lower mind, one to give them assurances and comfort while I see the work actually done."

"Hang on, that's what you think I'm here for? To act as your 'normal person interpreter' and block all the crap that gets flung your way?"

"Ideally, no. The true job of a Watson is something far more important. However, I see very little chance of you ever successfully filling that role. For someone of your limited capabilities, simple diplomacy is a task you can possibly handle."

More deep breaths, more reminders that it wasn't intentional, as Watson drove further into the night.

9.

As a rule, dreams were something that only existed in the off times, when Watson allowed himself true rest. When on a job, he would fall into a light, empty sleep to prioritize mental recovery over all else. His pills and nightmares were set aside, devotion to the job perhaps the only thing stronger in him than his demons.

Tonight was an exception, as Watson found himself in an all-too-familiar dreamscape. He was walking through a village. The name was lost somewhere in his waking mind, yet he could still recall every feature. Gentle wind rustling the trees, sunlight warming his face, the scent of a goat dish he'd grown fond of being cooked not far off. No matter how many times he had this dream, nothing changed. He would go into the bar, meet with Poole, and end up bleeding on the ground while that traitor escaped. Not because he hadn't sensed something was off, but because he trusted a supposed ally over his own instincts.

Ready to get it over with, Watson shoved the swinging door of the bar open. Only, to his shock, Poole wasn't waiting for him. Instead, Sherman was sitting there, swigging from a bottle of gin. Where would he have even found that here? Sherman's eyes, those far-too-intense eyes that Watson couldn't properly forget for even a moment, swung in his direction. As he moved to greet Watson, the gin bottle tipped over, sending splashes of liquid to the ground.

A lot of liquid, in fact. Way too much for a single bottle. It sounded more like a full-on rainstorm. The bottle turned on the counter, spinning as it lost its contents before tumbling down and shattering loudly on the ground.

For the first few seconds, Watson didn't realize he was awake. That was forgivable, largely because the noise around him remained the same. It still sounded like a rainstorm, a fact that made sense considering it *was* raining outside. As he shook the sleep from his head and took in the room, even the volume of the rain fell into place. Having the balcony door wide open sure seemed like an excellent way to get a listen, while also leaving them considerably undefended. One more blink, and Watson noticed what should have been his first realization.

Sherman was gone.

Up in a flash, Watson pulled a gun from near the bed and made his way to the door, checking it carefully to make sure no one was waiting on the other side. They'd broken into a room on a higher floor, limiting the avenues of entry, but Watson had used that same sense of security to his advantage when others leaned on it too hard. Scaling buildings wasn't as hard as everyone wanted to think, especially when properly motivated.

Bracing himself for anything, Watson peered around the corner of the door frame, out onto the modest balcony most guests used for smoking.

Slowly, the gun went down as Watson tried to understand what he was seeing. There was no threat. Not a physical one, at least. Sherman was still here, in a manner of speaking. He was seated on the balcony, stripped completely naked, with his eyes closed and an expression of… peace? It was the most relaxed Watson had seen the man since they'd met. Even when sleeping, there was something frenetic about Sherman, like his brain was mad about the wasted time. Nudity aside, with his eyes closed and the calm expression, Sherman could have been mistaken for any normal person.

There was a twitch in that serenity, a tremble along the eyebrow. "I suppose you've emerged to tell me this is needlessly dangerous, and I should come inside at once before catching cold."

In honesty, that was exactly what Watson should be saying. Sherman was a one-of-a-kind oddity that the government wanted to duplicate. His health was of paramount concern. Hell, that very health was why they had to continue indulging all his whims to keep him mentally active. This, whatever it was, seemed like the opposite of stimulation. A good bodyguard would check in with Gregson, seeing what the new development signified. A great bodyguard, on the other hand, would appreciate that running every problem up the chain only made building any level of trust more difficult. If he could get Sherman to listen, even a little bit, it would make the remainder of the job far easier.

Besides, Watson knew what it was like to have trouble finding peace. He didn't feel the urge to yank such a feeling away from someone else, especially someone like Sherman. "Just promise to take a hot shower when you're done. Warm back up. You need anything out there? Umbrella, towel, bottle of water?"

"Frivolity? From you, Watson? Perhaps one of those oafs last night landed a blow I missed." Cordial as ever, peaceful expression or no. Except Sherman did seem a little less acerbic with his words: more like he was going for friendly ribbing. Maybe that was always what his tone intended to be; guessing the inner workings of Sherman's mind was plainly a game without winners.

It wasn't as if Watson would be going back to sleep out here, so he decided to play along for a bit.

"I'll have you know I'm considered one of the funniest secret guard mercenaries in the government's employ, second only to the guy who does impressions at the company holiday party."

"A word to the wise, Watson. If you wish to deceive someone regarding the art of humor, do not cast your top talent as one who dabbles in impressions. It's a lower art, barely above whoopee-cushions, and everyone knows it. Ventriloquism, that's where the true talents set their sights."

It was impossible to know if Sherman was being serious or joking around, but this might well have been their longest talk without Watson feeling the urge to strangle him, so there was no strong inclination to push the issue. Instead, he watched for a little while longer as the rain poured in, feeling a sense of pride that he'd spent the extra time to park under a carport. With weather like this, the car would have been soaked, maybe bad enough to get through the canvas roof. How could this not bother Sherman?

"Do you like the rain?" The question earned Watson a single eye opening halfway, staring at him, then closing once more. Fair enough, that had felt like a stupid question the minute it left his lips. "What I mean is, does it help you like the heavy metal music?"

At first, he thought this question was earning him more silence, without even the courtesy of an eye opening. There was no change in Sherman's visage once he finally did speak.

"Imagine you are in a crowd. A crowd of people, yelling things at you. Around you. And you can't ignore them, not truly, despite your grandest of efforts. Sometimes, you hear them clearly. More often, you only get pieces of what they are saying or misunderstand them completely. At best, you find ways to cope with the sound, distractions to keep the voices at bay. There is a tipping point, however. If the crowd gets large enough, loud enough, the sound becomes a roar. When it is impossible to hear the voices, your brain finally stops trying to understand them."

Sherman's right hand extended, catching some of the many raindrops along the palm. "Each of these tiny oceans slamming into the ground with their own speed, velocity, composition, history… it's simply too much. Not even my incredible mind is capable of tracking such a cacophony of information."

"Silence through noise. Peace through chaos." Whether it was the early hour, the unexpected dream, or too many years doing this job, Watson got it. In the field, sometimes silence made his teeth sit on edge. Noise, action, there was a sense of certainty in that. The next step was always right there: survive, extract, neutralize. It was in the still moments that fear and doubt crept in.

"A simplistic encapsulation, but not wholly inaccurate."

Getting a tad snippier. Was he wearing out his welcome? No, Sherman had never invited him here to begin with. He saw Watson as an overseer, just like Watson had been viewing him as a burden. The smart move would be to back off now and build on what they'd managed so far in terms of civility. Watson wasn't much of a fan of the smart move, not when the stakes were this low.

"Is that what it's like when your enhancement window kicks in? The voices shut up?"

"Quite the opposite. The 'cognition enhancement window' as those dullards termed it, does not silence the voices at all. It… tames them."

"Tames them?" Watson asked. He was having trouble picturing how that might work.

Sherman's right hand lowered from its extended position, going back to his side. "Same scenario, Watson. Crowd of people. Only now, they aren't shouting. They're helping. Any conundrum you wish to analyze, any information you need to recall, the information is right there, ready and waiting. Within limits, of course. Were I someone with no knowledge of medicinal science, I wouldn't be able to puzzle out a cure for cancer just by thinking about it. But those limits will be less than you might imagine, once I've gained mastery over the skill."

Based on what Sherman had described, Watson wasn't sure the tradeoff was a worthwhile bargain. Especially since no one was actually sure Sherman *would* be able to completely control his mental enhancement. Breaking into a car was a neat trick, but it didn't prove one had an intellect capable of tremendous feats. Mostly, it meant someone had basic dexterity and access to a tutorial video. Still, it was hard not to be curious what that kind of power could actually do, when properly wielded.

"Today's stop is that county fair you wanted to check out." Watson glanced over at the clock on the nightstand, while confirming the time on his wristwatch. "I'm not telling you to come in. I'm just letting you know that if you want to be there in the afternoon when all those crafting demonstrations are going on, we need to leave within an hour and a half. Do with that information as you choose."

It was time to try a new approach with Sherman, Watson had decided. Guidance, rather than orders. Based on the lab and the set of instructions he'd been given, it seemed like Sherman hadn't been in charge of much about his life since the drug changed him. Some people took well to structure; others would balk if ordered to jog a mile but would power through a marathon wordlessly so long as it was their choice. That attitude didn't work for all every charge being escorted; however, in Sherman's case, he could afford a little more leash. It wasn't as though it would make him that much more troublesome.

Even aside from all of that, there was another reason Watson opted to be gentle. His dream, strange as it had been, was a reminder of something. Seeing Sherman instead of Poole had been confusing, yet also a relief. Watson didn't especially care for Sherman, with good cause, whereas Poole had been charming from day one. The two had clicked near-immediately, working seamlessly together on an assortment of missions. Sherman had a lot of faults, many of which seemed aimed at Watson specifically, but he didn't appear capable of lying.

Between working with an honest jerk and a charming traitor, it was no contest. Sherman was the better choice every time. Of course, that didn't mean Watson was giving up on a more congenial environment for the remainder of the trip. This morning had been a good start. Hopefully, things would go smoothly during the afternoon.

Even as he had the thought, Watson tucked a spare clip into his bag. Hope was for civilians; he needed to prepare some contingencies.

10.

As much as the prior night had not gone to plan, Tom didn't consider it a complete bust. True, they'd missed an opportunity to grab the target, but in the process they'd learned some important facts about the bodyguard. He was more dangerous than he looked, he knew how to at least attempt diplomacy, and he was willing to do whatever was necessary to protect his charge. That was, ultimately, why Tom and Jenny had intervened. It wouldn't do for those two to leave a mess of broken bodies that would lead to local authorities asking questions.

"Found them."

Jenny walked in from the rain, shaking off her umbrella as she did. Tom had scouted the southern section of the area, which took less time, allowing him the first chance to dry off. "Her hunch was right, they doubled back here later last night."

Something unfamiliar, a flash of fear, danced in Tom's eyes. "You reached out to That Woman? We're supposed to stay disconnected during the job whenever possible."

"We're also supposed to succeed, so I called up *her* representative and got some help, although they weren't especially friendly about it," Jenny admitted. "The working theory is those two probably broke into an empty room. They've got their car tucked in an out-of-way carport at the edge of the property. We can hunt the room, or just watch their ride."

One glance to the clock made the decision for them. "It's almost time for them to be moving; makes more sense to watch the car. So far as we know, they don't have any vehicle changes planned."

"I'd feel more confident about that if our internal source had proven to be a little more reliable. We got nothing about that detour yesterday, who knows what other details they forgot to pass along?"

That was Jenny, one eye open, looking over her shoulder for betrayal at all times. Given the people they often were forced to work with, it was a reasonable habit – one that had saved their lives on occasion. But it could also make her over-worried, seeing conspiracies where there were none.

"You saw how the target was acting last night," Tom reminded her. "I think… we have to be more adaptable on this one. He's a chaotic element, and the bodyguard seems to be enabling that behavior. My money says that was the cause of the detour. Something happened, and it may well happen again. We stay loose and ready to act whenever the chance arises."

Jenny finished shaking off her umbrella and reached for a dry towel set near the door. "Good. I don't like dragging this one out. Besides, we're getting further west. A few more days, they'll get where they're going and he'll be out of our reach."

"Don't worry." Tom reached under the bed to grab his gear. They needed to able to move as soon as their target did. "We're not letting them get away."

* * *

"I see. Still no progress?"

Dr. Dunaway looked annoyed, which was worrying for the messenger delivering this news. Some personnel in the organization had a habit of visiting Dr. Dunaway and never turning back up. He probably wasn't just murdering them outright – although, given the value he represented, the higher ups might just be letting that slide. The people Dr. Dunaway worked for and the strange drug they offered was an entity all to itself. The only thing that mattered was access to the serum. Once it was ready, whoever had it would hold the world in their hands, waiting to squeeze.

"Correct. The contractors we hired are in pursuit, however they've yet to see an opportunity for clean extraction. As ordered, they've stayed back rather than risk tipping their hand."

Dr. Dunaway looked at his watch for a lingering moment. "I think we've given all the time we can afford to doing it cleanly. Getting him without a ruckus would be ideal and make our job easier, but we can't risk losing the opportunity entirely. Send word to the other teams. Pay goes to whoever brings us our target, alive and unharmed. That man's brain is worth more than this entire country. It is not to be sprayed across a parking lot because some goon got trigger-happy. Be *very* clear on that point."

The man taking the orders, one who would have described himself as tough in other situations, gulped. Fights, stabbings, shootings, he could handle all that. A half-mad scientist who kept making co-workers vanish, on the other hand, was deeply unnerving. "Yes, Dr. Dunaway. I'll put the orders out immediately."

"Excellent." Dr. Dunaway looked at him, almost like seeing him for the first time. "And once you're done, feel free to come back. I have a new formula that I think you would love to try."

Another gulp, followed by a nod. "I will keep that in mind." He would, too. He'd keep it in mind next time the order to deal with this wacko came down, and then he'd pull whatever favors needed to make it someone else's problem. He missed normal crime. The sooner Dr. Dunaway and his mysterious cabal were far from this place, the better.

*　　*　　*

The County Corn Carnival was a local favorite. The midway was busy, the food was almost like home cooking, and a small stage was hosting a country band. The carnival stoked a touch of nostalgia in Watson's heart, more than he expected from himself.

"Not a bad choice, Sherman. I mean, logistically this place is a safety nightmare, but at least it seems like one where we can get a churro." Seated in the car, watching people walk through the gate, Watson found himself slightly eager to head inside.

"A benefit to assisting the world's greatest detective. You are swept up in my waves of genius." Sherman was at his side, also watching the crowd. "I do spy one predicament in our path. The general attire of the average attendee is a stark contrast to our own garb. If we wish to blend in and sample the culture as true locals, there is only one solution."

Personally, Watson didn't think it was a big deal that they looked out of place, he in slacks and a button-down while Sherman continued his pairing of jeans, a long coat, and that ridiculous deerstalker hat. Out-of-towners came to these events all the time. Then again, even for a "city-dweller," Sherman did stand out. Blending in was probably a good idea, especially knowing that was likely a question of when, not if, Sherman would cause some kind of scene.

"Okay, I'll bite, what did you have—?"

"Disguises!" Sherman thrust his finger into the sky like he was trying to poke out the sun's eye. It drew a few looks from passersby, although none stared for long. Carnival season meant the town got some weirdos; it was just part of the bargain. "We shall have to don complex disguises and conceal our true identities."

This was the most excited Watson had seen Sherman get. Was this some piece of his past self shining through, or did it just make sense that a person with so little self-identity would relish trying on new ones? Either way, excited Sherman beat surly Sherman, and Watson could admit that it might be easier to get through today if they blended in.

"Disguises, huh?" Watson turned the car back on, savoring the sound of that engine humming to life. If he weren't in the doghouse, he might have asked about keeping the ride for his next assignment once this one was completed. "I saw a mall not far back. Betting we can find ourselves some jeans and plaid. Maybe even get daring and go for a pair of overalls."

To his surprise, Sherman considered the suggestion like Watson had just proposed robbing a bank, an expression of severe contemplation on his face. "Possible, yet I think we shall have to wait and gaze upon the selection for ourselves. To wear overalls is a great commitment. They are a battle garb donned only by those ready to put their life on the line."

And just like that, Watson found himself at a crossroads. The day was going pretty well, for them. Strange as the nude balcony discussion was in retrospect, it appeared to have afforded them a sliver of understanding toward one another. Watson didn't want to risk that. But on the other hand, if Sherman really wanted to function in society, he'd have to make peace with being corrected. His condition made it unavoidable. That wasn't necessarily his bodyguard's job, though. In the end, Watson decided the best choice was just to ask Sherman what he wanted. It couldn't earn a worse reaction than flat-out correcting him.

"Remember this morning, when we talked about how sometimes the voices, the information, can get jumbled? If I notice that happening, do you want me to tell you, or would you rather I let it slide?"

The question earned him a hard stare at first, one that softened slightly after some silence. "That is a problematic area, Watson. I know that my mind often observes more than it can process, so there are situations where an error could occur. At the same time, there will be occasions when I am seeing details and information that others are missing, so we can never work from the assumption that I am truly mistaken."

"How about this, then. When these moments happen, I won't tell you that you're wrong, but I will tell you what the common understanding of something is. That way, you can decide for yourself whether you're seeing deeper or crossing wires. Never hurts to have more information, right?"

Sherman was already removing his hat and tucking it under the seat for the ride, leaving his dark, erratic hair exposed to the air. "I suppose there is value in such a perspective. It might be beneficial to the know the perceptions of possible suspects. One issue in that proposal, though, Watson. If I am taking your word about those common understandings, it means I am trusting you."

"I'm already the man in charge of your safety on this whole trip, how much more trust can you give?"

That earned him a snort. "I did not select you for this job. Were it in my hands, you are quite possibly the last candidate I would have chosen. But I suppose you do raise a point. In the grand scheme of things, I am handing you no more power than you already have. Very well, Watson, you may inform me of common understandings in contrast to my own, when such situations arise." He paused, eyes out the window. "You really do not see why trusting you is a dilemma?"

"Can't say I do," Watson replied.

"Then your intellect is less than I initially suspected." Sherman took out a fresh book, this one about common tomato gardening techniques, and started to read. "Even children know trust is meant to go in both directions."

11.

While Sherman had raised a semi-valid point, the real reason Watson went along with the suggestion for disguises was that it demanded erratic behavior. Going all the way to the carnival parking lot, then turning around and heading back to a store? That was the sort of nonsensical routing that only Sherman could come up with, meaning anyone else doing the same would stick out like blood on porcelain.

Watson's eyes were peeled as they made the drive away from the carnival, entered the store and made their purchases, then drove back. Nothing stood out. No signs, no signals, nothing. Aside from one car making a communal exit with them the day prior, there had been zero evidence to suggest that they'd been compromised. Yet Watson couldn't quiet his instincts, the raised hairs on the back of his neck that demanded he take the potential threat seriously. The sorts of jobs Agent 221 had done before he was Watson were dangerous, messy, and often highly confidential, but they did have the benefit of teaching him to trust his instincts. If his gut said someone was on them, then that was how Watson would proceed.

Until that person or persons revealed themselves, there was still Sherman to deal with. His new ensemble consisted of overalls, a plaid short-sleeve button-down, and a wide-brimmed straw hat that kept a vast amount of sun from his face. Although it was perhaps a touch on the nose, none of the other patrons gave Sherman so much as a sideways glance as they ambled up to the gate. Maybe he'd done a better job choosing a disguise than Watson realized. As for himself, he was clad in simple jeans paired with a shirt distinguished from Sherman's by the lighter coloring and longer, rolled-up sleeves. Together, they more or less looked roughly the same as the other attendees, allowing them to blend into the crowd – another reason Watson had agreed to disguises.

Making it into the carnival was a brief affair, largely consisting of trading viable currency for tiny tickets that could be exchanged for food, games, rides, and other assorted distractions: an ingenious scheme that had people spending more than they realized as they handed over tickets rather than cash. The beauty of this hustle was that, even knowing what it was,

Watson was still forced to participate. To him, that was the hallmark of an excellent scam.

Sherman had little appreciation for the shady economic manipulation. His attention was on the sea of sights and smells that greeted them. Well, "sea" might be overly generous, as he scanned the size of the carnival and realized it only took up a few city blocks, at most. Corn mascots wandered around, some in cob form, others popped. One poor employee who'd drawn the short straw was dressed like a bowl of creamed corn—a wide white bowl base filled with some gooey, gelatinous looking substance, with a cheery false head on top, all of it poorly balanced.

"Watson! There is the flesh of a cow upon a stick! Let us test the mettle of this culinary adventure!"

Right, Sherman still didn't have much experience with eating. Not that he could remember, at least. Maybe this trip could be good for more than shaking out any hidden tails. Here, they'd be able to test a variety of different foods; deep-fried and unhealthy, yes, but foods all the same. Finding a favorite dish would also provide Watson with one more motivation tool. Once Sherman had things he wanted, Watson could reinforce positive behavior with them. They only had a few days together to go, but Watson would consider it a gift to whoever had this position next.

"Cow on a stick? Sign me up."

Watson smiled at the man working the grill as he handed over his tickets, receiving a polite nod when the man handed back a pair of skewers with sizzling steak stuck on. Credit to Sherman's nose, this did smell pretty good. Generally, Watson preferred a little more sanitation and security in his food prep; however, he'd long ago had to cast aside those preferences in the field. Food was sustenance, and sometimes that meant finding it wherever possible.

Together, they strolled along the midway, noting the townsfolk enjoying themselves. It was a pleasant view of rural living, almost enough to make Watson fully homesick for his own childhood. Almost, but not quite. The thought did make him wonder about Sherman, though. What must it be like to have no childhood, no adolescence, no past to draw from whatsoever? Even without his condition, that would be disorienting enough.

"Ahh, that pig just defecated, Watson. That's how you can mark a good one." Sherman had discovered the petting zoo and was wildly pointing to a swine still midway through doing the necessary. Perhaps Watson was worrying more than needed, for whatever his origins, Sherman appeared semi-functional. He must be dealing with it somehow.

"All pigs defecate. Part of being a mammal," Watson replied.

"But not all pigs do it in front of an audience," Sherman shot back. "Or do you have no respect for the theatre and those who seek to entertain?"

Watson truly had no idea how to respond to that sort of statement.

Thankfully, something new caught Sherman's eye in that moment, releasing Watson from the conversation. "Oh ho now! What's this? The perfect opportunity for the world's greatest deductive mind to prove his mettle and refill our stores of snacks? Truly, this day is a wonder!"

Already rightfully worried, Watson's eyes scanned around them before ultimately settling on a display advertising the chance to win one of every food item at the carnival if a contestant could correctly guess how many corn kernels were inside an enormous jar. Entry was a full ten tickets, which felt greedy, even by carnival standards. Were it up to him, Watson would have vetoed the idea without hesitation. Sadly, as with much of his life at the moment, the decision wasn't his to make.

"I shall best your challenge. Watson, pay the man."

Apparently, Sherman's love for disguises didn't extend to acting differently around others, or even not using names. He loomed around the jar, looking it over from several angles, getting near enough for his breath to fog the glass without ever actually touching the surface. The attendant looked uncomfortable with the whole process, but Sherman wasn't breaking any stated rules, so the burly worker let it slide. He probably imagined it would make no difference, and in any other circumstances, Watson would have agreed. But Sherman was something special. Whether that would be enough or not remained to be seen.

"I believe I have an adequate grasp of the dimensions. All that remains is to put the pieces together." Sherman took a slow breath after his declaration, eyes locked on the jar. Barely audible, under his breath, a few words were whispered. "Time for a case!"

If one wasn't watching, the changes were easy to miss: a momentary strain of the body's muscles, eyes fully dilating then returning to normal in under a second, the clench in Sherman's jaw, like he was trying to wrestle some unseen monster to the ground using purely willpower. Fleeting, all of it, yet unmistakable to the bodyguard told to watch for precisely these sorts of sudden signs. Unless Watson's assessment of the situation was way off, Sherman had just activated his enhanced cognition window. Right now, supposedly, he was driving the most powerful brain on the planet.

"What... what was I doing?" Sherman looked around, and for once, the burning intensity in his eyes was gone. In its place was bewilderment and uncertainty. Seeing Sherman like that, he appeared closer to normal, perhaps even vulnerable. "I had... a task. Focus."

Two quick slaps to his own face, and Sherman looked a little less lost. "That jar. I need to say how many kernels are in there. Such a simplistic equation, though... was that truly my only task? The calculation was done before I'd finished focusing on the object, it's so simple. No, clearly, there's a great need, I'm getting it wrong again. I need to—"

"Sherman. It's just the jar." He had no idea if this would help or not, but Sherman appeared to be on the verge of spiraling. With a mind like his in an unstable condition, that was dangerous... to the government's research, of course. So it was natural that Watson tried to help, a part of his job. That's what he told himself, at any rate. "No bigger purpose. We just wanted to get some snacks. All you have to do is say how many kernels are in that jar."

"But it's a mere sixty-two thousand, nine hundred and twenty-seven kernels. Is that truly of significance and worthy of my true attention? At least last time was for justice, a cause one can always find purpose in."

While Sherman was speaking, Watson noted the stall worker's shocked expression as the number came out. Either this carnie had done a tour on Broadway, or the reaction was genuine flabbergast. Clearly, Sherman had gotten it right. Whatever else might be true of his condition, it really did appear to amplify his brain. Nice to know they weren't going through all of this for nothing, but at the same time, Watson felt a twist in his stomach.

If this ability could let someone like Sherman do that much mental math in the span of moments, what would it allow people with Watson's training to accomplish? Nothing good, which was all the more reason to keep Sherman safe and happy until the scientists could figure everything out.

"You heard the man, and given the face you made, I know we got it right, so pony up." Watson moved close to the worker, making sure he couldn't be ignored. The faster they got this resolved, the better he'd feel. This was the opposite of avoiding standing out, but a lucky guess wasn't quite so incriminating and memorable. At most, they would be a fun local story about the lucky jerk who guessed right on the nose. "I'm guessing we'll get a book of coupons or something, unless you're going to bring everyone over for a cookout."

"Look buddy, I don't know how your pal pulled that trick off – and I definitely think there's something suspicious going on – but we run an honest carnival. He got it right; he gets the prize, fair and square. Can't give you the coupon book, though."

"Why not?" Watson asked.

"Because we only give prizes to the actual winner, and your buddy took off running a few seconds ago." The man pointed over Watson's shoulder.

Spinning around, Watson could just make out the shape of an oversized straw hat darting to the left, out of the midway.

Without pause, Watson took off at a dead sprint, nimbly weaving and dodging his way through the crowd. It took some real doing, but he slowly pushed past them, hot on Sherman's trail. There were any number of reasons why he might have bolted, especially in this state. Maybe something spooked him, or Watson inadvertently committed some kind of offense. Was he trying to escape the program entirely? No, the gas station had been a vastly better opportunity if that was the goal. There had to be more going on.

As Watson rounded the same corner that Sherman had less than a minute prior, his stomach dropped even while his feet picked up the pace. Smoke was coming from farther down the path, paired with a growing crowd of people milling about, some yelling for help. Technically, it could be a coincidence. That thought gave Watson little hope as he sprinted, knowing it might already be too late.

Where there was trouble, there was bound to be Sherman.

12.

Most major accidents were, in fact, a series of small factors all going wrong simultaneously to create a specific outcome. Or, in rarer cases, a man wearing a creamed corn costume losing his balance while passing a ride, slamming himself, the ride's worker, and said worker's lunch all into the console simultaneously. The combination of soup, soda, and blunt force trauma had done quite a number on the equipment, causing the ride to increase in speed unexpectedly. On most attractions, that was bad enough, but this ride, The Spin Doctor, featured lots of rotation. Low-end results would be a lot of vomit to clean up, and if the speed kept rising, people might begin to lose consciousness.

All of that was immediately evident as Watson ran up on the scene. What he was less sure of centered on why Sherman would go racing in this direction from so far off. How'd he even known this was happening from where they'd been? Scanning the crowd, Watson quickly spotted Sherman. He was trying to get closer to the console, being rebuffed by some burly men with serious expressions. While a carnival was, by default, about fun and games, this situation was turning more dangerous with each passing moment. Putting on an extra bust of speed, Watson raced up to Sherman's side.

"—and I am telling you the cognobble switch needs to be cauterized!" Sherman declared, yelling it triumphantly in the face of a man blocking his path.

"Buddy, half those words were nonsense, and the other half wildly misused. Stay back while we get this sorted out." The carnie was unbothered by the yelling; in this environment, a little shouting was probably background noise. His concern was solely for the ride, which was going even faster.

Balling up his hands in evident frustration, Sherman spat out a reply through gritted teeth. "The words are just words, placeholders for ones I'm too busy to find at the moment. If you would just move out of my way, I can *fix* this."

Could he? Checking his phone, Watson saw they were still well within the five-minute window. Sherman *did* have some augmented thinking power in his current state, but this wasn't merely a jar full of corn kernels. This was a complicated, damaged machine that Sherman should have no experience with. Most likely, he was only going to make things worse. Better to leave this one to the professionals.

"Come on, Sherman. The men know what they're doing; let's stop getting in their way." Watson laid a comforting hand on Sherman's shoulder, and for a moment, the message seemed to get through. Sherman turned with him, taking several steps away from the ride's entrance.

As it turned out, that was nothing but a trick. No sooner had the guards relaxed than Sherman was off like a shot, barreling past them in a combination of tumbling and falling that somehow coalesced into functional movement. He dashed along the metal grating, slamming into a trio of people clustered around the control box with his considerable height and roughly shoving them out of the way. Watson was right behind him, protecting Sherman from the pursuing carnies.

"The ankle bone's connected to the knee bone. The knee bone's connected to the skull bone. The skull bone's connected to the wing bone. The wing bone's connected to the goat head, and that's how chimeras are made."

"What the hell are you singing?" Watson asked. Around him, everyone Sherman had slipped past or knocked aside was gathering, all with worry and anger in their eyes. If they started to move, Watson wouldn't get to play it gently like at the bar. They were coming to deal some hurt; Watson would need to do the same.

"Rhymes help people keep information in order, Watson, it's the one of the first learning tools we're given as children. I just needed to remember exactly how all of... this... fit... together!"

At his last words, Sherman began to struggle, until finally jerking on something so hard that he fell back out of the console, mass of wires in his hand. Instantly, furious hands began to reach for him.

Then, a new sound took priority. Screeching could be heard from The Spin Doctor as brakes kicked in and the whirling mass of metal and guests finally started slowing down. All attention swung to helping people off and making sure they were okay, the babbling intruder momentarily forgotten by all but the man he'd arrived with.

Moving fast, hoping no one would have gotten a good enough look at them to make a description, Watson grabbed Sherman and began heading for the exit in a brisk, yet calm, manner. They needed to get clear before anyone started wondering who that weirdo that saved the day was.

"You seem bothered, Watson."

"A little, yeah. We're not supposed to stand out, remember? Disguises, blending in, all of that? Yet you left an impression that they're going to talk about for years to come."

To his surprise, Sherman suddenly halted in place, refusing to move another step. "If you're about to suggest that I should have ignored the cries for help when I knew it was in my power to give aid, then you can right well leave me here and now. I have tolerated your ineptitude for the job out of necessity, however I will *not* allow a man like that to wear the title of Watson. I am the world's greatest detective, that means I am duty-bound to help when needed. Make peace with that or get out of my sight."

It was quite possibly the most coherent statement Sherman had made since they met, and at the worst possible time. Whispers were rippling through the crowd, eyes searching for the mysterious helper who saved the day. Of all the times for Sherman to find a functioning train of thought, it had to be now.

"I'm not angry that you helped people in need. But you could have taken five seconds to tell me what was happening. Protecting you is my job, so if you'd stop doing things like running into danger, picking fights, and *planting your feet during an escape*, I wouldn't be so annoyed. You want to help people, fine? Just don't run off like that. Let me help you."

"Yes, Watson, you were a true help back there, taking their side and trying to convince me to back off. Without your aid, I can't imagine how I would have managed." Sherman was moving again, thankfully, although Watson noticed his movements were getting jerky.

They barely made it out of the area with rides before Sherman threw an arm around Watson's shoulders. "Rejoice, Watson, you'll get to be of actual use. My time is nearly done, and once the enhancement window closes, I'll need some rest to recover. Usually a good hour nap will do it. Until then, I'm afraid I'll be slightly less func—"

Sherman went near-limp without warning, his weight shifting heavily over to Watson, who propped his charge up without so much as a missed step. A quick glance at his watch showed that roughly five minutes had passed since Sherman activated his enhancement. While the effect wasn't exactly what Watson expected, he couldn't deny it got results.

The instant kernel calculation, the way he'd known exactly how to shut down The Spin Doctor, that version of Sherman was certainly more capable than the default one. He wasn't quite sure it was worth the tradeoff, however. While he was impressive during that five-minute run, Sherman was virtually useless the rest of the time. Assuming the scientists even could manage to reproduce the effects safely, every agent like Sherman would need a team of handlers, and at that point were the benefits still worthwhile?

On the other hand, so far as Watson knew, the window was an unexpected side effect. The real goal of whoever was cooking this drug presumably had to be a version that put people permanently in the enhancement window, or at least came with fewer drawbacks. Now *that* was a terrifying idea, and all the more reason to keep Sherman safe.

They made it back to the car with little incident; Sherman's insistence on disguises ended up quite the boon to their escape. Watson loaded him in carefully, clicking the seatbelt across Sherman's chest to keep him propped up. Making his way into the driver's seat, the bodyguard spared a moment to look over his charge for any signs of injury.

So far as he looked, the "world's greatest detective" was asleep, passed out in an almost peaceful manner, if one ignored the occasional snores that burst from Sherman's throat. Staring at him, Watson's mind flashed back to the carnival, the glare in Sherman's eye when he'd given Watson that ultimatum. Inadvertently, Watson's hands tightened on the wheel.

Who the hell did Sherman think he was? Did he have any *idea* the things Watson had done to keep this country and the people in it safe? So maybe, *maybe* sometimes he focused more on the job than outside distractions. That was how jobs got done. Block out everything else, keep your eye on the task, ignore the non-essential… like people screaming for help, apparently.

Looking back, Watson wasn't entirely sure at what point he'd become okay with that trade-off. It would be nice to say it was after The Incident, to lay one more thing at Poole's feet. Truthfully, though, Watson wasn't entirely sure that was true. Out there, in the field, the lines were muddier. It was hard to say exactly where right ended and wrong began.

But Watson had barely even considered those people in the moment, and Sherman noticed. Perhaps that was why it stung more than the usual barbs. This job was throwing Watson off; he was making mistakes that would never normally occur under his watch.

Only a few more days. A bit longer, and Sherman would be someone else's problem after which Watson could get back to doing real work.

Firing up the engine, he pointed them back toward the highway, more ready than ever to see a day finished.

13.

Tom and Jenny's original plan was to strike between the carnival and that night's hotel. Ambushing mid-freeway was expensive, flashy, and kicked up a lot of interest. Smaller roads, the sort one might have to take to visit the County Corn Carnival, were another matter. A downed tree or sudden hole didn't raise quite as much suspicion from the locals.

That *was* the plan, from the time their target entered the fair until Jenny let out an annoyed snort from her side of the car, typing away on her phone. "I can't tell if I'm more annoyed by betrayal when I see it coming, or when I don't. Looks like word finally went down. Despite us telling them upfront it would be a careful, slower-paced job, someone got antsy and put out a broader contract."

Tom's hands flexed against the leather of the steering wheel as he pushed back a wave of anger, forcing himself to stay clear-headed. "That's going to complicate things. How long ago did word go out?"

"From what I can tell? Looks like they've had some people on the back burner; this was their go signal. Assuming they receive the same intel, we should assume we've got competition from this evening on."

This new development put them at a crossroads. While the chance to grab Sherman on the backroads was tempting, it had also been something of a long shot, the sort of play they would set up but make the actual call in the moment if they thought it would work. Now they had to assume that – starting very soon – Watson would likely realize he had new tails on him. That could make him more cautious or call for backup. Of course, the incompetence of the others might also open up opportunities for Tom and Jenny. The one thing that couldn't happen, under any circumstances, was one of the others succeeding while this team was on the job. Their real payday depended on being the ones to make the grab.

"New idea." Tom fired up the car, wheels turning in his head. "Basically, the same as the old idea, but we do a much worse job of it. Let the less capable ones run our duo down and wear them out. Just have to make sure the target's guard is ready for an attack; can't risk someone else getting lucky."

"The competition will be mad if they find out." In spite of the warning, Jenny had a keen look of danger in her eyes. She loved this kind of play even more than he did. "How bad do we make it?"

"Competent, but hurried. The sort of believable mistakes a decent operative might make when crunched by time. We don't want him thinking they're being pursued by true idiots and completely letting his guard down." Tom headed toward the nearest hardware store, shopping list already in mind. It had been a while since he got to work with his hands, might make for a pleasant afternoon.

* * *

It was a testament to Watson's focus that, even after the mayhem of the carnival, he was still alert enough to catch the telltale signs of a waiting ambush. They were on one of the many smaller roads leading back to the highway, an out-of-the-way option Watson felt certain no one else would select. Either the attacker was reacting fast, or they'd correctly guessed Watson's route. They might also be laying traps along every road, only springing the one that got their prey, but that spoke to a large commitment of resources over a short time. While it was certainly possible, someone with that kind of backing could probably find a better move to make.

Tire prints in the mud near the road, shattered branches tucked almost out of view, the way something in his stomach said the woods were too quiet. Individually, all elements that were easy to explain away. Pity for the attacker: Watson long ago learned to trust his instincts, and he already had an idea of what trap was waiting.

In a situation like this, with heavy woods to either side of the roadway, the best option was to drop a tree down in the middle of the street. Then, when Watson stopped, they would drop another behind his car, locking him in place. Spike strips might be easier and faster, but they had the disadvantage of being obvious and out of place. Trees fell on their own – inconvenient yet true. Still, other drivers used this road, so the attackers would have to drop the log just as he approached.

Spotting the signs of impending attack early, Watson had two immediate options. He could either stop and back up – which would most likely alert the ambushers that he was onto them – or speed through.

Increasing speed was the safer, more practical choice, and had absolutely nothing to do with the juiced-up engine those scientists had tossed under the hood. Watson, a trained professional, had obviously not been waiting for just such an opportunity to cut loose and see how fast it could go. That would be his report, at least. Suddenly in a dangerous setting, he'd opted to take the more expedient method of escape available. If that also happened to be the raddest possible option, well, he liked to think of those as happy coincidences.

With one eye on the road, one on Sherman, and some third layer of shared vision scanning his surroundings, Watson pressed down on the gas. Instantly, he felt the convertible spring to greater life. Several days of tooling around the highway, keeping it constrained to blend in with traffic, all faded away as he tapped into the vehicle's true potential. Normally, vehicles escorting high-value targets were armored, mildly at minimum. Sherman's need for an open roof would have made such a feature pointless for this model, therefore speed and maneuverability had been emphasized instead. While the car wouldn't hold up for long under heavy fire, a skilled driver should be able to get them out of trouble.

Flashes of green whipped past as they moved even faster. Watson was surprised by how much pick-up the seemingly cumbersome vehicle had. Their speed reached a point where even Sherman mumbled something in his sleep, although what it might have been was lost to the wind roaring past their faces.

Had he not been on guard for it, Watson might have missed the giveaway. Sure enough, as he scanned ahead of them, there it was. A single log, leaned against a sapling, ready to "accidentally" fall in the road as soon as someone pushed it. Whoever had been on duty clearly wasn't prepared for a convertible to come racing past the ambush point.

Gratifying as the sight was, Watson didn't feel inclined to savor it, not even as he found his way to a more crowded road, settling in with the normal traffic. For one thing, there was no way to be sure that was the *only* trap awaiting them. From this point on, Watson was going to have to assume they were under attack at all possible moments. That would be hard enough on a normal escort job, let alone with Sherman in tow. Then again, that very well might not be his problem for much longer.

A trap confirmed one thing for sure: the plan to keep Sherman an unknown had failed. Somebody was after either him or Watson, and if they knew who Watson was then they would deduce Sherman to be a target of value. Either way, the initial idea had been blown. What came next would be up to the people who made Big decisions, but given that this was punishment, odds of Watson being peeled off were low.

He was allowed to dream, though. Especially with Sherman loudly snoring in the next seat.

* * *

Tom watched from a hidden spot in the woods as the car blazed past. Predicting the route hadn't been easy; in fact Jenny was set up half a mile away on a different road with another fake ambush. The effort had certainly proven worthwhile, thankfully. Now, the bodyguard knew something was up. On the one hand, that should have made things harder, since their target would be alerted. The trouble with that was, no one could stay alert forever.

With other teams now in the mix, Watson and Sherman would have to deal with multiple attacks. True, that risked someone else succeeding, but so far the duo had been smart and careful. Tom had faith they'd be able to endure at least a few kidnapping attempts. Each one would wear them down, and the need to be on constant watch would erode their concentration. Much as Tom disliked having interlopers working his gig, they did make a useful tool for softening up a target.

Grabbing his phone, he fired off a quick text to Jenny before starting the trek back to their car, stashed halfway between their respective stake-out spots. They'd be at least an hour behind their target once all was said and done, yet there was no feeling of concern. For right now, the others could take their swings. When they failed, his team would be ready to exploit any openings they created. And on the off chance one of them succeeded... well, their job was to kidnap the target. Nowhere in the agreement did it say who they had to kidnap him from. If anything, snatching him from a lesser crew might be easier than getting around that careful bodyguard.

All of that was in the future, potentials to be ready for. Today, he needed to focus on getting back to the car and on the road. Lagging behind a little was fine, under the circumstances, however he didn't want to miss the evening's festivities.

It shouldn't be too long now before the others were in position to start making moves.

14.

This was a tough phone. In his career, Watson had broken quite a few. Some on purpose, others as collateral damage, but either way, he had a respectable base of knowledge regarding the topic of cell phone durability. The fact that his current one hadn't snapped under his straining white knuckles spoke to just how well-crafted it was. To his credit, he was keeping what he considered to be a fairly cool head, under the circumstances.

"Paranoid?" He'd said the word twice already; the third iteration came out more as a curse than anything.

"You saw tire tracks and a log in the woods," Gwendolyn replied. "Because of *that*, you want me to scrap our entire transport plan, marshal additional resources, and make this into a big production."

Watson paced around the hotel room, keeping an ear on the shower where Sherman was cleaning up. Or maybe he was building a toilet bomb for all Watson knew, and cared, in this particular moment. "You can't be serious. I know what an ambush looks like. How many have I seen, or set, just on *your* operations?"

A beat of silence, then a tired sigh. "What do you want me to tell you? Even a year ago, this report might have carried some weight, but lately you see traps and traitors everywhere. I'm working hard to keep you in, and every time you make one of these false flare-ups, that job gets a little more impossible. Maybe it would be different if your asset could confirm the story – *maybe* – although with his issues, I'm not sure even that would be enough."

Muffled noises came from the other side of the receiver, a sound Watson recognized as someone getting close to the phone so that no one else could overhear.

"Listen, this job is important to some major players, so if you are absolutely sure the operation has been compromised, I'll make the report. But if you're wrong, that's it. This is already penance; if you mess it up, I can't protect you. My advice is to wait until you have something more substantial."

Hours ago, Watson would have sworn on his life that they'd been made. But Gwendolyn's words gave him pause. What had he seen, really?

Logs and tire tracks, that was all. Maybe an ambush, *probably* an ambush, yet was he sure? Watson wasn't dumb; he understood that since The Incident he'd become warier. The idea that he couldn't trust his own intuition anymore – *that*, more than anything else, scared him. He wanted to be right, despite what that would mean for him and Sherman. But when put in the crosshairs, Watson found he wasn't confident enough in himself to make the gamble.

"Let me sleep on it for now. In the morning, I might think of a new detail or figure out how to get you some proof. Can I at least request extra security at our lodgings? Even just a few black-and-whites patrolling the area would give me something to work with in a pinch."

"I'll put in some reports of vandals in the respective areas, make sure they up patrol without telling them why. It *should* go without saying, but make sure to keep civilians, even law enforcement, out of this as much as possible. They don't have the kinds of clearances to know what's going on."

"Clearance might not matter much as soon as they're around Sherman. He's not exactly the discreet type." At Watson's words, the shower turned off, his signal to wrap up the call. "But yes, I'm not planning on dragging cops into this unless absolutely necessary. I just want a little extra cover on the off chance I'm not being 'paranoid'."

"Act as snippy as you want. You're being treated the way your behavior has determined you should be. Want different treatment? Try different behavior." The line went dead with no more than that, one final chiding from Gwendolyn as a parting gift.

Carefully, aware that he only had so many spares, Watson set the cell phone down on a simple wooden dresser. Their room, and the hotel as a whole, had a deeply rural theme. A field of corn was painted on one wall, dotted with cows and sheep near the edge. All of the furniture was wooden and rustic, the sort of faux-rough look that evoked ideas of simplicity. Even the name was on-brand: The Hayloft Hotel, with a big red barn on the front sign. Staring at the room as a whole, Watson found it easier to release his dying rage. Fuming in a place so cartoonish just made him feel ridiculous.

The bathroom door flew open to reveal a newly energized Sherman. He was back in his usual ensemble—jeans, shirt, oversized coat, and the hat matting what was clearly still-wet hair against his head. In a way, after the weirdness of the afternoon, it was almost comforting. For a terrible instant, Watson realized he might be getting used to the regular version of Sherman.

"Watson! Send my regards to the pipe-gnomes. The water pressure here is truly outstanding. They have permission to dance under the berry moon tonight."

Well, that more or less dissuaded any notion that there was a "regular" version of Sherman, although Watson did notice he wasn't quite so put off by the bizarre orders. "I'll pass on word to the staff that you were satisfied. Any preference on dinner tonight? No restaurant here, plus after yesterday and our afternoon, I thought delivery was the easier option. Got a new food you've been eager to try?"

It was supposed to be a simple question, yet Sherman sat down on his bed heavily, rubbing his chin as if there was a beard to stroke. "The dilemma of sustenance. While I have been reading about many different kinds of cuisine, one dish keeps recurring frequently in many books, shows, and podcasts. Apparently, a great many people hold deep reverence for this pizza, and I confess my curiosity has been piqued."

Oh, wow. Watson somehow hadn't taken the time to consider it, but a total lack of food memory did mean Sherman would have no reference point for pizza. Initially, he'd planned to just grab something from the nearest chain, however this changed things up a little. It wouldn't hurt to do a little online research and find out which nearby spot had the best reviews. Since it was going to effectively be Sherman's first bite of pizza, Watson felt he should at least make it a good one. Despite their harsh words near the end of the day, Sherman had helped saved people in trouble. If there was any behavior to reward, that was definitely it. One day, if he ever got full control, Sherman might be capable of truly terrifying things. Better to condition him early and often toward decency.

Strangely, Watson realized even as he picked his phone back up that it was a minor concern. Sherman was brash, rude, and often incomprehensible, but so far, he'd never actually been cruel. Hell, the only way he'd used his enhancement window was to stick up for some kid and help save a bunch of strangers. And analyze a jar of corn, Watson recalled, although that had taken a quick second place once Sherman found trouble.

If Sherman were in control of himself, he might be a decent guy. As it stood, Watson took comfort in knowing that the worst parts of his personality were, most likely, involuntary. Under it all, he seemed to have a good heart. For everyone's sake, Watson hoped it stayed that way.

"Pizza is a definite good call. It's available all over, and virtually every place delivers. Let me do some research for a good spot, then I'll get us a spread. We'll say a pepperoni, a cheese, and a veggie, just to give you the basics."

"I have also heard much debate about the existence of a Hawaiian pizza. Many people have strong opinions on whether it is good or bad. As the world's greatest detective, I shall put it to bed at last," Sherman declared.

Watson paused his thumb mid-typing, glancing up to Sherman. "What is it that you think detectives do, exactly? Because you've been putting a lot of stuff under that umbrella."

"Detectives solve mysteries, seek justice, and help those in need. Obviously, determining whether the pizza is delicious or not will solve the mystery of pineapple as a topping. Do try and keep up a little, Watson."

"I'll try to do better," Watson replied. "Okay, so that's a pepperoni, a cheese, a veggie, and, of course, the Hawaiian. We'll need to find a place that splits up the toppings or makes tiny options, otherwise we'll have way too much food." Turning his attention to the practical issues, rather than worrying about whether or not he'd really seen an ambush, helped Watson keep a clear head. Until this was over, he had to learn to live with a little insanity.

At least it came with decent meals.

* * *

The delivery driver for Give Me Amore had just finished loading the order into his car when he felt the cold press of metal against his back. With an annoyed grunt, he held up his hands. "You're supposed to wait until I've traded the pizzas for cash. Is this your first time robbing a driver? Going to have to step up that game. We see better than this from half-scared newbies."

"I'm neither scared, nor new." As the female voice spoke, the driver felt the pinch of the needle entering his neck. The warmth flooding his veins, then his brain, made continued talking more effort than he could muster. He slid gently down to the ground, caught near the end by a pair of surprisingly strong arms.

Had he turned around and seen her face, she might have felt the need to kill him, but he'd kept his eyes forward the whole time. At this point, murder would just be adding more work to her plate, what with bodily disposal and cleaning. The drugs would keep him loopy for hours. By the time he came around, she'd already be done – and in less than a day since getting the job. She might even set a personal best, if she hurried.

Working methodically, she dragged the delivery man around to the side of the building and stripped off his uniform. It would wear big on her – she kept a lean frame, prioritizing speed over brute force – but the illusion had to last just long enough for a door to be opened. Pants and shirts went on quick. Normally, she would toss the name tag aside, however this one bore the name "Andy." Since it worked across all genders, one more component to sell the lie was welcomed into her ensemble.

Redressed, the new Andy stepped out from the side of the building. She paused, walked over to her car, and pulled out a thick blanket. While a job was a job, seeing someone exposed to the elements struck a tad too close to home. Tossing it onto the drugged-up driver, Andy got into the car without so much as a glance at the directions.

She knew precisely where she was headed.

15.

Watson was prepared. Weapons hidden throughout the room, including several within easy reach. A mattress was propped up near the door, a quick hidey hole to duck into if someone opened fire. The mattress wouldn't be enough to fully stop some rounds, however anything with a spray, like a shotgun, would be halted. Best he could do on short notice, and the superior plan was not to let such an incident occur. That might be out of his hands, unfortunately. How this exchange played out would be dictated by the intruder coming to their room.

If nothing else, at least Sherman had gone into the bathroom. It had taken some convincing, especially to leave the shower running, but he'd finally agreed. An unknown element coming to their room was bad enough; Watson could hardly risk exposing the asset.

When the knock came, his hands flexed involuntarily. The afternoon had definitely gotten to Watson; even now he could tell he was going overboard. Such was the trouble with paranoia: even knowing you were probably wrong didn't lessen the need to take precautions. Still, Watson worked to keep a neutral expression on his face as he opened the door.

"Hello! Give Me Amore Pizza, Pasta, and Seafood here with three pizzas for Mister Doyle."

Wordlessly, Watson handed over the cash, cost of food plus a generous tip. The woman – Andy, according to her name tag – counted the bills twice, messing up halfway through the first time. When she reached for change, Watson shook his head.

"All for you."

Not saying anything more, he shut the door, locked it, and shoved the mattress completely flush with the knob, so it fully blocked the doorway.

Seconds later, Sherman came bursting out of the bathroom, on a crash course with dinner. Instantly, Watson blocked his path, holding up a hand for him to wait.

Methodically, Watson replayed the interaction in his mind. Sorting the truth from the details his brain wouldn't stop screaming about wasn't an easy task, but it had been essential for him to keep working in the field.

And Watson did *whatever* was essential. Yet, for all the drawbacks of his endless suspicion, there was at least one tangible benefit.

Being paranoid meant that when someone did make a move, Watson caught the signs.

Flipping over the first box, he ran his fingers along the cardboard, checking for any incendiaries. They needed Sherman alive, so bombs were a long shot, but that was definitely not a surprise he wanted to miss. As he checked, Watson quickly explained the situation to Sherman.

"These are probably poisoned. That delivery woman didn't quite fit in her uniform. Add in the barest hint of an accent, the way she shifted her weight when I leaned in with the money… Just take my word for it, something was off. She didn't try to force her way in, so smart money says she's waiting until these zonk us out before coming in for the extraction."

To Watson's shock, Sherman didn't fight him. Instead, he merely nodded excitedly, causing that ridiculous hat to bob atop his head. "Quite an eye for detail, Watson. You may just have the makings of a detective in you. Tell me, what course of action do you suggest?"

The words alone were enough to bring Watson up short. "Hang on, did you just ask me for input on something? Me, the dumb, terrible Watson?"

"Cease being so dramatic. Just because you are a terrible Watson does not mean I am incapable of seeing the other skills you possess. Between the two of us, you are undoubtedly the more experienced in attempted kidnapping scenarios. Until my own expertise catches up, you offer the greater chance of survival."

If he really picked that all apart, Watson felt he might just find a compliment buried somewhere within. Fun as it might be, they had much larger issues to deal with at the moment. Going by what he would do in the same situation, Watson estimated they had around five to ten minutes, at most, before she tried to collect her prize. Against a simple motel door, one breaching round could easily destroy the lock, and she'd knock the mattress over when she came charging in.

The sole advantage they had was that Watson had seen the trap coming. Assuming she was smart – and her approach had been so far – she wasn't going to assume success. Andy would come in ready for a counterattack. Luring her into a false sense of success was the best option.

"Sherman, grab those spare pillows from the closet. I've got a plan."

In earnestness, it was more half-cobbled strategy and wishful thinking, but in the field, Watson counted those as plans.

Working fast, Watson yanked off the pants and shoes he'd been wearing, jamming the spare pillow down the legs. He laid the trousers down between the double beds, as though he'd managed a perfect field goal when collapsing. There was barely enough time to open the top pizza box and throw a few slices in the trash, along with donning new pants—their time was running short.

Surveying the room, Watson felt confident they'd set a good stage. It sure looked like they'd dug into the first box and dropped hard within minutes. But props didn't sell a production; for that, they would need an actor. Since Watson had to do the actual ambushing, that left one option.

"Sherman, I need you to lie on the ground, still, like you're passed out." Watson pointed to an area not far from his own fake legs, one purposely clear of debris.

"Then we have a dilemma, I am afraid. Stillness is not my strength, as you well know, and I highly doubt I would be capable of such a performance under the best of circumstances. Amidst the chaos of an intruder, there is virtually no chance I would capable of selling such a ruse. Yet I do agree that your plan holds merit, Watson, and I will not be the one to cause its failure."

An interesting ending, seeing as Sherman sure sounded like he was turning it down. "So, what's your solution?"

The condescending look shot in Watson's direction was a nice reminder that, cooperative or not, Sherman was the same man he'd been riding with this whole time. "Quite obvious, do you not think? If the plan relies on my appearing to be drugged, and I am incapable of pretending, then the simplest solution is to not pretend."

In a movement faster than Watson was ready for, Sherman grabbed a slice of pepperoni, jammed half of it in his mouth, then gave a dangerously low number of chews before swallowing. All Watson could do was watch in mute shock as the person he was supposed to be protecting put unknown chemicals into his body.

"Not sure if it's the poison or the pepperoni, but I can see why people were so keen on this dish." Sherman appraised the food once more as he went in for a smaller, more savored, bite.

At this point, it was more on Watson for being surprised than it was on Sherman for acting erratically. He had to keep Sherman alive, but all the same... Well, it was done now, there was no yanking the pizza out of his stomach. If that was their situation, might as well make the most of it.

"Don't eat much more of that, we don't know how strong it. And lay down in your spot. We don't want you falling when it hits."

Sherman complied, although he also brought his slice to the ground with him. Much as Watson wanted to object, it added an air of authenticity to the scene. Not to mention, he had far more pressing matters to deal with. They didn't have long left; Andy should be coming by to collect them any moment.

* * *

While many in her industry liked to enter with a bang, Andy was one for more subtle tactics. Yes, the right ammo would make short work out of a motel lock, but the same could be said for a competent hand with a set of lock-picks. This method did, admittedly, come with a higher risk if her targets hadn't yet been poisoned; however, it also didn't demand entering with a bang that might wake them.

Listening at the door, she heard nothing. Moving quietly, she pulled the picks from her pocket and went to work. In under a minute, the lock was open, and with the benefit of not alerting everyone in the building that a kidnapping was about to go down. Pushing gently, she felt the door stop without warning. Cautiously, Andy peeked through the sliver of an opening she'd created. What greeted her eyes was the faded white of an old mattress.

The bodyguard wasn't completely incompetent; he'd blocked off the door. Smart move, just not as effective once one was unconscious. Waiting a tad longer, listening for any sounds other than steady breathing, she decided that there was no moving forward without risk. From her boot, she produced a small gun – a purposefully chosen low-caliber, just in case a bullet found its way into the target. While that certainly wasn't the plan, shootouts could be unpredictable.

In one motion, Andy slammed a shoulder into the door, knocking over the mattress as she came barreling inside. It thudded against the floor, nearly clipping the sprawled-out form of Sherman, her soon-to-be prisoner. A slice of pepperoni still rested only inches from his mouth, nearly finished. Impressive; she'd laced the food with enough chemicals to put down the average person after a single bite.

Behind him, largely concealed by the double beds, a pair of pants stuck out. Tempting as it might be to assume she'd succeeded, Andy instead crept forward. She would call it a success only when she saw the bodyguard down with her own eyes. She crept along, gun at the ready, drawing steadily closer.

Just when Andy was about to peer over the lip of the bed, she felt a strong hand grab her left arm, the one holding the gun, while at the same time cold metal touched the back of her head briefly. Crap, he wasn't even holding it close enough for her to snatch. This guy definitely was no amateur.

"Didn't think the decoy would really work, just needed you distracted enough to sneak up behind." Watson's voice rang as he gave her arm one good shake, her warning to let the gun drop. "Next time, check for rear exits. A smart enemy will use them to get the drop on you."

"I did. This is the third floor, and there's nothing to climb down." It was a sheer building with what looked like nothing more than cheap siding along the surface. Had this guy really managed to scale down it in so little time?

Another shake of her arm, this one noticeably firmer. He was getting impatient. "That's my other piece of advice. Pick an easier target, if you do more jobs. You're not ready to play in my league yet."

That was it. Whether he got the drop on her or not, she was a professional. Andy would ensure this punk understood exactly what that entailed. Her entire body went limp as she turned to dead weight, falling faster then he'd be able to adjust the aim of his gun. She tried to turn her own weapon with the force of the fall, angling back in Watson's direction, but his grip was too strong. The moment her back touched the ground, Andy prepared to swing her legs up in a kick. If she could force him to let go, get a little distance, this could be a proper fight once more.

Unfortunately, no sooner had Andy landed than Sherman sprang to life, throwing himself atop her. As she struggled, she became aware of something hot and gooey only inches from her face. There wasn't even time to scream before the item was shoved into her mouth. Andy refused to chew, yet her own cunning betrayed her. She'd chosen a concoction that didn't even need to be swallowed; touching the inside of the mouth was enough to let the toxin into the bloodstream.

From Watson's perspective, he merely saw Sherman jump into the fray and jam the rest of his slice into Andy's maw. Seconds after that, her struggling halted as a dazed, vacant expression filled her eyes. Watson looked from Sherman to Andy, then to the pizza, trying to put it all together.

"Her drugs wear off that fast?"

"Unlikely. The more viable explanation is that my altered brain chemistry does not process outside forces the same way as most people. I did feel an unexpected quiet in my body, a sense of floating, however my mind remained roughly as active as usual. To be frank, if she hadn't struck when she did, I might have broken into movement soon. Even with the drugs, that was an ordeal."

Whatever tolerance Sherman had, it didn't apply to Andy, whose pupils had begun to dilate noticeably. Watson could kill her, technically. She'd knowingly tried to kidnap someone from government custody, and given that she'd walked in with a gun, no one would know she hadn't been killed in self-defense. Well, the official report would contain the truth, but he suspected those were burned as soon as they were written.

Tempting as it might have been, Andy had come in carefully. No needless shots, no putting civilians at risk: a quick and concise plan meant for safe extraction. She was a criminal, not a monster, and the justice system was designed for people like that. Eventually. Right now, she was the first lead Watson had found, and he was eager to get some information.

"Sherman, help me tie her up and load her into the car. This location is obviously compromised so we need to go, and I would love to learn more from this nice delivery driver once she comes to."

Just as Watson leaned forward to take her arm, a gunshot rang out. On the nearby dresser, their television exploded, sending both him and Sherman diving to the ground.

It seemed that poisoned pizza was only the beginning of their night.

16.

A sniper was *bad*. For one thing, snipers were like roaches: if you saw one then there were more lurking around. Assuming they were competent, of course, although based on that shot, Watson worried he might be giving them too much credit. Firing into a room when there was a target to recover was poor form, no matter how sure the shooter was in their aim. That pizza woman had come in smart, attacking with a plan. Didn't mean everyone after them would try the same tactics.

"Sherman, strip the sheets off the bed."

Grabbing the poisoned woman's heel, Watson dragged her across the ground, sandwiching her in between the beds where his false legs were still lying. She hadn't come in shooting, so leaving Andy to the mercy of snipers didn't sit right in his gut. There was a certain amount of professional courtesy one had to observe in these jobs.

Of course, he did still rifle through her pockets as he moved her. No identification, which he'd expected from someone this good. Keys, although to what, he didn't know. Could be a car – she may have driven here, which might be useful if their own ride had been compromised. There should have been an alert sent to Watson's phone if the vehicle was touched or tampered with, but he wasn't in the mood to take anything on faith.

Aside from the keys, all he found was a piece of paper with their motel room and address scrawled across the top, along with a phone number Watson didn't recognize. Maybe they'd just gotten a clue from Andy after all. That would have to wait for later. Their primary concern was getting clear from this room. As things stood, they were pinned down, positions revealed, with no open routes. Even scaling the back of the building was out; Sherman couldn't be expected to manage that. Besides, there might be more snipers on that location by now.

Front door it was, then. Reaching forward, keeping as low as possible, Watson inched along the dirty carpet until his fingers gripped a section of door. Shoving as well as the angle would allow, he moved the door closer to the frame. Another bullet burst through near the top, partially moving it back open, but Watson was already prepared. He caught the door on the rebound, shoving it again, this time all the way to the latch.

It wasn't going to stop anyone determined, but at least they didn't have an open view to shoot through anymore. That would give him and Sherman time to move. Yanking his phone from his pocket, Watson began to dial.

"Hey Sherman, any chance that brilliant mind of yours can see materials for an impromptu fire? Preferably something that will burn in the tub."

"They are already in my hands," Sherman replied. He held up the sheets, but since he was also crouched, the armful of linens barely cleared the top of the bed.

"We're actually going to need those for something else. Keep looking."

Much as Watson wanted to dial Gwendolyn and rub this all in her face, survival came before gloating, as personal policy. Instead, he punched in 9-1-1, though he didn't connect the call just yet. Best to make sure they could set a fire before reporting one.

A soft thump jerked his eyes from the phone. Sherman was still low, grabbing pillows off the bed and tossing them over in Watson's direction. "Based on materials, quality, and their general odor, I presume these will all burn nicely."

Odor? Watson gave the pillow a test sniff but got nothing aside from the motel's cheap detergent. Probably not the time to dig into that. Fabric and stuffing would do just fine for his purposes. They needed to get ready, however. Once the sirens came, that was their shot. If they missed it, they were going to be stuck, and in danger of choking to death on smoke.

"Bring me anything you need to take. I'll stow everything non-replaceable; the clothes we brought up aren't worth the effort of hauling. Then wrap the sheet tightly around yourself, especially the head. On my signal, we run like hell. Whatever happens, Sherman, do not let them see your face."

"Your point is made, Watson. No need for theatrics. Next you'll say my very life depends on me not revealing my face."

"No," Watson corrected. "*My* life depends on you not showing yourself. They only need one of us alive. If they can tell which one is which, they'll pick me off then scoop you up once your protection is gone."

Sherman's face pinched, he seemed to sift through those words more carefully than most. "Could they not just fire into our legs as we escape?"

"Sheets will also make it harder to track our limbs, assuming they're sure enough to take that kind of shot at all. One stray bullet and you become worthless to them. Besides, I'm getting us a distraction." Watson grabbed the mound of pillows and took out a flask from inside one of his bags. Although not an especially hard drinker, sometimes the nightmares needed persuading to leave. Dumping the vodka onto the pillows, he moved them about, getting the best coverage possible.

Still low, he dragged the booze-soaked lot into the bathroom, tossed it all into the tub, and then struck a match. He punched the "Call" button on his phone just as the flames began to spread.

Sherman crouched in the doorway, observing the indoor bonfire carefully. "Pillows burn well. A fact I shall keep in mind."

Even Watson had to agree; these things were roasting much faster, and smokier, than he'd expected. As the call connected, his voice changed, becoming frantic and uncertain. "Hi! Yes, um, I'm sorry, I've never called emergency services before, not sure this qualifies, but I'm at a motel on the interstate and there's smoke coming out of a room. A lot of smoke. Uh huh."

Watson paused after giving the operator their address, covering the receiver as he looked over a shoulder to Sherman. "Hurry up and grab the sheets. We've got a few minutes at most before we have to move."

"Quite true," Sherman agreed. "I am curious to see if our distraction will arrive before the entire room fills with smoke."

Although Watson wouldn't say it, he'd been thinking the same thing. "Oh wow, I just saw flames through a window! You folks might want to hurry." With that, he ended the call. They had the address and the emergency; they'd be here soon. Until then, Watson had hurrying of his own to do.

* * *

The needle went in smoothly. Seconds later, the sniper lying in wait near the target's car slipped gently off to dreamland. Jenny checked the man's airway and breathing for any signs of a reaction. Just because they didn't want someone else to get the prize didn't mean they were going to kill him over it. Making sure these idiots didn't accidentally shoot the target's head off before anyone could collect on the bounty was in the common good, as she and Tom saw it.

"Can we get to any others?" Jenny flipped the sleeping fellow over, emptying his gun and pockets. No sense in not bolstering their own supplies while the chance was there.

"Perhaps, but I doubt it." Tom tilted his head, listening. "You can just make out sirens in the distance."

Based on the motel's distance from the local fire and police stations, one of many countless tidbits they'd looked over in prep for this job, that gave them less than five minutes until some manner of authority figure was on the scene. "Guess that means you don't want to grab them at the car?"

"Tempting. Very tempting," Tom admitted. "But after all this, they're going to come out with frayed nerves, aware of even the wind shifting. No chance we'll get the drop on them, and I don't want to deal with that bodyguard head on. If we can keep a gentle tail, we'll grab them when they stop for rest."

"And what if that bodyguard drives straight from here to the nearest secure facility?"

That was a reasonable point to ponder, given the events of the night. Plans would have to change from here on out. Even if they didn't hole up in some safe house, the way these idiots had all blundered in at once made it clear the target's location was compromised. Anyone with half a brain would throw out the old plan, assume there was a leak, and change things up. From here on out, they couldn't be sure where the duo was heading or stopping.

"We have to chance it," Tom ultimately replied. "Unless you've got a way to surprise them, I can't see an approach that's worth the risk. Getting shot won't help us collect, so my vote is we keep playing it smart. Plenty of others are handling the direct approach for us."

"I can't see a safe tactic here either, so I guess that makes me a ditto." Jenny finished checking over the unconscious man's effects, yanking out a card that was punched to ribbons. "On the plus side, looks like somebody is getting a free frozen yogurt."

Tom sighed, keeping it quiet and contained just to be on the safe side. "Is that necessary?"

"Free froyo is the cheapest way he can pay for my services," Jenny shot back. "After all, I just gave this gentleman a very good lesson in the importance of paying attention to his surroundings."

* * *

The biggest problem was Andy. Initially, Watson was planning to leave her, perhaps more in plain view so the firefighters would see her right away. Given her low position and the short time they expected her to be unattended, it was a minor risk. But that was before the pillows started smoking like a 1950s diner. Whatever they were made of, it was sending dark, acrid smoke up, the kind Watson wasn't quite so sure wouldn't have lasting effects.

Were it down to a life-or-death choice, Watson would have left her behind without a glance over his shoulder. They weren't quite that far in yet, and there was professional courtesy to consider. In the end, they grabbed a mattress sheet, wound it around Andy as best they could, then split the load of carrying her between them, Watson on shoulders with Sherman on legs.

While Watson alone could have handled it alone, doing so would have marked him as the bodyguard. They stood like that, covered in sheets by the door, holding an unconscious woman, as the room filled with more and more smoke. At last, sirens flooded the air, followed shortly by a shrill buzzing that sounded all through the motel. People began stumbling out of their doors in various states of wakefulness and dress, most deeply confused about what had awoken them.

That was the signal Watson was waiting for. With practiced speed, he yanked open the door, leading himself and Sherman out of the room, Andy gripped between them. It was a curious sight for the normal motel residents; however, this was generally not the sort of place one went to ask questions. True, the police might be curious about a pair of sheeted figures carrying a third, so Watson intended to be long gone before that happened. Every move, every step, was as fast as he dared move.

At least they'd made it ten steps from the door without getting blown open. Between the normal people, the arriving cops, and the inability to tell which person was the target, Watson had made the equation too complex. That didn't mean they were in the clear by any means, but it did feel good to have cover again as the crowd pressed around them on the stairwell.

Hurrying, they ran down to the bottom before pausing to gently lower Andy into a small alcove. She would be out of the way from fleeing patrons and the first thing firefighters saw when they came through in a minute or two. Not the safest place in the world, but she *was* a kidnapper, so this would do.

With her gone, that only left them a sprint back to the car. Well, it was a sprint for Sherman – less so for Watson, who easily matched his pace. Sherman turned out to be a fairly decent sprinter, his long legs and lithe frame helping support his underdeveloped cardiovascular system. By the time they made it to the convertible he was panting audibly, yet neither had suddenly discovered bullet holes in their body, which made it a success.

Giving the phone one last check, Watson said a silent prayer of hope that Gregson's people were as good as they thought. They had no time to stop and scout; if the car was rigged, they were screwed. Much as Watson loathed betting so much on the word of others, in this case he had no choice.

They dove into the convertible, staying low as Watson fired up the engine and slammed them into drive. Tires squealed in an unintended peel-out before finally catching, jerking the car forward before settling into its usual smooth motion.

Yanking down his impromptu ghost outfit, Watson scanned as he drove out of the motel parking lot, keeping a close eye out for any potential threats. After a poisoner and a sniper, he was expecting anything up to and including Bigfoot to come charging at them. The roar of sirens started to fade as they got back on the highway, quickly putting distance between themselves and the motel.

Unwinding the sheet from his body, Watson took a long breath, the first since that shot rang out. No question about it now: their cover was blown. Somebody knew who Sherman was, and they wanted him. If nothing else, the police reports and fire, along with however much Sherman's testimony counted for, would back up his earlier reports that they were in danger. Hectic as the night has been, it might just be worth it for the chance to shove all this back in Gwendolyn's face.

"Watson, from the gleam in your eye you seem to be celebrating; however, there is a dark shape quickly catching up to us."

As if on cue, bright lights flared behind them. Watson had just enough time to wonder how they'd given themselves away before the sound of a cranking engine reached his ears. How Sherman had seen that shape with so little light was its own mystery, one that was of far less importance than the problem behind them.

The pursuing vehicle was a huge, black truck on wheels that couldn't possibly have been factory issue. Not quite a monster truck, but certainly more than any commuter could possibly need. This was a vehicle for battle. Specifically, battle on the road.

"Sherman, you should probably buckle your seatbelt." Watson followed his own advice, clicking the belt into place before checking the truck again in his rearview. Definitely gaining, and fast. But it wasn't like they'd been showing everything this baby could do.

On a near empty highway in the dead of night, Watson slammed the gas down and braced for things to get crazy.

17.

Open highway, no route in mind, little chance of backup, being actively pursued by a team they had to assume was working with superior firepower. Not the worst chase Watson had been involved in, but also not a candidate for the top five easiest. He tossed his phone over into Sherman's hands.

"We need to find somewhere to go. Preferably a large police station, the sort they wouldn't try to assault directly. If we can hunker down, I'll get us reinforcements."

"Hmm. An interesting hypothesis." Sherman was typing as he spoke, which was an unexpectedly productive swing. "Five more miles, then you shall see an exit for a farm road. No one will be expecting you to use that one, but if you're open to some creative driving, we can cut a fairly direct route."

Without question, Watson knew that Sherman was leading him somewhere strange. He strained to glance at the phone's screen, which was quickly tilted away. They had no choice. He was going to have to follow Sherman's directions and cross his fingers this was one of those less-crazy moments. Sherman didn't seem like he wanted to be killed or capture, so if nothing else, Watson knew he wouldn't intentionally steer them wrong.

That thought should have been more comforting than it was.

Their situation wasn't improved by the bright lights staying on their tail. No matter how the convertible moved, that huge truck kept on them. They could hear the roaring of the engine too well now; it almost sounded like there might be more than one tucked away inside that stalking vehicle. Whatever they'd done, it probably destroyed that thing's gas mileage – a small comfort to Watson as he continually failed to lose their pursuer. He did still have some options, but he was holding on to them for now.

Getting a lead in this situation wasn't especially useful. With flat, open road, they'd easily be able to track any movements Watson's car made. If he couldn't outrun them with just gas and driving, then he needed to wait until pulling away would mean something, or until they got desperate and did more than follow, necessitating escape. In his younger, more impulsive days, Watson would have felt uncomfortable going this long with an obvious threat and no engagement. That was before he'd learned the value of patience, and in picking the right time to strike.

In no time, five miles had passed. Watson saw the sign for the exit and waited as long as possible to make the swerve, diving for the off-ramp and hoping dearly that the truck would be going too fast to follow. Unfortunately, whoever was on their wheel had skill, as the cumbersome beast lost a sideview mirror on a guardrail but otherwise made it off the highway unscathed.

Although it had been hoping for a lot, Watson was still somewhat disappointed to see their move not shake the truck. Worse, they were now on a barely-paved road with fields on their right, plenty of places they could be knocked off the road or into a ditch.

From behind, the truck roared, as if it were having the exact same thought.

"After one more side road, you'll take a sharp right," Sherman informed him.

"Wait, so right at the next road?"

"Use your ears, Watson. I said *after* the next road. You will not be turning onto a street."

Just as Watson was about to ask what the hell that meant, they passed the road in question. Up ahead, Watson could see what looked like a mound of dirt and some warning signs. Of course, of course – Sherman led them to a dead end. At this point, their only choices were stop, plow into the block, or turn into a field full of corn.

With an unspoken apology to the poor farmer whose next morning they were about the ruin, Watson spun the wheel and took them into the fields. Instantly, visibility turned to nothing as they thudded through stalk after stalk of corn, all of them slapping across the windshield. They drove in deeply, then slowed to a near crawl to see what would happen next.

On the road, they heard the truck rolling to a stop. Their pursuers hadn't seen this move coming and were halting to figure out what to do next. Unhappy as Watson was with their situation, it was the first hiccup they'd caused the truck so far. Not that it would help, if this was as far as Sherman's plan went.

"This isn't a police station."

"Truly Watson, your deduction grows by leaps and bounds daily." Sherman tossed the phone back over into Watson's lap. "Your plan was a poor one. We would once again be trapped, perhaps endangering innocent officers in the crossfire. I devised a method more suited to your skillset, without drawing in anyone else."

Knowing he would regret it, Watson still found himself asking the next logical question. "Is there more in mind for this than driving around a corn field?"

"Of course. I am the world's greatest detective. I have an excellent plan, although I should offer caution, as it places the majority of the risk and danger on you, Watson."

"Just tell me what you're thinking." Watson glanced back once more to the truck, which was already turning to give chase. "At this point, I'm fairly open to ideas."

As it turned out, Watson was right. He definitely regretted asking for the rest of the plan.

* * *

Thick, scarred knuckles gripped the leather of the truck's wheel. Despite its rough appearance, the inside had surprisingly nice features. Originally, before being stolen and repurposed, the vehicle had belonged to someone with a taste for comfort and luxury. It meant more room in the cab for weapons, bullets, and other accoutrements suited to the job.

This one he had to be careful with, unfortunately. No pay unless the target was alive, with an undamaged brain. If not for that, he could have run them off the road miles ago, or broken out one of his louder toys.

Idling in the field, that blue convertible waited. They were up to something – probably hoping to lose him in the coverage. Stained teeth appeared as his smile stretched wide. This was perfect. Out here, off the highway, he could take out their wheels or engine. Once they were stuck, he could pick off the bodyguard then grab the prize.

From the passenger seat, he pulled a rifle into position. Punching through a spinning tire required serious stopping power, more than he'd dare hope for with a pistol or shotgun.

With a rev of the engine, he gunned the machine forward, diving into the endless stalks of corn shooting up from the ground. No sooner was he moving than the convertible spun its wheels, flying into motion, shooting off to the left. Those thick knuckles kept a tight rein on the wheel, following the prey as it darted off.

The convertible turned, suddenly jerking to the right, but the truck's weight and all-wheel drive kept it rooted while driving roughly the same path. Smaller car meant more maneuverability, but that wouldn't be enough to make up the difference – not so long as he stayed on its bumper.

Swerving around, whipping wildly about, the convertible continued careening through the corn, never quite going too fast, yet swerving enough to make a difficult target. Sometimes, it would slow down tremendously, almost luring him into taking a shot, before bursting forward in a fit of speed. On the third rotation, he realized they were driving in a circle. Well, square was more honest given the roughness of their angles, but the point remained. The car wasn't trying to escape after all, so what was it up to?

Drumming those heavy hands on the wheel, his eyes drifted over to the display on his dashboard. The *gas*. Clever. They were stopping and starting, making lots of turns, purposely working to drain his tank and take advantage of their better mileage. If they could run him to empty, they'd have a clean shot out at escape, assuming their own fuel supply held. That changed things. He was going to have to start taking some riskier shots. True, it came with the slim chance of going wild and ruining his payday, but at least he'd have the satisfaction of not letting them get away.

Chipped nails ran along the rifle, making sure the setup was ready and comfortable. Once he got close enough, the shots would all be one-handed, using his open driver's window as a rest for the barrel. Although hardly precise, this method would send the bullets in the general direction he wanted. For now, that would do.

In all his attentiveness, he missed the figure creeping through the shadows, slowly, quietly slipping into the bed of his truck. The figure had just settled when the rifle adjusting was done, narrowly missing being thrown into the truck's gate as the whole vehicle burst forward in pursuit. Such a powerful vehicle, in fact, that the driver wasn't even aware he'd taken on a whole extra person's worth of weight.

*   *   *

"Our pursuer sees us a singular entity. The breadth of work and effort placed into that vehicle betrays a strong sense of identity tied to it.

For someone like that, the idea of leaving a car in the middle of a chase would never even occur. Therefore, our optimal tactic is for you to approach on foot while I provide a distraction."

It was a testament to how deep in they were that Watson had allowed himself to even entertain the notion at all. Firstly, he didn't even know for sure that Sherman *could* drive. As it turned out, the answer to that question was proving to be "kind of." In an open field, with nothing to hit but more corn, Sherman was doing well. On a street with other cars, Watson might want him to take a few more lessons first.

Even that part wasn't so crazy – not compared to the idea that he was supposed to leave the car and find a way to board their pursuer's truck. The circular route and varying speeds were his suggestion for Sherman to make the task easier, but it had still taken several passes by Watson's hiding spot before he'd seen a viable shot. Add in that Sherman had no real idea where Watson was, meaning he might drive right through him at any moment, and the whole ordeal had made for a very tense, stressful last ten minutes.

Worse: that was theoretically the easy part. He still had an aspiring abductor to deal with.

When Watson had dared to ask how, exactly, he was supposed to do all this, Sherman had merely looked at him the same way one looked at a wild animal defecating in the street before replying. "I realize that some aspects of this job will forever lay beyond your reach. However, I had hoped you could at least handle the tertiary duty of your role: figure it out."

For some reason, that grated Watson. Maybe because "figuring it out" was what he'd spent the majority of his adult life doing. Dealing with Sherman meant eating a lot of guff, but there was no way Watson was letting that one stand. Sherman wanted to see if he could solve the problem; that's exactly what he would do.

Moving slowly, staying steady above all else, Watson began to dig through the bed of the truck and take inventory of his situation. Pulling back the first burlap sheet, he found himself staring into a familiar black case: transportation devices designed for highly-sensitive materials, the kind Watson had handled himself many times in the past. Just to be sure, he flipped a latch and peeked inside.

Four grenades, what appeared to be plastic explosives, and a few sticks of actual, honest-to-goodness dynamite. Watson couldn't remember seeing any of those outside construction projects and cartoons, but this box alone had enough to leave a sizable crater in the corn field, stored loosely, with several other types of dangerous explosives. And there was a lot more than just one box in the back of this truck.

Watson swallowed hard as he carefully lowered and re-latched the case's lid. So, the person pursuing them was driving around enough destructive power to blow through a dam. That complicated matters somewhat.

The gunshot rang through the night, forcing Watson's attention back to the car chase. A rifle poked out from the driver's side, bopping and weaving along with the turns. Of course. The truck bed of explosives wasn't enough; now the guy was sending wild bullets toward Sherman. It would take more than one lucky shot to puncture their tires – thank goodness for the armoring their car had – but a stray or ricochet could easily end up hitting Sherman. Which meant on top of the truck-that-wanted-to-be-a-bomb, Watson now also had to get this all handled before a random bullet made it into the convertible.

Figure it out, indeed.

18.

There was one major factor in Watson's favor as they sped through the corn field, shots ringing out, and it was that very rifle being used to try and kill Sherman. Between the gun, the driving, and the explosives, the man chasing them was definitely not observing the same professional courtesy as Andy had. That was fine. This was a messy business; people didn't always get to play nice. However, the fact that this man had ignored such decorum left Watson free to do the same. He could solve this problem in whatever way was most efficient.

The first, most obvious solution, was to simply set off one of the explosives in the bed of the truck, ideally after giving himself plenty of room to run away. Tempting as it was to light this fellow up with his own ludicrous supply of destruction, there was too much back here, all of it tied down under multiple layers, ensuring he couldn't lower the gate and kick everything out. Without knowing how far away the truck would be from Sherman, the blast might easily be large enough to get him too, and that was ignoring the amount of shrapnel that would hurl through the air. If he absolutely had to, it might suffice, but definitely not good enough to be a first plan.

Shooting through the rear of the cab was Watson's major hope, however he only needed a careful glance to know that was out. Unlike their vehicle, this one had taken the full-armor route, including the clear section of bullet-resistant glass between him and the driver. With a high-enough caliber, it would still be doable, but Watson didn't have a prayer of punching through on one shot with only a handgun. And it had to be the first, because once he was made himself known, this entire situation changed. It became a fight, and Watson much preferred an ambush.

In theory, if he swung around, Watson might be able to get a shot through the open driver's side window, where the rifle was poking out. Jamming his arm, and only weapon, into the cab at that angle was dangerous. It left him vulnerable, and if this man had any decent training or saw the approach, it could all go very wrong in a matter of seconds.

Another gunshot, this one followed by the ring of metal, brought Watson out of his head and into the moment. That last one hit the convertible's bumper, leaving a visible hole. Those bullets were getting closer. He had to get this truck stopped, because if a tire did get shot out, Sherman would be sitting prey. Unfortunately, none of the practical options were presenting an ideal path forward.

Time to get impractical, then.

In his observations, Watson had noted one other key detail: the passenger side door was unlocked. Given how intently the driver was going after Sherman, there was a chance Watson could make it over before he noticed. And even if not, the downside to rifles was that they were hard to adjust in small spaces. If he was quick, and sure, Watson could probably get inside without being shot. He hoped.

Before making the move, he reopened the case he'd dug through, taking a pair of dynamite sticks and a pair of grenades. There was no plan for those items yet; Watson simply preferred to have them and not need them rather than needing and not having them. This night was taking a lot of turns; next time Watson might like to have a surprise of his own to dish out. Tucking the supplies into his pockets and belt respectively, Watson crept back over to the side of the vehicle, trying hard not to look at the speeding ground. It would make him dizzy and disoriented; he'd done this more than enough to know that much already.

Of course, the last time he'd done something quite this crazy had also been before a bullet carved up part of his right leg. The pain in that limb worsened without warning, throbbing, telling him he wouldn't be strong enough anymore. Watson shoved those doubts away. He'd done his physical therapy, conditioning, and countless hours of work to recover. His body was still capable; it was his mind trying to turn traitor. Sometimes, it got the better of him, but not in moments like these. When he could see the goal and understand the problem, Watson could brush his doubt aside.

No more stalling.

The truck slowed down as Sherman's car did the same. Their pursuer still had no idea whether Watson was onboard or not. In this case, it worked out well, offering Watson a chance to leap forward, balancing on a chrome foot bar probably meant to help shorter people when climbing in. The foothold gave Watson enough balance to swing open the passenger door, sweep the arsenal of weapons off the seat, and jump inside. The door swung closed behind him, though that was due to momentum rather than showmanship.

It had all happened in the span of seconds, so fast that the burly bald man glaring over from the driver's side was still yanking on his rifle, trying to pull it in. Watson pulled the hammer back on his pistol. True, there was no practical effect or reason for the move; however, the gesture *did* draw his opponent's attention to the firearm, which was the real point of the display.

"Drop the rifle out the window, or I shoot you in the gut."

"Fire that thing in here, we'll both be bleeding from the ears." The driver's voice was coarse and rough. He was a man who'd seen too much; Watson knew the look by heart.

"Mostly ringing and pain, not much blood. More pain for one of us than the other. Rifle. *Now*. Last warning."

From a reasonable perspective, the fight was done. He had the drop and the gun, so anyone with sense would yield, take the loss, and live to work another day. However, reasonable people also didn't typically drive around with an armory's worth of guns and explosives on hand. Expecting this man – or anyone else, really – to act with reason in a high-stakes situation was setting one's self up for failure. People were wild, unpredictable beasts, all the more so when cornered.

Several things happened all at once. The driver dropped his gun, just as Watson demanded. At the same time, he jammed a foot on the gas, sending them on a crash course for Sherman's car. While his foot was occupied, he slung his substantial arms forward, trying to grab the gun out of Watson's hands. In terms of pure strength, judging by muscle size, there was a good chance the driver was stronger. That was why Watson never gave him the chance to turn it into such a contest.

Ready for the dive, Watson responded not by shooting, instead by using his free hand to punch the driver dead in the nose. A gun was good for more than just shooting; they also made handy distractions.

The punch staggered the driver, buying Watson enough time to bring the butt of the weapon down onto the driver's face. There was a wet *crunch* as several teeth broke or went flying, following by a prolonged slurping noise as he tried to cope with the blood now filling his mouth.

That might have been the end of things, if they hadn't suddenly smashed into the left rear of Sherman's bumper.

Braced though he was, the crash still sent Watson slamming into the door at his back. No, he quickly realized that was wrong: the momentum had actually pushed him entirely out the door. Apparently, it hadn't latched when it closed behind him.

Dragging himself up from the grass, too aware of a fresh wave of pain in his leg, Watson looked back into the cab and felt his heart stop.

From the glove compartment, the driver had produced a lighter and what appeared to be some kind of cloth. What it had been soaked in was a mystery, but at a glance, Watson knew what it was for. He started forward, feeling for his gun and finding it gone, lost in the corn field when he'd been tossed. Crap: that left him with only one option.

Bolting as fast as he could, given the conditions, Watson forced his way into the convertible, where a stunned Sherman was still staring at the wheel. "I fear the traction on this road is quite lacking, I wasn't even able to make my last turn in time."

"Doesn't matter, we need to go." Watson shut his door, firmly this time, and slapped the dash. "Right now! Pedal to floor, gas in gear. That entire truck is full of explosives, and he's about to blow himself up just to take us with him."

With a surprisingly adult sigh, Sherman took hold of the wheel again. "Really, Watson, you have got to be better about sharing this sort of information. While you can only make some use of it, in my hands, we could discern—"

"He's got the cloth lit!" Watson could see telltale flickers through the now-cracked front of the driver's window.

"See, that is an excellent example of telling me something I absolutely need to know," Sherman agreed. They finally started forward as he pressed the gas. It was gentle at first, necessary to get traction yet agonizing as Watson watched their enemy light some unseen fuse.

Mercifully, the tires caught quickly, rocketing them into the corn field at an ever-increasing pace. After ten full seconds of driving, Watson looked back to make sure the whole thing hadn't been a feint. That vantage point gave him an excellent view of the explosions which tore through the night. Not every device triggered at once. A wave of them echoed out from the epicenter, sometimes in spurts, sometimes in unison. It was a brief, bright, loud affair that left a hum in both men's ears for the next hour.

The upside, though, was that this threat was definitely neutralized. Even if he'd run for it after lighting the cloth, his legs wouldn't get him far enough.

After a few more seconds, Sherman let the car begin to slow down, gliding to a halt in the middle of the corn field. "As I am unfamiliar with our travel plans, Watson, you must guide us from here. What next?"

That was the million-dollar question.

They were compromised, no question there, but by how much had yet to be determined. Protocol said get the asset to a safe house. Unfortunately, any safe house location could be just as compromised as their motel. Until they knew who to trust, they would play it safe. Right now they needed to eat, rest, and send word that the operation had hit fresh complications – all without alerting anyone else as to their location.

"What's next is you and I switching seats," Watson told him. "We'll have to find a place to hunker down and sleep, but first, we never did get to have dinner. Seeing as I promised you pizza, let's find a late-night spot and get you properly acquainted. Things always look better after a meal."

19.

Once, Gwendolyn had high hopes for Agent 221, now known as Joel Watson. Bright, observant, resourceful, and stubborn to an almost mythical degree: everything about him pointed toward a legend-in-the-making, the kind of agent she'd use as a story prop to shame and inspire those who came after.

Poole had changed everything, though. All that stubbornness turned inward; Agent 221 was so mad at himself for being fooled that he closed off rather than make the same mistake twice. Talent turned to liability, observation into paranoia, and his own willfully stubborn nature became the inability to move on. Poole had aimed for the leg and spared Watson's life, but he'd killed that all-star agent-in-the-making just the same.

In spite of the mistakes that piled up, Gwendolyn felt a fondness for the man, and part of her nursed the hope that there was still a way back. That one day, Watson would become capable of growing past his failure and becoming the kind of asset he was meant to be. Maybe that was why she'd gotten Watson assigned to the bodyguard detail: something new, something different. Any tactic that might help the true Watson find a way back. Or, failing that, success would at least give Gwendolyn some ammunition to take back upstairs. It was supposed to be an easy win.

The prior night's call had set Gwendolyn on edge. Although she couldn't afford to indulge Watson's worries directly, it was hard to fully shake off what he said. She'd been doing a little poking around when the second call came, hours later.

Gwendolyn, as a rule, hated admitting she was wrong, but not even someone with Watson's current record of crying traitor could obscure the facts before them. Somehow, their location and situation had been leaked. Given that Watson's suspicions of being tailed earlier now had a *lot* more credence to them, the conclusion was simple: they had a leak. Not their first, not their last. When one dealt with people who could be tempted to this kind of work, there was always the risk that same nature could allow them to be compromised. The higher ups tried to suss these things out; however, training professional liars meant they were all fairly good at getting away with treachery.

In Gwendolyn's opinion, this was almost the worst situation: knowing there was a leak with no leads on who. The *actual* worst was what they'd just been in with Poole, having a leak without being aware. Still, their current predicament was hardly ideal. As of now, Watson had no one he could trust. Any call in could get them traced, any planned location had to be assumed as compromised. Even contacting him was risky; with the right permissions, someone could get a tap on his line. Gwendolyn wasn't sure if the leak was above or below her in the hierarchy, so running it up the chain was dangerous as well.

Thankfully, Watson already knew what he had to do as soon as they talked; the call was largely just notification. He and Sherman were going into the wind. They would ditch everything they could, checking with Gwendolyn only when safe. There was only one question she'd needed to answer: what next?

Ultimately, Gwendolyn told them to keep heading toward the new facility. If someone was striking while Sherman was in transit, then that likely meant the destination was more secure. Plus, it would still take them several days to make it, possibly more with a new route. That would be Gwendolyn's time to do some work of her own. Despite how she felt about Watson's habit of seeing turncoats everywhere, he and Gwendolyn did share an opinion on the subject: neither of them had any mercy in their heart for traitors.

Gwendolyn would root the source out, and make sure everyone knew what happened to one of their own who decided to betray the others.

*   *   *

The morning sun found Sherman and Watson sitting on the hood of the convertible, parked in a near-empty strip mall parking lot, eating breakfast sandwiches. Last night's eventual pizza, while nice, didn't quite satisfy with the mix of worry, adrenaline, and nerves in Watson's stomach. He was too busy scanning every corner and entrance for a surprise attack to savor the meal – unlike Sherman, who'd eaten all of his own food and the majority of Watson's.

With a few hurried naps under his belt and a night to think, Watson was a little more stable. Getting the situation reported to Gwendolyn helped. At least now if he or Sherman died the leak would still get what they deserved. Gwendolyn had the harder job: sniffing out the problem. Their only task was to stay alive and keep driving.

Swallowing harder than was needed for the meal, Watson's eyes trailed down to the convertible. In a perfect world, he'd ditch this, steal something else, and be back on the road before rush hour. The issue there was the utter lack of convertibles they'd passed so far. If they'd needed a truck, Watson could have stolen them a fleet, but go figure that a rural farming community didn't have as much demand for convertibles as for cars that could get actual work done. There was also the matter of the car's extra capabilities. Having lost their entire plan, along with access to most resources and safe houses, tossing away one of their few advantages gave Watson pause.

"Sherman, after breakfast, we need to find a body shop. That bullet hole in the bumper is too conspicuous, plus we need to change out the license plates. I'd like to get a paint job, but we can't spend days hanging around here. I'll need to sweep it for trackers too. Can't risk someone pinging our ride."

"Fascinating. Tell me, Watson, do you have skill or experience in checking for such devices?"

"More in planting them. I figure it's basically the same thing, just reversed." He took another bite of his breakfast, racing the lowering temperature before heat could stop masking subpar ingredients. "Speaking of skills, that was nice driving last night. Forgot to say something in all of the chaos, but I was impressed."

Sherman nodded. "Yes, it is almost like I am not the incapable child everyone is set on treating me as." The strangest part of the sentence was how bored and neutral he sounded about the idea. Sherman wasn't angry about it, more mildly annoyed.

"Good news, then: you're going to have plenty more chances to prove yourself in the next few days. As of now, we are cut off from everyone else until Gwendolyn gives me the all-clear. That means it's just you and me, so I'm probably going to have to start leaning on you more. If nothing else, someone needs to figure out where we should stop to eat and sleep."

"A task that will be more difficult without access to a phone," Sherman pointed out. Watson had made a point of breaking both their old phones, then running them over with the car, then dumping the remains in a bucket of water.

Finishing his food, Watson hopped off the hood and walked over to the convertible's rear. After roughly a minute of rummaging, he returned to the front and handed Sherman a new smart phone. As it powered up, the display showed that it had even been fully charged.

"I presume these are not assets provided to you."

"Yeah, stopped being on board with only having approved tech years ago. I prefer to keep a stash just for situations like this one. Never been used, no connection to me. Got a few parts missing and some others added to keep them from being easily tracked. Let me fire up a new one as well and we'll trade numbers." Watson produced another phone, identical to Sherman's. "Make sure you only call *me*," Watson added. "Anyone else learns that number, and they've got a path to finding you. Until we get the all clear, that's the way it has to be."

Turning the device over in his hands a few times, Sherman appeared satisfied with the replacement, tucking it into his pocket. "I must say, I find it fascinating."

"That I keep spare phones?"

"That you trust this Gwendolyn so much," Sherman clarified. "On an ordinary person, it would be quite mundane, however for you it is a genuine curiosity. You do not trust. One can hardly help but wonder what makes this woman so different."

Sometimes, Sherman's odd nature made him come off like a jerk. Only now, Watson was realizing that might not be so bad. There was something to be said for a companion who told the truth as he saw it no matter what.

"Gwendolyn is an old friend. She could have betrayed me more times than I can count. And I trusted her before... before."

"Pity, here I thought we were finally going to talk about why you favor that right leg of yours."

This time, Watson's eyes did widen a hair. He hadn't expected Sherman to catch such a minor detail or put together that it was connected to his paranoia. Just when he thought he had a handle on this guy, some new aspect popped up.

"Not really the time for that kind of story. We've got work to do. If possible, I'd like to be out of here by the afternoon. We're several towns away from last night's fun, but I'm not going to relax until we're out of this state."

"Please, Watson. You know my policy on lies, and we are both keenly aware that you *never* relax, regardless of what state you are in." Sherman was looking up at the blazing colors of the morning sky, something not quite a smile, yet close, on his face. Was it possible that Sherman was making a joke?

"Hey, you try relaxing when you're carting around the world's greatest detective. That's a lot of pressure."

Eyes drifting down from the sky, Sherman looked Watson over for the umpteenth time. "As it should be. Although I will confess, after seeing your skillset last night, perhaps you are not quite the most incompetent Watson possible. Some of that was appropriately impressive for a man of your position."

"You have high expectations for a bodyguard," Watson noted.

The snort from Sherman's nose was so loud it verged on becoming a honk. "Nonsense. You are no mere bodyguard, Watson. You are the assistant to the world's greatest detective. I have every right to expect greatness from anyone filling such a position. Consequently, I also have a duty to acknowledge the occasions where such expectations are met. Last night was one such incident."

It took a little work, and peeling back some delusions, but Watson realized that there was a fairly sincere compliment buried among all that hullabaloo. Bit by bit, he was starting to get a sense for Sherman. Not quite an understanding, yet quite a degree of progress from where they'd begun things. Him pitching in to help the night before hadn't hurt either. Watson knew that when things went sideways, some people stepped up while others wigged out. As a rule, he was fonder of the first group.

"Thanks. You were pretty good yourself. Now let's hope our luck holds out, because we're going to need to find an auto body shop that opens early, asks no questions, and works cheap. From this point on, you and I are cash only. No paper trail. I can't tell you how many people I've found that way."

"You may as well," Sherman said, sliding into the passenger seat. "With those limitations, I am going to be searching quite a while for a suitable repair shop. Besides, learning what mistakes to avoid will help me, should I ever need to go on the run solo."

Hard to argue with that. Next time Watson might not be around to bail him out. And, for all their differences, he didn't want to hear about somebody cracking open Sherman's skull, even when their job was done.

"Let's see, we've covered cars, phones, and sticking to cash. The dos and don'ts of using fake names should get us through the first couple of searches."

20.

"You *sure* this isn't a bullet hole?" The woman in a gray jumpsuit was staring at the bumper, which had been popped off for repairs. "Looks like a bullet hole to me."

"Weird how gravel thrown by a tire at just the right speed and angle can resemble that." Watson looked up from digging around inside the engine, giving her a pointed stare. "You know how these things go."

There was a pause, as she considered the damage once more. "Uh huh."

Despite spending a fair chunk of the morning, they hadn't succeeded in finding a repair business that fit their parameters. In a place this small, there wasn't much of a black market, so under-the-table cash deals were met with an appropriate amount of suspicion. What they did stumble upon, through persistence and a dash of search-engine fortune, was a local high school with an auto repair curriculum. Mechanics might be doing well enough to turn down cash in exchange for discretion, but teachers being underpaid was, sadly, a constant Watson could count on.

The name on the gray jumpsuit said "Terri," though whether it was hers or not was open to interpretation. She didn't offer a name, nor did he ask, since she didn't probe for his. He had no idea if she was a custodian, a teacher, or someone else doing secret car work. She'd just been there when they made the approach. It was a simple exchange: facilities, help, and silence in return for a few thousand dollars that had been tucked away in one of Watson's bags. His philosophy was that it only counted as over-preparing if one didn't need the resources, and these habits had saved his neck more than once.

Sherman was busying himself with some textbooks piled up in a corner. There were stains, torn pages, and missing covers; these were obviously the ones taken out of circulation. None of that dulled his interest as he spread them out along the floor, reading in spurts and sections, sometimes following a line across three entirely different textbooks, mumbling to himself all the while. It was disconcerting. However, considering it was Sherman, this was one of the best outcomes Watson could have hoped for. So long as he stayed out of the way and didn't insult their host, he was welcome to read every old textbook in the state.

For the moment, Watson's major concern was finding any trackers hidden in the convertible. There would be a few – redundancies on top of redundancies, especially considering the dangerous components inside their transport. Governments weren't generally fond of their assets being abandoned for anyone to find, so they'd want to pick this up even if the mission went bad. Fair and reasonable, until one realized that anybody with the right clearance could get the car's location in a few clicks. Enemies wanted to hunt down the target he was protecting, fine; that was part of the dance. But he wasn't going to make it *that* easy on them. Tracking him was going to take real effort.

The remainder of their morning was spent working and reading, respectively. School was out, since it was a weekend, so they didn't have to worry about any kids wandering through. Of course, knowing that made Watson's hair stand on end every time he heard a car drive past, sure that this was the next squad coming to strike while they were occupied. As the time wore on, he only grew more tense. Staying somewhere this long, especially knowing they could still be tracked, went against his instincts. Watson tried to focus on the work. They had to get the car fixed, then they could proceed more safely. Smaller risks now to negate larger ones later.

By the time Watson was sure he'd checked every nook, cranny, and seam, he'd pulled out five devices. Some he knew for certain were remote GPS locators, others simply had enough components to potentially fit the mold. All of them went into the same pile. Maybe some functions would fail, but he was sure the car would still run. It was a necessary roll of the dice; no single gadget or tool was worth giving away their location.

He didn't destroy the trackers as he worked. Once those were broken, anyone monitoring them would immediately know the GPS game was up. Depending on their resources, they might launch an attack on the last known location, striking before Watson and Sherman could get away. Better to use them more carefully than give their enemies information. When the last was collected, Watson swept the lot into a small canvas pouch and zipped it up.

Terri was nearly done reattaching the bumper. There was visible warping where the hole had been, a rushed patch job that couldn't compare to a proper repair. At least it no longer looked like the car had been shot.

At worst, someone inspecting very closely might mistake the imperfection for a dent. On the highway, flying past, it would be utterly invisible.

"Nice work," Watson said. "Especially given the time. If I'm ever back this way, I'll look you up."

"Part of me really wants to say you shouldn't, but I'll probably need the money again." She hesitated, a worried expression barely being kept off her face. "I know life occasionally gets strange and all. Just… could you at least assure me that I'm not helping bad people get away with something? While you don't seem the sort, the longer I worked, the more I had to wonder."

"Fear not, noble educator." Sherman had popped up from the floor at some point, the pile of textbooks all sorted neatly behind him. Watson did a double take, wondering if they'd all been read in the relatively short time here. "Not only are we not wicked, we are firmly planted on the side of justice. I am the world's greatest detective, and this is my humble assistant. Our ambitions are to enrich the world, not lessen it."

Creases appeared in Terri's forehead as she puzzled through Sherman's attempt at reassurance. "So, you're cops?"

"Not exactly, but we *are* on the side of the good guys," Watson confirmed. "Sherman is right about that."

A few more moments of uncertainty, until Terri finally let the tension fall from her shoulders. "I guess you would be pretty weird for criminals. Fine, give me a hand with the last parts and let's get you on the road. No offense, I'll just feel better once you're out of here."

Watson felt an unexpected sense of comradery with the woman in that moment. "Trust me when I say, you and I are exactly the same page."

*   *   *

The aftermath was something to see. Between the fire in a bathtub, a few people reporting gunshots, and the explosion that burned down half a corn field, Sherman and Watson had really done quite a number on the area.

Tom and Jenny's original plan had been ripped through by that giant, cumbersome truck that tore out from the shadows as soon as the target was in his car. They tried to do a distant follow at first, letting the more obvious threat draw attention, but even that failed once the chase exited the highway. In a situation like that, their only option was to drive on and regroup.

After a few hours searching the area, hoping to get lucky, the duo had returned to the motel. Dedicated or not, they were human, and both needed occasional rest at minimum. Once refreshed, they'd dug into the fallout from the night before, hoping that perhaps the cops might have a lead on the strange pair that fled in the night. Sadly, there was no such luck. Either Watson really knew how not to leave a trail, someone up top was still protecting them, or both.

The one thing they did know for sure was that all of their old information was officially trash. An attack like this left nothing to doubt. Nobody as capable as Watson would be dumb enough to keep using the planned stops. It all came down to how much had been figured out. Assuming Watson realized his information stream had a leak, he'd go into the wind with the target. That was, oddly, the better scenario for Tom and Jenny. Otherwise, Watson would bring Sherman to a safe house, and no one would get to scoop him up.

Jenny let out a groan half-muffled by the muffin in her mouth. "I'm going through everything we've got, and there are no solid leads on where they might run to. My best theory is closer to a wild guess."

"If the wild guess is yours, then I want to hear it," Tom replied.

Coming over from the modest table and thinly-cushioned chair where she'd been working, Jenny brought her laptop over to Tom's seat on the bed. "Since we can't trust the itinerary, I started wondering if there was anything we could trust, a place to start from. All I've come up with are the detours. We know they aren't part of the plan, but they've been happening, obviously at the target's request. If they're now cut off, with no route to follow, there is a slim chance they might take a path that lets them hit more of these tourist traps."

For a wild guess, Jenny's idea held quite a bit of merit.

"That's not bad. They'd be using the same roads as other cars from various states, meaning lots of cover and non-native license plates to blend in with. Probably be assured decent crowds if they chose their destinations with a modicum of care. I think you might have something. And even if not, I've got nothing better, so we may as well chase this for now."

"There is another alternative." Jenny's hand tapped the eastern edge of the screen's map. "We could cut our losses and let this one go. I know the money is good, but this job is getting more knotted up by the hour. Something is off. I know we were warned dealing with these people would be messy, and I'm starting to agree. This kind of money for a simple snatch-and-grab, not to mention the people they let onto the operation… I don't trust it. We're in deeper than we realize, so this is a good time to take stock and make sure we want to keep going. With *either* side of the job."

"All very fair, reasonable points," Tom agreed. "Personally, I was originally just in for the payout, but now I'll admit, my curiosity is piqued. While I could walk away from the cash without hesitation, we may never get an in with that woman again. This is our shot. My instinct is to keep trying until there's a concrete reason to retreat."

"Same here. Glad we're on the same page." Turning the computer back around, Jenny considered the map before her carefully. "Of course, that means now I have to try and figure out which of the countless highways and backroads they might be taking. Go get the car gassed up. Once it's time to move, we'll want to be ready to go."

Tom did as instructed, snatching his keys from the bedside table and leaving Jenny to work. There was no guarantee she'd succeed. Some games were lost; that was the nature of playing. If anybody could suss it out, though, he knew she was the one to do it. Jenny's talent for analysis was so exceptional it had carried her into the freelance world and her partnership with Tom. Nobody won forever, but Jenny came out ahead more times than not. Hopefully, this would be one of those occasions.

And if not, perhaps that wasn't so bad. Curiosity or not, she hadn't been wrong that this whole situation stank. Losing the target would hurt their bottom line and cost them a new connection, but they could recover from that. Getting tangled in the wrong net and drawn in with their target, now that was a fate to be consciously avoided. Ideally, they'd be able to still grab Sherman. Failing that, maybe it would be time for a vacation.

Just nowhere that required lots of driving to reach.

21.

The destination was northwest and only a few more days' drive; it should have been a simple run for the safe house. What complicated matters was the obvious fact that if someone knew where Watson and Sherman were spending their nights, then they likely knew the ultimate destination as well. Even if Gwendolyn could ensure the new facility was actually safe, she wouldn't be able to lock down all the roads between here and there. Meaning it was time to make a choice.

This wasn't a whole army they were against: so far just a few freelancers. There were far too many roads to have people on all of them, so if he chose a direct route, it was theoretically possible to slip past. Going south or east would put them out of their way, yet also give them the chance to lose their pursuers entirely. But if he could see that move, then so could they, which meant he shouldn't assume those routes to be safe either.

In the end, Watson decided to lean on the only element he had that was truly unpredictable: Sherman. When asked where he wanted to go next, there wasn't even hesitation. He merely rattled off the address of a dairy farm from some ad or brochure that Watson hadn't paid attention to. It was in the next state, not far from the border, and to the southwest. A direction they should go mixed with one they shouldn't seemed as good a tactic as any.

After the farm, they would have to make a serious decision. In terms of major highways, they were nearing a breaking point: a fork in the road, where one direction would aim northwest right at their destination, and the other straight west. If they took the latter, they could still go north once they ran out of west.

The sun dipped low in their eyes, forcing both to look away. In spite of last night's rough activities, the car was running fine as they finally got out of town. After a real rest, they would do the dairy farm and then decide which direction to take. Part of Watson was thankful for the delay, nursing a small hope that Gwendolyn would get things sorted out. Probably not – these things took time – but it was nice to hope.

"How did you hold up sleeping in the car last night?" It was, in retrospect, a question Watson should have asked much earlier. Those things were just hard to consider when staying alive was on his mind.

"Where I sleep, if one can call those half-dozing fits such, makes little difference. A soft mattress or hard stone, once my thoughts turn inward, I would not be able to notice either."

About what he'd expected. Good to know they could sleep in the car again, if needed. He wasn't sure where they'd rest for the evening, or what resources would be around. Best to play things loose for now, be ready to change and improvise at a moment's notice. But the words stirred something in Watson: a memory of Sherman's endless tossing and turning, something his own nightmares had inflicted on him multiple times. It wasn't the same thing... probably. Watson realized, perhaps for the first time, that he'd tried to learn very little about what Sherman's condition was like. He'd read the reports and noted the odd behavior, true, but outside of their rain conversation, he had no idea what it was really like inside that mind.

"Up front, let me say if you don't want to talk about this, that's cool. I was wondering, though, how does it feel? Your brain, I mean. What is like to see the world the way you do?"

"Like holding a hungry tiger on a leash." No pause. He'd either been ready for the question or had an answer locked and loaded at all times. "My brain is ravenous, willing to jump on anything and devour it. Noise and reading keep it soothed – fed, in this analogy. That is deeply essential, Watson, because when the tiger has nothing else, he will devour me instead."

"You know what? That was a bummer and it's my fault," Watson said. "You and I are both living a little too much in the past and present. Let's look toward something cheerier: the future. These last few days, you've basically been ingesting information constantly. Learn about anything interesting you might want to try? As a man with no past, you get to discover what you love all over again."

It could have Watson's imagination or the glint of the lowering sun in his eyes, but for a moment he thought Sherman appeared slightly more interested. "Many things, Watson. Many things indeed. Leaping from a plane with only a thin canvas sheet as salvation seems an especially potent way to spit in the face of death. There is also the habit of standing on boards in the ocean while taunting the local shark life, which could be enjoyable with proper preparation. Tell me, as a man experienced with firearms, what model would you recommend for doing battle with a shark? Presumably in the sea – best to prepare for worst-case scenarios."

For longer than he was proud of, Watson was tempted to answer with a joke, but part of him worried Sherman might take any offered advice literally. Odds of his new overseers ever letting Sherman surf were slim, but the man had a knack for ending up in unusual situations. Best to assume anything was possible.

"If you absolutely *have* to fight a shark underwater, you want to use a spear gun. More ideally, just don't fight sharks at all. They rarely attack surfers, and when they do, it's just a misunderstanding."

"Ah yes, I forget you cannot discern the evolving pattern in their strikes. Mark my words, Watson. The shark rebellion stirs. Within twenty years they'll make their push for the shores unless they are stopped."

Ignoring his initial instinct to push the idea aside, Watson opted to see where it led. They did still have a few hours of driving left. "Okay, so how are the sharks going to get on land? And what happens when they do?"

"Clearly they have been hauling off the corpses of their victims for dissection, learning how the lungs work, endeavoring to find a way that they can leave the ocean at last." Sherman flipped a few pages in his book, far more than would be needed if he was going in order. "Of course, the moment they step foot on land, they will be gunned down by our military. Breathing apparatuses do not turn creatures bullet-proof, and when it comes to the science of killing, there is no animal on this planet that could dream of contesting with mankind."

Watson had no counterclaim to offer. Humanity was especially adept at killing. Even a drug that could theoretically help the entire species evolve to the next level was considered a weapon, first and foremost. People were terrified of what Sherman, or someone else like him, could be capable of. Considering that such a drug should be offering just as much hope for the future, for what leaps forward they might make as a species, it said a lot about humanity in general that everyone's initial reaction was to assume the worst.

It said even more that none of those reactions had been wrong so far.

"Anything else plotting against us I should be aware of?" Watson asked.

"Obviously the orangutan mafia is still hard at work behind the scenes, but they have long since learned to not get their own hands dirty. The network of cats still schemes, however they took control centuries ago, so nowadays it is more a social club. And I do not trust sparrows."

Watson waited for a few moments to see if there would be more elaboration on that last point. When none came, his curiosity got the better of him. "Why don't you trust sparrows?"

"I lack a concrete reason as of yet, however a great detective must trust his instincts. Especially when they are the world's greatest detective's instincts. The sparrows whisper, and one day I shall uncover the reason why."

It made as much sense as any other part of Sherman's declaration, which was to say very little. That cat line had come a tad too close to feeling true, though. Who knew, if there was a drug that could radically alter a brain this much, perhaps some animals truly were smarter than humans realized? Watson had seen strange occurrences in the field – experimental science and things lost to time. He wasn't exactly a believer in anything so much as he was fluid in what he considered to be real. The job he did required adapting to new information rapidly, so it was hardly surprising the attitude had bled over into his normal outlook.

"Do you think they want more food? Or better nests?"

"My working hypothesis is that they seek to undermine the cats' victory and place themselves as the dominant life form. A difficult task, no question, especially without soft fur to stroke. They also lack the decades of forging peace with canines, humanity's great protectors, which would create high diplomatic hurdles. That means they will likely strike using force, presuming my theory is accurate. With so little to go on, even I must be open to the possibility of error."

The longer Sherman talked in that serious tone, treating the idea of sparrows plotting as reasonable, the more Watson found himself scanning the trees they drove past, just in case. Probably best to change the topic before they both wound up too unstable to drive.

"I'll watch for wings. In the meantime, we either find a place to crash, or we stay in the car again. Not against that second option entirely, but it's been two days. We need a shower before the dairy farm, or we'll draw too much attention." Also, Watson disliked wearing the same clothes multiple days in a row. He'd had to do it several times, but an operation where he spent a full week in the same outfit and the baking sun had given him a taste for freshly laundered apparel.

"My earlier assessments of the maps indicate there is a small town less than an hour away with ample wooded areas where one might park undisturbed, along with a local gym. Presuming your infiltration skills to be on par with the rest you have displayed, I trust you'd be capable of gaining us entry easily enough. Should none of the available lodging suit our needs, that location permits a secondary plan."

That was... pretty good, actually. A town big enough to have hotels and small enough to also have spots they could park for the night gave them the best of both worlds. "You know, for someone who claims to be the world's greatest detective, you're pretty cavalier about breaking laws."

"Laws have no bearing on my discipline," Sherman shot back instantly, even looking up from his book. "They are simply rules made by the powerful. A true detective does not serve rules, for they are inherently corruptible, since they were made by humans. We serve only the ideal of justice. Uncover the truth, reveal the guilty, protect the innocent. Anything outside of those three parameters is variable, and stealing a shower is a victimless crime. If it soothes your conscience, we can leave a dollar to pay for the water we shall use."

There was no way any actual detective would sign off on Sherman's definition of the title, but Watson found he didn't hate it. The thesis of his chosen vocation was doing right and helping make things better, a sentiment someone such as Watson could heartily get behind.

Part of him wondered about the man beneath the brain, the person Sherman had been before turning into an unwitting experiment. Who had he been? What dreams, what past, what life was lost when his brain got scrambled? Whoever else he might have been, Watson suspected he'd gotten a measure of the man's nature, something that bled through even without memories. For the first time on the trip, he realized that protecting Sherman wasn't just his job: it was what he wanted to do.

Craziness aside, Sherman tried to do the right thing, as best he could. Maybe that wasn't such a rare trait, but Watson had met fewer people with it than he would have liked. He was fond of that type, the ones who gave a damn.

One way or another, he was going to get Sherman delivered safely. Anyone who had other plans than that could get out of his way or be cleared by force.

22.

Dr. Dunaway raised his eye from the microscope, certain he must have heard incorrectly.

"Lost? He cannot be lost."

One of the nameless grunts – who very much did in fact have names, if Dr. Dunaway had cared enough to learn them – had come into his lab to deliver the news. The same grunt was still standing there, stoic and expressionless, as the dangerous doctor slithered from his stool.

"Do you understand our arrangement, you replaceable cog? The criminal organization you work for is providing my employer with resources and assistance. In return, when the formula is perfected, the leaders of said organization will be the first to receive it." He was looming over the grunt, despite being physically frailer by a substantial margin. There was something unsettling about the way Dr. Dunaway moved, like one could never truly be sure what was going on in that head.

"Now, at the simplest level, that means your bosses want this target found even more than we," Dr. Dunaway continued. "Maybe one day we can crack it without that brain, but if we do, we'll owe your people nothing. On the other hand, if you can get me that sample, stable living brain tissue that survived the dosing process, it will unlock so much. With it, research would shoot ahead years, perhaps decades. There is no monetary value you could place on such a discovery – which is why it is not acceptable to tell me that you 'lost' the target and all information has dried up. So go out there and spend however much is needed to cover those roads in eyes until someone spots them."

Dr. Dunaway paused, looking the grunt over again, a new gleam in his eye. "Failing that, should your minds prove incapable of the task, then we can start expanding them. Let the others know."

The terror that darted through the man's eyes was palpable, and he vanished back through the lab's thick door with only a curt nod of understanding.

Dr. Dunaway watched him go, idly wondering how long it would take a brain like that before it folded in on itself and self-destructed. With no living subjects to study, he'd been forced to content himself with noting the different ways and speeds at which his subjects died. Tweaking the formula altered the results somewhat; however, much seemed to come from the individual's size, sex, diet, health, and so many other factors that there was no telling for sure what was interacting with what. That was part of why Dr. Dunaway was so eager for more people to test the serum on: the larger his sample pool, the better the data.

Of course, he also just enjoyed that spark of light in their eyes right before the end when the drugs catalyzed, finishing their work, opening the person's mind in ways never imagined. Even without the brain scans showing him all the sections lighting up, he would have known the process was working in those moments. The clarity, the awe, whatever they could see or understand was unlike anything else. Dr. Dunaway burned to know the answer, to hear what it was like to touch that realm. So far, only two known subjects had seen that vision and returned. The first was long since past their reach, which made Sherman the doctor's only hope.

Hearing about it would be a start. Then, once they took some samples and fixed the formula, he would see it for himself. That great, glorious vision that would mark the end of any mundanity in his life. At last, Dr. Dunaway would be elevated – perhaps, dared he to dream it, gaining such brilliance that he might surpass the formula's inventor.

Instantly, Dr. Dunaway scoured such a thought from his mind. Even in success, attaining the enlightened state he'd worked so hard to help create, no successful subject could hope to surpass the creator. They would all be shadows of his greatness, extensions of the daring new science the great scientist had gifted to the world. And once the creator could take the formula himself – the best of them made even better – entire new universes of scientific progress would be opened.

Returning to his microscope, Dr. Dunaway rummaged around until he found a notebook with carefully maintained records and charts swelling its innards. Untold entries, subjects, victims. Some had been personal, others part of mass-dosings to test new formula configurations. Great losses, each and every one, yet a necessary toll on the road to progress. Knowledge, power... these things didn't come without sacrifice.

There were few limits to how many Dr. Dunaway would sacrifice to see the creator's vision made real, and the boundaries that did exist were largely technical in nature. It was difficult to dose thousands at once, after all – not that he didn't have a few ideas cooking, in case they were needed. When the prize was the collective evolution of humanity's intelligence, Dr. Dunaway didn't see how any price could be too high.

*   *   *

Sherman tried to ride a cow. Truthfully, it could have gone much, much worse, Watson continued to remind himself. He'd jumped on the back of a cow, and not a bull. Said cow was also massive enough and so intent on the patch of grass she was chewing that she barely seemed to notice him. Had she bolted, Sherman could have been hurt when he fell, because there was no way Watson was giving him odds of hanging onto a running cow.

Their dairy tour *was* cut short, however. It seemed the owners had firmly held ideas about the inappropriateness of leaping onto farm animals not bred for the task, which was a bit of a murky distinction, Watson had to admit. But they had been quite clear that Sherman and Watson were both banned and not to return. By that point, Watson had seen enough cows and grass to be grateful for the kerfuffle, so he was in an unexpectedly cheerful mood as they got back on the highway.

A good night's sleep and a hot shower had that effect on some people. While the gym plan was useful as a backup, they'd been lucky enough to find an out of the way motel that took cash, asked no questions, and had a parking lot not easily visible from any major roads. With the car and themselves stashed, they'd taken the evening to fully recover, a much-needed respite after the prior night's antics.

With the end of the tour, however, the pair had arrived at the first major crossroads. They wouldn't be locked in to a path by any means; with a good map and back roads, they could change highways easily enough. The larger issue was what this represented. South meant they were trading speed for stealth. There was a major town only a few hours down the map, big enough that it would certainly have enough convertibles for Watson to "proactively borrow" one. They would disappear, ideally, and slowly trek their way to the destination.

With most targets, that was the call Watson would have made without a second thought. Sherman presented some unique challenges, unfortunately. Attempting to steal a cow was an excellent reminder that no matter what they wore or drove, Sherman stood out. The longer they were exposed, the greater the chance of being discovered. With no backup or resources to call on, Watson couldn't hold off threats forever. They could very well end up in a race for their lives anyway, one where they didn't even have this much of a head start.

However, if they took a direct route, they'd almost certainly be spotted. Nobody who sent three freelancers after a single target in one night was going to give up this easy.

"Hey, Sherman, any feelings on which route we take? Keep heading there directly, or use the west coast to mosey around and hopefully avoid making new friends?"

So far, relying on Sherman's unpredictability had worked; his first pick had gotten them out of town without issue. Maybe Watson couldn't rely on Sherman for every crossroads they met, but he decided Sherman should get a vote, at minimum. This trip might well be the last chance he had to see the world for a long time.

Looking up from a book about the reproductive cycle of the emu, Sherman blinked the sun out of his eyes a few times before finally managing a reply. "Keep the course straight, Watson. While I do enjoy our diversions, let us not draw the trip out quite that long. The longer I permit myself this holiday, the more people need my aid. We'll head to our destination directly so that I can commence my work all the sooner."

Watson was taught to see the truth of the matter as it lay before him, regardless of whether he liked it or not. Here, the truth was obvious: Sherman thought he was going to be some kind of detective instead of a lab rat. Maybe they'd even find a way to make it sort of true, giving him files to look at, permitting a consult, that sort of thing. Not what Sherman was envisioning, even though Watson wasn't sure he could imagine that himself.

"Straight for the goal it is. Any leads on what tomorrow's detour will be? Need to know if I should stop for supplies. Could have used some shoes I cared less about when we were walking around those fields."

"Watson, I daresay you verge once again on impressing me. Here I thought after new developments and today's unfortunate misunderstanding you would require convincing to continue our educational excursions. Have faith, I shall deliver us the best possible stop for tomorrow. Something enjoyable enough to make even you relax."

There was little chance of that, especially knowing they had people hunting Sherman, but Watson merely gave a nod and kept on driving. Things were already screwed: giving him a few glimpses into the outside world didn't really put them in substantially more danger than they already were. At least outside of the convertible, they might be less recognizable. Good thing Sherman had reacted so positively to disguises; those were going to be necessary moving forward. It wouldn't keep Sherman from being himself, but maybe it would buy them a few extra minutes.

Regardless, Watson was currently in the wind. With no clue about the way things were going on Gwendolyn's end, it didn't matter where or how they spent their time, so long as they arrived safely. As Sherman's bodyguard, Watson decided that practice mingling with normal people might help him blend in when it counted. If that happened to ease a growing sense of guilt about the life Sherman wanted versus what he would get, then Watson considered that a happy coincidence.

It might have worked, too, if only he hadn't been so cursedly bad at self-delusion.

23.

Jenny ran her hand along the keyboard, comparing results, routes, reviews, and every other tidbit she could mine about the various tourist traps still between them and the final destination. There were so many, and the larger a section of the map she had to search, the more results had to be filtered through. They were going to have to choose a course; there was no way around it.

"Based on those two, you think they'll make a break for it or try to move carefully?" She looked over to Tom, who was sorting their gear on his bed. Hers was on the other side. In the beginning, they'd gotten different rooms. Over time, though, enough trust developed that such expenses were no longer necessary. It was also nice, on occasion, when things got complicated. Easier to fight their way out with someone to cover her back.

"With the target at his side, they've got little chance of going unnoticed once he opens his mouth. The bodyguard is smart, he'll figure that out. The question is whether he's going to bet on his ability to keep Sherman under control or outrun everyone after them." Tom slipped a large knife back into its sheath, carefully tucking it away in the right bag. Resorting the on-hand equipment was necessary as situations changed. Infiltration demanded different tools than tracking, or extraction, or any number of potential operations.

Tom raised a good point. The target was too unpredictable to transport without drawing any attention, and a trained guard would recognize that. When viewed through that lens, the outcome became more predictable. Someone as good as Watson had proven to be must have both training and experience. His first inclination would be to trust in those exceptional skills, rather than wrangling someone he'd known for mere days. Whether or not he could overcome that, she didn't know. But they had to make a choice, so at a certain point, it became a matter of accepting the odds.

"Let's assume they take a straight shot, trying to reach the new lab. Starting from there, I can find a few potential stops. The trouble is, without knowing where they are, we can't be sure the timing would line up. However, if we go ahead, past where they can possibly be, then we can set up and wait for them. That puts all our eggs in the basket of me being right, though. If they don't stop, we'll miss them entirely."

Barely looking over, eyes still trained on the bags, Tom gave a soft nod. "That's fine. Running the roads would just be us hoping to get lucky. Your baskets have held plenty of eggs in the past. I'd rather trust you than chance. Tell me what you're thinking."

Lifting her laptop, Jenny brought it over to the bed, clicking on the entry in question to make it fill up the page. Tom looked it over, pausing a few times to double-check certain paragraphs. By the end, he was letting out a gentle chuckle as he shook his head.

"Can't fight you on that one. If the target sees that place, they'll definitely be stopping."

* * *

Most people did the work for money. Other because it was all they knew. Even for the money folks, however, there was wisdom in occasionally working for favors. Racking up the right credit with useful people could make other jobs, the ones with *real* payouts, far more achievable. Lose a little upfront to make more on the back end. Not everyone had the right outlook and mindset for that tactic, though.

The man known professionally as Cauldron – so-called for an infamous incident amidst his old crew in which bodies had to be disposed of – was one of the rare few who could manage it. When the head of a biker club got robbed and needed the cash back, Cauldron could have held him over a barrel. Had word of the theft gotten out, his employer would have lost quite a bit of face, and probably his very position. Instead, Cauldron did the work on credit, earning a useful favor while also making sure to collect enough proof that he could destroy the biker, should the man fail to live up to his word.

Such efforts had not proven necessary. While the club had fewer members in the center of the nation, they still managed to rally and spread the word with exceptional haste. Already, they'd spotted a few convertibles, one of which sounded like it could be a match. With the schedule blown, everyone was hunting for the target in their own way. Cauldron was keenly aware that he might be the only one who'd spotted them, or he might walk in on a parade of competition lining up to take their shots.

After what had apparently happened at the Hayloft Hotel, it was obvious no one was coordinating. The prize was too big. All niceties were out the window – not that this profession lent itself to many in the first place. Usually there was at least enough respect to keep everyone from tripping over one another, yet sometimes greed blinded their better judgment.

Most of his competitors wouldn't have the means to hunt down the target, not so soon. They would likely cluster closer to the final destination, hoping to lie in wait rather than hunt the roads. If he wanted a shot at the target with as little competition as possible, this was the time to strike. It was possible this was a dead end; the pair might have changed cars and Cauldron could be chasing nothing but ghosts. Wasn't like he had something better to do, though. Besides, even if he was wrong, he could always head out further west to try an ambush.

Rising from his seat at a coffee shop, Cauldron donned his simple hat, paid for his meal while leaving an average tip, and walked calmly out to the gray sedan in the parking lot, virtually identical to two other cars nearby. Generic car, generic color, generic man driving it. The only thing interesting about Cauldron was, by design, his nickname. A single, unique aspect for his enemies to focus on. Even that was intentional. A name like Cauldron had no associated gender or distinctive physical characteristics. Anyone could take a name like that.

For as much as people had talked about that incident with the actual cauldron, it was mere chemistry. The right solutions mixed in the correct amounts yielded a predictable, reproduceable outcome. What should have scared them, had they been a tad wiser, was that after the fact, none of them gave the same description of the man who had filled the cauldron. No one was quite sure of the details – his height, face, any of it.

Cauldron could be anyone. Often, he was right next to his targets for quite some while, striking when the time was right, catching them totally unaware. Things probably wouldn't go quite that easily tonight; anyone who could survive the hunt for this long had powerful survival instincts. Still, they'd be slowing down as the constant grind wore them out. With care and precision, Cauldron could handle this with his usual brand of rapid precision.

Otherwise… things might end up getting messy.

*　　*　　*

Gorgeous Views Motel was a master class in technically not committing false advertising while coming as close as conceptually possible. Tucked away on the fringes of a smallish town not too far from the major highways, it was one of few buildings residing in a more industrial space. In what Watson was trying to see as a humorous twist, the concrete and construction all around them made it among the worst views they had seen on the day's drive. Much as he wanted to complain, making waves was out of the question. Plus, they weren't really lying, if one got down to it.

Across the street from their motel was a worn-down warehouse that looked as if it predated whatever current economic shift was washing over the area. The Gorge was a seedy-looking club that stoked an odd sense of nostalgia in Watson, some part of him remembering the endless dives he'd had to comb through for people or information. In the motel's defense, the rooms did all have excellent views of The Gorge, so Watson couldn't say the name was entirely a lie.

Truthfully, by the time he and Sherman had hidden the car, gotten their bags in, and unpacked enough to rest, that bed had started whispering in his ear, urging him to lie down. After days of nonstop driving sprinkled with bouts of adrenaline, he was beginning to feel frayed. This was by no means the furthest Watson could push himself if needed, but he tried not to reach that point when possible. Rested and ready was always the ideal way to enter a new situation.

Tempting as it was, Sherman clearly didn't share the same sentiment. He'd been holding up well, especially considering the circumstances of their last forty-eight hours, but was growing visibly more restless as the day wore on. Arrival at the motel had only made things worse. He was currently reading a book on the history of radishes with his right hand while picking apart the threads of a pillowcase with the left. There was more to it as well, minor ways his eyes roamed and face twitched, telltale signs that Watson hadn't even realized he was learning.

"You need anything?" Watson wasn't at all sure he could help but trying didn't hurt.

"Unfortunately, what I require is not so easily obtained." Sherman didn't look away from his book, however his left hand did increase its thread-picking speed. "Although the distractions do their jobs to a degree, I still need enough peace to keep myself centered. A mind lesser than mine would have cracked already from the endless influx of information. Such a prize is not so easily won. Thus far the only stimulus that appropriately affects me has been running water. Rain works the best, and showers can do, to a lesser extent. With less stimulation and excitement, they would be adequate."

"The rain is best," Watson said, turning the conundrum over in his head. It was strange, when he stopped to think about it. What was it about the rain specifically?

As his eyes looked over the room, they fell onto the deerstalker hat resting atop Sherman's skull. Something in his mind itched, an idea half-formed and ambitious to become more. All of this personality – the obsession with a fictional character – was theoretically because of that hat. Nobody knew for certain where it came from, only that he'd imprinted on the object deeply during whatever happened to his mind. It wasn't this particular hat that was special; they'd packed a few spares and Sherman didn't treat it with any extra care. It was the concept that it represented, something Sherman had taken deep into himself.

So… was it just a coincidence that they'd found him dancing in a downpour of sprinklers, and rain was the only thing he'd found that truly soothed him? Or had they all underestimated just how open to influence Sherman was during his brain's alteration? On a conceptual level it was interesting to ponder, while the practical side had less to offer. Why rain worked was less important than the fact that it did, until rain wasn't available.

Watson had read the file about the night Sherman was discovered. He knew there had been one more major element on the scene. The music. Headphones and speakers weren't going to be enough. If they wanted to test this out, to see if sound could do the same as rain, they'd need something comparable to what Sherman experienced: huge speakers, booming noise, the kind that went down to the bones and only came out with the blood. It might not work, but it was unlikely to make Sherman worse. They had several more days to drive, and no rain in the forecast. Trying this was better than watching him struggle.

"Drop the book and get ready." Watson jerked a thumb toward the window. "With views this good, I can't resist the temptation. We're going to check out The Gorge."

24.

Whether an upscale yachting club half a world away or the dive bar down the street, entering a new place had some universal constants. First, be aware of the crowd, and one's relation to it. Different spots had different cultures, which affected who they welcomed and who they were hostile toward. On that account, Watson wasn't too worried. There were no distinctive gang markings anywhere in sight, so they didn't need to worry about anything as simple as wearing the wrong colors or holding a dangerous allegiance.

The vast majority of the crowd was Caucasian: no shock, given where in the country they were, although many had hair colored all across the spectrum. Dark clothing was clearly the default, though not quite so committed as to cross the line into older Goth territory. Taking a stab, Watson guessed they were going for something like a punk aesthetic, or perhaps something local and so specific he'd never entirely put a finger on the concept. On the plus side, they were able to get in without much fuss about their outfits. Watson was dressed slightly more casually, while Sherman had made no alterations whatsoever and at a glance fit in better with the crowd.

Watson's next step in entering a new place was a classic: clock the threats and exits. Boring as it might be, there was a reason it was a fundamental, and Watson didn't dare dream of skipping it. In what had to be a fire hazard violation, The Gorge had a modest entrance, leading into a large open section hosting two bars on opposite sides of the room. Directly across from the entrance were a pair of large double doors, barely holding back the sea of music pressing at its seams.

One major entrance and exit, with a funnel point before they'd be able to step outside. Definitely not up to code. Watson would scan for any extra doors, but given the age of the building, his hopes were minimal. It wasn't all bad; there was something to be said for one way in and out. Limiting the ways potential enemies could get in had benefits, and Watson did enjoy the idea of seeing exactly who came and went.

As far as threats went, aside from a few bigger boys with a glint of violence in their eyes, Watson didn't see any serious concerns. Even the drunks would need more courage before the brawling began, and he wasn't planning to stay for that long. That didn't mean Watson could relax, unfortunately. They were being pursued; he couldn't be sure any of these people weren't just waiting for the chance to spring.

The last of Watson's initial evaluation protocol, before he moved on to the less glamorous secondary evaluation protocol, was to assess relevant environmental factors. A place with unusual elevation, heat, or local customs could change how he needed to handle an operation. Here, the obvious environmental aspect was the very reason they'd come: the music.

Through the door, all Watson could hear was the deep thud of the bass. Someone must have spent a lot of time soundproofing the building; it held the roaring sound in with surprising power. Once the seal broke, however, so too did the separation between them and the music. Standing there in the lobby, looking things over, Watson almost didn't notice when a couple took their drinks up to the double doors and carefully yanked one open.

Instantly, it became clear why the bar and dance floor were separated. Commerce would have been utterly impossible with the incomprehensible storm of sound that came bursting through. No one could place an order in that sort of environment, let alone carry on any manner of conversation or, hopefully, string two thoughts together.

A strange expression rested on Sherman's face as the heavy door closed once more, cutting off the noise as suddenly as it had begun: not just curiosity but true intrigue danced in those unsettling eyes. "Watson, what manner of music was that? I do not entirely recognize it, yet it calls to me."

"From what we just heard, it sounded like techno. Sort of like the club music where you were found, only without lyrics."

"Or any sense of coherency and logic." Sherman certainly didn't sound like those were bad things as he started forward on a direct course with the huge doors. He was nearly running by the end, grabbing the handles and flinging them wide, letting the sounds bowl over them in one powerful wave.

With a better vantage point, Watson could see into the actual dance floor. For the most part, it looked like what it was: an old warehouse. Through the years, tech had slowly accrued on the walls and ceiling. A dozen different flashing lights in various makes and styles lit up different sections in seemingly no prescribed order. Speakers lined the walls, corners, on top of a medium-sized stage near the back, and in any other nook they could find a place to shove one. Seating was minimal—a few busted stools near the back. The rest was open space being used to dance, mosh, or otherwise celebrate, with methods changing depending on where one walked.

After the long stare, Watson realized the doors were closing again. Sherman had merely flung them open, not held them in place, and he was too transfixed by the spectacle to bother taking hold of either handle again. By the time they shut, permitting even the concept of conversation once more, Watson felt like he'd gotten more than enough of what this place had to offer... until he looked over to Sherman.

Tears fell from Sherman's eyes, not in abundance, but neither were they hidden. "It is... noise, Watson. Pure, beautiful, pointless noise. It is like the antithesis of thought made real." Without warning, one of his large hands clapped down on Watson's shoulder, squeezing it hard.

"Thank you. Truly. I needed this more than I realized."

With that, Sherman whipped the doors open again and flew through them, submerging himself completely in thrall of thundering techno music. If not for his height and that ridiculous hat, Watson might have feared losing his charge. As it was, he hung back as much as felt safe, for the most part allowing Sherman the freedom to do whatever he needed. And as it turned out, what Sherman needed was to dance.

Watson quickly realized that "dance" might not be the right term for what Sherman was up to. True, his body was moving, though not to any discernable rhythm. Shaking, hopping, spinning in a circle at some points, Sherman was truly moving to the beat only he could hear. It looked more like a standing seizure than any sort of dancing, which oddly did help him to better blend in with the rest of the crowd. While they weren't quite as bad as Sherman, it was a closer contest than it should have been.

Setting his back to a wall, Watson chose a position where he could watch the double doors as well as Sherman, just in case they got any unexpected company for the evening.

Coming out here had been dangerous. In his younger days, Watson might not have taken the gamble. He'd have told Sherman to power through, tough it out, in favor of keeping their exposure as limited as possible. For all the baggage Poole's betrayal had given him, it did have the benefit of showing Watson just how powerful the mind could be. No longer did he assume every issue could be handled with determination and gritted teeth. Sometimes, there was no other solution besides a break. However brief it might be, he'd found a way to give Sherman that for tonight.

In a few more days, once the job was done, Watson intended to take a nice long break as well. He was definitely overdue for a little down time.

* * *

A club was hardly ideal. Noise, people, chaos, so many factors that were unpredictable. Of course, those same factors were what made it an opportunity that Cauldron couldn't afford to pass up. The bodyguard was careful. From the way they'd stashed the car to how his head stayed on constant swivel whenever they were exposed, he wasn't some amateur with a gun. But with the madness of a dance club, not even he could be aware of every person who approached the target. Add in the camouflage of dim lights and thundering sound, and the whole thing almost became too easy.

So easy, in fact, that Cauldron feared it could be a trap. Putting the bait out in the open like this set his nerves tingling. He had to remind himself that it wasn't as though they knew they'd been followed. Both probably assumed themselves to be moderately safe. All the same, Cauldron would go into this carefully. Scan the area, find the weakness, exploit it, escape. A simple plan, admittedly, but one that required patience and expertise to properly implement.

Checking the black leather pouch he'd set on the next seat, Cauldron ran through his tools. Plastic needles and syringes – something he had made custom for slipping through metal detectors – along with bright liquids inside. Zip ties, for when chemical means failed. A ceramic knife, in case the plan went completely awry. Two antacid pills. Those didn't have a nefarious purpose; blending in at these places just usually demanded drinking, and more than one beer would trigger Cauldron's reflux. Age was a monster that spared no victim, regardless of how skilled they might be.

Making his way in was simple. Adorned in rustic clothing purchased from a thrift store, he had the aesthetic of someone who wore what they had and that was all there was to it. In fact, the ensemble actually risked mimicking a few of the other outfits Cauldron passed when stepping into the bar. He noted the lack of a metal detector, which meant he could have brought a gun in. That wasn't especially relevant; in a situation like this, he would have chosen the same tools again in a heartbeat, but it was a fact he had to keep in mind.

Just because he hadn't brought in a gun didn't mean no one else had. Especially that bodyguard, who might very well be strapped down with an entire armory after what they'd been through. Most in his position would be armed to their teeth, and that was ignoring that virtually no other bodyguard would have taken their asset to a location like this without extremely good reason.

That was what happened when things went off-script. People turned to improvisation, which was the same as getting sloppy. Sure, a little wiggle room in a plan was essential for adapting to changing variables, but throwing it out entirely was a step too far. With them this flustered, it should make snatching the target relatively simple. First, he'd have to scout the area, then find a way to ensure the bodyguard was distracted.

Cauldron yanked open the double doors, standing in the torrent of sound for several seconds before shutting them and walking over to a bar. If he was going to spend time in that room, the very least he owed his ears and mind was a drink for protection. One brief scan showed that this establishment served bad beer and worse liquor. Choosing the lesser of two evils, Cauldron selected the can of beer he saw the most people drinking. Every little bit of camouflage helped. As he ordered, Cauldron took out his antacid pills and swallowed them dry.

Based on the volume and the music, this would definitely be a more than a one beer kind of job.

25.

After a while, Watson found his ears grew essentially numb to the thundering sounds bursting from the myriad of speakers. Some years back he'd taken minor eardrum damage when a bomb went off early, and this felt like a lesser version of that experience. Too long in here might have him using the TV subtitles for a while.

Besides, the minor discomfort was worth the trade-off to see Sherman so visibly relaxed. His dancing had slowed from the earlier fever-pitch, though his face did still have a telltale sheen of sweat. Now, Sherman more swayed and sashayed, continuing to move to his own beat, just not quite so aggressively. Physically, he looked the same as always, only with dampness running across his skin.

Mentally, it was a whole different ballgame. The constant tension that surrounded Sherman, the squirming like he'd eaten a squirrel that was endlessly trying to claw back out, was severely diminished. He might not quite pass for normal, but it was plain to see this experience had been a release for him, like the rain before it.

Watson would make sure to tell Gregson about this during the handoff. It could be a potent tool for helping Sherman adapt in the years to come. Really, it was a little strange that no one else had considered the idea. Maybe they hadn't needed to; with lower stress and presumably good water pressure, the showers were probably enough. Or… perhaps they just hadn't cared enough to dig that deep. Gregson seemed like an okay guy, but he was only one person in a large facility.

To most of the people studying Sherman, the sole thing they would care about was his brain, not his mind. So long as he was controlled enough, soothed enough to stay pliable, then that was all they needed. From an operational perspective, Watson understood such a sentiment completely: minimize resources expended on anything non-essential, prioritize studying and understanding the physical alterations that his brain had undergone, and, of course, spend all available energy on helping Sherman develop that enhanced cognition window. Because *that* might be useful to them down the line, so it mattered.

That was why Watson had never been such a fan of the operational perspective. When humans were reduced to numbers, feelings into factors, it became too easy to lose sight of where the lines were. He'd seen it happen to too many agents already; one in particular still sent pangs through his right leg. More than a few people in Watson's industry tried to bury their humanity, sealing it off so they could do what was sometimes necessary. For his part, Watson liked to think he'd held on to his, but some days it was easier to be sure than others. Looking at Sherman and realizing that he was delivering the asset to people who would spend the rest of his life treating him like a lab rat, Watson truly didn't know whether all of this was good or evil. It was a concern for later. Right now, his job was to keep Sherman safe, and that much he could do without any sense of conflict.

Then, like a fin jutting up from the calm surface of the ocean, Watson noticed the sudden movement rippling through the dancers, causing them to shift. If someone had enough presence to make this crowd get out of the way, they were either a local celebrity or inherently terrifying. Given the way their luck had been breaking as of late, the answer was almost too obvious.

Bolting forward, Watson arrived less than twenty seconds before the ripple reached Sherman. As it turned out, Watson's instincts were spot on. This was a big man, muscular and with a barely holding together tank top showing off his physique. Bald head, lots of tattoos, and a sneer meant to melt people's resolve. It was a good image, carefully built with purpose.

"Is there a problem?" Watson tried to keep his tone light, despite having to nearly yell over the noise.

Whether due to the music or lack of interest, the tattooed man didn't appear to hear Watson's question, moving to brush past him the same way he had the rest of the crowd. Well, that wouldn't do. Reaching up, Watson pressed his palm against the dark fabric of the man's tank top, a symbolic gesture to make him stop.

The reaction was a deeper sneer, followed by a casual attempt to shove Watson's arm aside. When it failed, Watson proving stronger than he looked, that face grew even angrier. The next shove was meant to send Watson sprawling. In a flash, Watson grabbed the man's arm and flipped him effortlessly into the air, putting an extra oomph into it as he slammed the fellow down, nearly clipping some other dancers in the process. Thankfully, the sight of this hulking jerk hitting the ground was more than enough to buy them all some breathing room. Watson shot a quick glance to Sherman, who was still swaying, uninterrupted, as if he hadn't even noticed the spectacle.

Tattoo Man had a small crew with him, all of whom had taken steps back when the big fellow went down. They were eyeing Watson now, thoughts so transparent they might as well have yelled them. Everyone was wondering if now was the time to strike. They could go after the boss if they had old grudges or ambition, or Watson himself if they wanted to display loyalty. None of that was permissible. It would force him to fight without holding back, and he wasn't sure these people deserved to be injured yet. Not until he knew exactly what was going on, or the situation became untenable, would he resort to that level of violence. There had to be lines he was hesitant to cross; it was one of the distinctions that separated Watson from scum like Poole.

They didn't know that, however, so when a lazy punch came toward him from the still-rising opponent, Watson wasted no time. People threw their hands around like they were hammers, not realizing that they were offering up dangerous vulnerabilities to someone with the right training. Watson easily caught the punch, jabbing the man's forearm with a strike of his own. As expected, the sudden pain caused the whole arm to loosen, including the fist. After that, it was just a matter of being fast and ready, both of which Watson definitely was. He grabbed the big man's thumb in a lock and applied immediate pressure. That was twice now this guy had swung at him; Watson's compassion was beginning to dim.

No sooner was the hold in place than the man's entire attitude changed. Gone was the smoldering anger. In its place was a person in sudden, unexpected pain with no idea how to deal with it. His other hand closed into a fist, so Watson briefly increased the pressure. On top of killing any ambitions toward fighting back, the move elicited a yelp so loud that Watson could hear it over the music. Hoping they now understood one another, Watson leaned in close enough to speak directly in the man's ear. Not pleasant, but also the only way they were going to talk over all the racket.

"You have ten seconds to tell me why you were coming after my friend. Take longer than that, and you get to experience the fun of life with a thumb cast. Trust me, it's even more inconvenient than you think."

For a moment, Watson feared the idiot would keep struggling. After a few seconds of failure, however, the fight seemed to go out of him. "A dude told me he was running his mouth about me and my lady. I don't stand for that kind of disrespect."

Were Watson in possession of hackles, they would have been raised. "A dude? What dude? Who told you that?"

"Same dude who walked off with him." A nod of that bald head caused Watson to spin back around. In the space where Sherman had been swaying, there was now total emptiness. He'd been distracted for less than a minute, if that. How had someone swept in that fast?

Because it was a matter of being fast and ready, just like he'd done in the fight. This whole thing had been teed up specifically to make him look away from Sherman.

Putting together a distraction like this on the fly – and having it work – spoke to someone with a tremendous amount of skill. Still, they couldn't change the reality of the situation. This was still a crowded club, with one central entrance and exit point. Getting out would take time, especially with someone like Sherman in tow. All wasn't lost just yet, but every passing second brought Sherman closer to danger.

There was no mercy in Watson's eyes as his grip tightened, pulling the man in even closer. "You're going to tell me everything about that 'dude' in question, and you'll do it fast."

*   *   *

In spite of all the drawbacks, there was one benefit to doing extractions from a club. The presence of alcohol offered an easy method of escape, even with an unconscious body. Cauldron made apologies for his drunk friend as he hauled Sherman's limp body back through the lobby and out the front door. He might have miscalculated the dosage; this guy had gone down fast. Hauling him around did help explain the mix-up; physically he was bonier than the huge coat let on. It made for an easier trip back to the car, though, so Cauldron was counting this one as a happy surprise.

Since they were still in view of the club, laying Sherman down in the back seat was a delicate affair. In truth, it probably would have been anyway, Cauldron bore the man no ill will and certainly didn't want to damage the goods. He might have added some zip ties, were there a way to do so inconspicuously, but given Sherman's condition, it could wait until they were a bit down the road.

Punching a few numbers on his phone, Cauldron only had to wait for three rings before the line connected. "Target acquired. Sending photo confirmation as soon as the call ends. I'll call later tonight with specifications for the exchange." He paused, listening to some rebuttal, before growing impatient. "Listen, with this much money in play, there are going to be safeguards – *my* safeguards, to ensure everyone walks away with what they want from the deal. Tell your people to make peace with that, or I'll toss this guy over the next bridge I pass."

Cauldron slammed the phone shut just as the sound of a closing car door drew his attention. Sitting upright, looking more bored than bothered, was Sherman. Moving fast, Cauldron yanked on the handle, but it was already locked.

"I must say, you are a great disappointment. I went to all the trouble of permitting you to drag me out here, hoping you would reveal *some* useful detail about your employer, and all I hear is a coded message and you throwing a tantrum. Curse my curiosity for permitting me to leave. When you filled my veins with that pointless drug, I simply had to see where things went."

Slapping his hands at his pockets, Cauldron hunted for his keys. A tap on the glass drew his attention back up, where he could see the jingling ring suspended in Sherman's fingers. "Quite easy to reach in someone's pocket when they are occupied with situating a body inside a car. You *could* break the glass. I can tell from the light and sound coming through it lacks reinforcement. If you think you have the time, that is."

They were on a clock, and both men knew it. Soon, Watson would realize Sherman was missing and come hunting. When that happened, if Cauldron was still between Watson and Sherman, then the job would turn messy, possibly dangerous. On the other hand, if he bolted now then this was the end of his best chance. While he could aim for an ambush farther down the road, they knew his face now – plus there would be others to compete with. Currently, he had the target isolated and in his vehicle. The chances of success weren't going to get much better than that.

Yanking out his ceramic knife, Cauldron flipped it around to the dense, rubberized plastic handle. In terms of pure damage, it wouldn't hold up to a metal hilt, however it was more than hard enough to shatter glass. In one blow, the window gave, crumbling into pebbles of safety glass that went running down along the floor. Sherman scooted away, putting his back to the other backseat door. A temporary solution; Cauldron could smash that window out as well. Were he a little smarter, Sherman would be making for the driver's seat, trying to get the car moving. It wouldn't work – Cauldron made a few adjustments to every car he drove for just such reasons – but at least it would have been proactive. This way, he was just waiting to be dragged out and tied up.

The soft crunch of gravel gave away the approach. Cauldron turned to find himself staring across the near-empty section of the old parking lot at a distinct figure lit by the back glow of The Gorge's neon lights. He couldn't make out much of the face, however the body language rendered such details unnecessary. Tight fists, elevated breathing, careful positioning: someone had come looking for a fight.

"Didn't expect you to catch up in time."

"Don't take it personally. No one can properly plan for dealing with Sherman." A step forward, firm and steady. "Why don't you go run screaming back into the night? I have had a long few days on what was supposed to be a simple assignment, and I'm really not in the mood for this. Take the loss, regroup, live to fight another day."

"Tempting, but the money is too high." Cauldron flipped the blade around in his hand, getting a comfortable grip. "You could always just leave. He's an assignment, nothing more. Everyone fails an assignment sometimes. With how many people are after you, I doubt they can even hold you accountable. Your whole operation was compromised from the start. This was the only way it could ever have gone."

Another step, and now Cauldron could see that face better. He could make out the confidence, the danger, and the awareness, all things he'd been expecting. But there was something more, an unanticipated addition. Anger. The bodyguard was mad, be it because of wounded pride or a real concern about his charge. Either way, that expression meant discussion was off the table.

One way or the other, this ended in blood.

26.

From the moment he'd been tossed into the car, Sherman had started boiling. Not literally, even if it the sensation was dangerously similar. It was Sherman's mind that was steaming, overloading as the walls tried to press against his sense of reason. Being in places like this, enclosed, limited – there wasn't enough information or variables. With nowhere else to look for distraction, his mind turned inward, trying to assess itself and their current situation.

In the early days, Sherman hadn't known the danger of these spirals. Whatever it was that allowed him to keep moving while everyone else died after tasting the mystery drug, the gift was tenuous. His own mind could overload and crumple in on itself just like the others'; they'd had the scans to prove it. Keeping mentally active helped stave it off in the long term; avoiding enclosed spaces was more relevant for moment-to-moment survival.

The shattered window helped, aided Sherman in keeping his cool until Watson arrived. Now that his assistant was finally on hand, however, even the presence of an attacker wasn't enough to distract him from his surroundings. Fleeing was an option, but a dangerous one. Putting himself into play could make Watson's task harder, and this particular opponent was so far proving dangerously competent. He couldn't linger in here either, unfortunately. Already, Sherman's body was sweating and visible tremors were shaking his arms. No good. At this rate, he'd crumple soon, become incapable of doing anything more than rocking back and forth. Only a single way forward, one version of him that was both useful and capable of existing in enclosed spaces.

Gathering his willpower, Sherman felt the strange pressure in his brain, a button that hadn't existed before his change. He'd never be able to describe activating the enhanced cognition window any more than someone could explain how they directed their limbs. It was simply there, a part of him, albeit one he didn't truly grasp yet. Turning it on wasn't the hard part.

"A case must be solved." The exact phrase didn't actually matter. Like a grunt while lifting weights, the words were simply a verbal component of a greater physical effort. Still, Sherman felt they weren't quite right yet. In fact, the phrase "not quite right" could effectively be applied to every aspect of Sherman's enhanced abilities.

As his brain shifted gears, the world around came into sharper focus. Blurry details, things he could barely make out, solidified instantly. Uncertainties turned clear, misunderstandings vanished. Most important of all: the world stopped screaming at Sherman. No longer was he assaulted by the information; now it stood, idle and ready, waiting for him to need any tidbit or detail.

It should have been perfection, an instantaneous evolution to a higher plane of intellect. But there was a nagging flaw; he didn't know what to do. Everywhere he looked, there were possibilities. Plans unfolded at every glance and thought, a dozen mental mice scattering in all directions. When the world became clear, Sherman lost his own focus. There was just so much to process. Even when the information was cooperative, it was still like trying to swallow an ocean.

If nothing else, Sherman could function inside the car again. He shook off the last of his tremors before looking out the window to see how Watson was doing. Immediately, Sherman was glad he'd already done the activation. Based on how things were looking out there, Watson was going to need some help.

*   *   *

While Watson did have a gun on his person, he was hesitant to draw. From their position across the street, a crowd at The Gorge could see the whole parking lot reasonably well. A post-bar brawl, they might not call the cops about. Gunshots were a different matter. On top of that, he didn't know if the enemy had one as well. Once firearms were brought in, there were all manner of other considerations to keep in mind. Bystanders, witnesses, police, to say nothing of the chance that Sherman could end up killed in the crossfire.

That was why Watson didn't reach for his pistol as the stranger approached, knife still in hand. Based on appearance, the guy was unremarkable: dark hair, bland face, and a build slightly too muscular for his mundane outfit to hide. No markings, no scars, nothing distinctive whatsoever. Given all that, the way he moved, and the skill with which he'd stolen Sherman, there was only one conclusion to reach.

They were up against a pro.

The others so far had been overreaching amateurs, playing in a league they weren't truly ready for. Not him. Nothing about this enemy spoke to fear or inexperience. In terms of combat, that made things harder, but it might at least offer a respite in one area.

"You seem like the kind who listens to reason. What do you say we keep this old-fashioned? No weapons, no random shots to get the police involved. Just two guys beating each other up outside of a bar. Also ensures my asset stays safe."

"Can't help but notice your proposal costs me a knife and you nothing," the stranger pointed out.

Wordlessly, Watson produced his pistol, keeping it carefully to the side so it wasn't yet publicly visible. With a quick motion, he popped out the clip, letting it fall to his feet. There was still one in the chamber, and both men knew it, just like they knew how much more complicated their jobs got once sirens arrived.

After a few moments of consideration, the knife tumbled through the air before vanishing into the shadows, thrown too far for either man to recover. Watson ejected the final shell and tossed it in the same direction as the knife. The gun he kept, tucking it back into his waistband. Leaving guns lying around was an excellent way to get set up and was just a poor economic policy in general, especially when he was already down one on this trip. Bullets and clips were much easier to replace.

"I'm going by Cauldron right now." With the knife gone, Watson's opponent had both fists raised in a tight, compact stance.

"Watson, at the moment."

Cauldron's eyes widened a hair, and his eyes darted to the car, where Sherman was softly shaking with his eyes closed. "Right on the nose with that one. Guess I've got no room to throw stones."

To a casual outsider, it might have appeared to be nothing more than banter. And there was, in truth, some element of ceremony to the introductions. It wasn't often one met others in the same profession out in the wild, even less so that they demonstrated noteworthy skill. Learning their codenames was important, because down the line, one never knew who might be an enemy or ally. The more information on hand, the better.

Of course, they were also doing more than merely talking. With every word, glance, and movement, they were assessing one another.

Gauging speed and mobility, guessing at fighting style, trying to unravel the riddle of their opponent before the first blow was struck.

It was Cauldron who moved first, coming in swinging with surprisingly heavy fists.

These were nothing like those amateur jabs from the club brawler. Blocking and dodging took everything Watson had; there were no openings for any sort of throw or lock. It had been a while since Watson fought someone who was actually good at this. As one of Cauldron's fists slipped past his guard, landing a glancing shot on his ribs, Watson had to wonder if perhaps it had been *too* long since a real fight.

Through the next minute, Watson made some important discoveries about the kidnapper named Cauldron. He favored his left arm over his right, dipped back just out of range when he couldn't block, and went for the sure hits rather than a flashy knockout that could be countered. The information might have been more useful if not for one other discovery: Cauldron was a better fighter than Watson.

It wasn't easy for him to admit. This was an area where he was accustomed to succeeding, but there was little point in denying the plain truth. As strike after strike went nowhere and his own sore spots piled up, it was clear to see who was winning this fight. Watson went for a sweep to the legs, only for Cauldron to easily sidestep it, landing a jab in the process. A punch only opened Watson up for the payback blow to another point on his ribs. Even a sudden charge led nowhere, as Cauldron nimbly avoided it with no visible effort.

Overall, Watson would have categorized the situation as non-ideal. However, that didn't mean he was out just yet. There were many different aspects to a fight, more than just the trading of fists. Cauldron didn't actually appear to be faster than Watson: he'd just been predicting every move before it was made. In plenty of ways, that was harder to fight against, but the flip side was that if he could stop Cauldron from predicting his moves, the bout would become far more winnable.

Another punch to the gut jerked Watson into the moment, reminding him that all the plans in the world were no good if he couldn't implement them.

A wayward turn of the head gave Watson an unexpected glimpse at Sherman, who was no longer trembling. In fact, his eyes were wide and bright, much too coherent to be mistaken for his normal expression. While he was still hesitant to unleash Sherman's unmastered mental abilities, Watson was grateful for any edge they could get. Sherman saw him take notice and hurriedly waved, pointing to the area near the car. He wanted Watson to lead Cauldron in closer. For what, was anyone's guess. Hopefully he wasn't going to try and run the kidnapper over; someone with those skills would leap clear as soon as the engine turned on.

Trying to predict Sherman was akin catching clouds in a pasta strainer: impossible and fundamentally ridiculous in concept. To his own surprise, that aspect made Watson open to the idea. So far, Cauldron was reading everything Watson could throw at him. If they wanted an outside chance of catching him by surprise, then Sherman was their best hope. The so-called world's greatest detective might be many undesirable things, but predictable was not among them.

Staggering back, pretending (not as hard as he might have liked) to be feeling the blows, Watson retreated a few steps toward the car. A break would be too conspicuous; it might raise Cauldron's suspicions. Losing, on the other hand, played into his ego. There was no telling how prideful this man was, although with skills this developed, there was bound to some amount to work with. If he thought Watson was losing ground, unknowingly retreating, then he'd most likely do what all predators did in such moments.

Cauldron would close in for the kill.

For the moment, he was continuing to play coy, staying back and hitting Watson at every opportunity. Never overexposing or getting greedy, Cauldron was clearly content to pick away at Watson blow after blow until he'd been chipped down to nothing. With a soft curse and a silent prayer, Watson allowed a few more hits to slip past his guard. Nowhere vital, but tender enough to sell the staggering.

Finally, after what seemed like ages but was less than thirty seconds, they were close to the car once more. Watson had no idea what was coming, nor his role in it. Anything would work at this point. A shove, a dirty look, a creative insult: anything that distracted Cauldron even the slightest amount could make the difference. Fist raised, Watson readied himself for a final stand. No more running now, not with Sherman so close.

All he could do was hope that oddball had come up with some kind of plan.

27.

Supplies inside the car were limited. This man – Cauldron had been the name he gave Watson – kept a spotless interior. No change, spare knick-knacks, or bags of groceries that might prompt inspiration. Although he had the keys, Sherman could effortlessly calculate Cauldron's speed versus the rate at which he could get the vehicle into hitting position, and it wasn't even a contest.

There was one ray of hope, however. The middle of the back seat folded down, revealing a direct path to the trunk. Inside Sherman was only able to find a dark bag and a spare tire. Ripping into the bag he found road flares, tire sealant, a pressure gauge, a small knife and other minor tools. It was a kit for road emergencies, but Sherman's brain itched as he devised a way to make use of it in a parking lot.

Initially, the situation looked dire. Watson was losing, and once he was down, there was little chance Sherman could best such an opponent. The physical work was part of what a Watson was for, especially since in a few minutes, Sherman would be largely useless. However, they did have some leverage. To start with, they knew Cauldron was here for a kidnapping, not a murder. That meant he needed to keep Sherman alive and would require some method of transportation for a presumably unconscious or restrained body.

Sherman had an idea. Catching Watson's eye, he waved for the fight to come closer. A good distraction only worked with lots of visibility, so Sherman would make this one impossible to miss.

Moving fast – quicker than he could have managed in his usual condition as every thought translated seamlessly into action – Sherman cut circular holes in the seats. Once he had four, one in each major position, Sherman tore open road flares one by one, hurriedly jamming them into the seats. Smoke starting spewing as the fire caught right away. Using the sealant, Sherman went around the crack in his nearest door, then moved up to the front. The only one he didn't bother with was the door with the open window. That was an intentional smoke exit point, a chimney to make sure this whole effort didn't pass unnoticed. Besides, Sherman needed something to yell out of.

"Duplicitous knave, your scheme is undone!" Sherman returned to the back seat and stuck his head out of the smashed window, taking a deep breath while he could. Even if this worked, he wouldn't get many more for a stretch. "I have set fire to your transportation, and with it, I have undone any hopes of fleeing with my unwilling form. Now surrender..." Sherman stuttered off, shaking his head. "Surrender to... my... surrender..."

With no more warning than that, Sherman's eyes closed as he fell – backward into the smoke-filled car that was growing steadily more on fire with every passing moment.

* * *

That absolute idiot.

Watson was hoping for a plan; instead he drew Cauldron closer to the car just in time to realize that Sherman set the whole thing on fire with himself inside. That was the opposite of a plan: it was what happened when unattended children were left alone with matches. Now, he'd not only drawn a *lot* of attention to what was going on, he'd ended up trapped inside a burning car. At least, that's the conclusion Watson would have jumped to a few days prior.

After everything they'd been through, he was sure, if nothing else, that Sherman didn't have a death wish. The man was living through constant suffering just to stay alive. And while it was easy to write Sherman off, when he had that gleam in his eye, he was capable of unexpected feats. Most important of all was that Watson had a well-developed internal sense of time, and he was positive it hadn't been five minutes yet. This was more than it appeared to be. Sherman was giving him an opportunity, if he was good enough to use it.

"Self-immolation. Been a while since someone went that route to keep dangerous information out of enemy hands." Physically, Watson forced himself to relax completely, as though the fight were done. "I'll make a note in his file. Braver way to go than I'd have expected from a man like him."

Cauldron's eyes were darting between the car and Watson, too experienced not to be wary, yet also keenly aware that his target was in serious danger. "So do your job, bodyguard. Pull him free."

"Secondary priority. If I can't keep Sherman from falling into enemy hands, I'm to execute him. We win by stopping your employer from getting him. Alive is preferable to dead, but jobs don't always go the way we want. And he saved me the trouble of bothering with a head shot. Fire should torch whatever is in his brain just as effectively."

It wasn't a bluff. It couldn't be. A man with Cauldron's experience would sense the deception. In that moment, Watson truly planned to do nothing, to let things play out as they would. Granted, that was only possible because he knew Sherman wasn't really out yet, but that truth permitted him to commit in a way that would have otherwise been impossible.

They locked eyes for several seconds before Cauldron's face broke into a snarl. "I've been playing nice and cordial with you. Come after me during this rescue, and that won't be the case anymore. Besides, we both know you don't want him dead." He dashed the short distance over to the car and yanked the door with the broken window open. No sooner had his face entered the smoke than Watson saw the trunk lid lift. It must have been quietly opened while they were talking, and Sherman held it to appear closed. As the lid rose, it all clicked into place for Watson.

Tempting as it was to go for the genitals, just because Watson's pride was still a little wounded from the fight, he did still believe in some manner of professional courtesy. So Watson's foot slammed directly into Cauldron's butt, sending him hurtling forward into the smoking car. The flames weren't quite so intense that he immediately began to burn, but the unexpected yelp gave away his discomfort.

Scrambling up, Cauldron grabbed the handle on the opposite side of the car, yanking it open momentarily—only for it smash against it his skull thanks to a well-placed kick from Sherman. The moment was just long enough for him to make out his prize was helping to keep him trapped, which elicited an unnaturally guttural growl. The growl quickly turned into a cough, a hacking one at that. By now, the heat and smoke inside the car had reached a truly dangerous level, and in the distance they could already hear sirens.

"Sherman, how did he get you out here?" Watson asked, delivering a kick of his own to the door Cauldron tried next.

"Needle in the neck. Had the same effect as the poison, however I suspected playing along might provide a chance to learn more about our pursuers." There was a gentle glaze coming over Sherman's eyes. Time was running out for him, and keeping Cauldron contained like this was definitely a two-person job.

"Okay, Cauldron, here's the deal. Come to the window where I can see you and inject yourself, then throw on some cuffs that I know you'll have for good measure. Do that, and we let you out. Don't, and our problem solves itself."

There were few things worse than being backed into a corner. Watson hated it; hell, everyone he'd ever met who did this job hated it. But it was a skill you needed to have – the capacity to recognize when you were beaten and live to fight another day. Someone as good as Cauldron, who'd lived to his age in such a dangerous profession, had absolutely honed the ability to understand when there was no way out.

In seconds, he was at the window, greedily sucking down air even as he fumbled with a leather pouch. He produced a plastic syringe, then a pair of zip ties. "Once I inject, I'm going to be limp, so at least drag me from the car if you're going to kill me anyway." That was all the preamble before he jammed the tip into his forearm, using every last drop of the liquid inside. There was virtually no delay as his movements grew sloppier, limbs acting like they were weighed down. Cauldron barely got his hands zip tied, pulling it tight with his teeth, before his head was nodding.

By the time Watson yanked him free, Cauldron was completely out and snoring loudly. He hauled the man several feet away from the flaming car, which was beginning to grow brighter as the flames spread. From the other side, Sherman staggered into looking like he might mimic Cauldron any second.

Dropping the kidnapper, Watson ran back and threw a shoulder under Sherman to keep him upright.

"That was crazy. You know that, right? Who lights a car on fire with themselves in it?"

"Someone in need of a maneuver no fully sane person would execute. I could hardly stay uninvolved, Watson. He was beating you quite thoroughly."

The analysis was accurate, if still a wound to Watson's ego. "I'm usually on top at hand-to-hand, but there's always someone better. Thanks for having my back."

"But of course. That is the natural state of our dynamic. You handle the mundane annoyances –food, lodging, survival, all of that drivel. Whereas I am required when we encounter the truly exceptional or a great enough need for the impossible. For all your failings, you do have well-developed martial skills. An opponent capable of manhandling you as such certainly qualifies as exceptional."

"I got in a few hits," Watson pointed out. He wasn't in love with how the fight was being remembered, even it was reasonably accurate.

As they talked, Watson was carefully leading Sherman away with a phone out like he was calling for authorities. The moment they turned a nearby corner, both would vanish into the night, but while the crowd was still watching, they had to play their parts. Sherman's time was up, so he was going to be more parcel than person until he had a recovery nap.

"Your blows must have landed while I was preoccupied with saving us," Sherman countered. "Credit and praise where they are earned… You have done a surprisingly good job at the secondary task of a Watson tonight: play along. I feared you wouldn't understand my plan, however you proved unexpectedly adept at grasping my intent."

"Maybe I'm not the worst Watson after all." They were far enough from the car that they'd become barely more than shadows, and as the duo slipped around a faded stone corner, the last of the lingering stares was lost. Speed increased right away; Watson half-carrying Sherman to keep him in step.

There was a delay before the response; words were coming harder for Sherman at the moment. "If only. You are a shrine to disappointment. So gifted in so many ways, yet you continuously fail at the most primary, essential part of the job. Even tonight, you looked my way only in absolute desperation."

"What, so my main job is to lean on you? Because it feels like we might have switched roles."

Watson glanced over to notice that Sherman was barely conscious, eyes fluttering as they logged step after step.

"Never mind, we'll talk about it later. For now, let's just get back to the car. After a spectacle like that, we need to be long gone by morning."

28.

Within any organization, there was attrition. In restaurants, that meant a constant turnover of servers getting steadily burned out on the job. For corporations, at times, it took the form of poaching by headhunters. Those who worked in the unsavory disciplines – be they part of legitimate organizations or the off-the-books sort that Gwendolyn ran – had their own form as well. Unfortunately for her and every other overseer of clandestine operations, in their line of work, non-fatal attrition most often took the form of treachery.

That was the nature of the game.

Want to hop over and work for someone else? Their first demand will be to stay in your current position and pump them information from inside. It was the same thing Gwendolyn asked of anyone who wanted to join her side, when circumstances would allow. The question of who was selling secrets could most often be answered by figuring out who wasn't happy. Anyone who might be looking for a change was a vulnerability.

Pulling on that thread had, in fact, led Gwendolyn to some analysts with peculiar financial activities. In doing so, however, she'd unwittingly unraveled a larger sweater than expected. Pushing on those transactions gave her the names of shell corporations and corresponding account numbers. Using that as a starting point, Gwendolyn had been running down everyone else with access to sensitive intel who'd gotten so much as a nickel from those companies. It wasn't a hidden conspiracy that dominated the whole department, but more of her people were potentially compromised than Gwendolyn would like.

Worse was that, mixed in with the fake stuff were some real, actual contracting jobs that had gone through proper channels. Without running down the details for each one, she couldn't be sure who'd been doing assigned work and who'd been lining their pockets by going freelance. It was the sort of convoluted obfuscation she taught agents to leave in their wake, which made her strangely proud and annoyed in equal measure.

Unknotting this should take weeks, probably months. She had days at the most. For the moment, all Gwendolyn could do was pull every person who had even the potential to be comprised away from Sherman's case. It was the best protection she could offer until they reached their final destination and would help ensure they were safe upon arrival. Until then, Gwendolyn needed to keep the pressure turned up. From time to time, a department required sweeping to keep tidy.

Clearly, this round of cleaning had been long overdue.

* * *

After a night filled with more fleeing and car-sleep, Watson was grateful for the simple joy of a quiet morning. Breakfast had gone over well, as Sherman both discovered he loved the local flapjacks then learned about the dangers of over-indulging on foods that expand in the stomach. Whether it was a full belly or weariness from the prior evening, he was wiped out enough to come off as practically normal during their detour.

The pitstop of the day turned out to be, after Sherman's promise of something more exciting, a museum of windmills: miniature handmade ones, designs along the walls, pictures, model recreations, and one huge actual windmill in the backyard. Watson had been subjected to chemical attacks that were easier to power through than the aggressive boredom of the tour; it took an exceptional amount of willpower to stay conscious. Sherman, on the other hand, absorbed every word with rapt attention.

Despite one minor incident during which Sherman found a wooden pole near some construction materials and tried to joust the backyard windmill, they'd made it out with minimal fuss. Even that part didn't seem to entirely take the patient guide off-guard; apparently Sherman wasn't the first to give such antics a whirl. While that did make Watson curious to know what sort of etiquette was in play at windmill museums, in the moment he was content to escape leaving as little impression as possible.

Thanks to their constant need for movement and a quick morning, Watson realized they were making decent time. The original schedule was blown from the moment they were discovered, but not by as much as he'd expected. Accounting for some delays, they had perhaps one-and-a-half more days on the road after this, which meant he was roughly forty-eight hours from freedom, being done with the job, and back to doing work that mattered.

Briefly looking away from the road, Watson watched Sherman pore over a book about the history of various sandwiches like he was learning the secrets of cold fusion. Mentally, Watson backed up a few paces. This *did* matter. Maybe not in the way everyone else thought, but it was important. Even if no one was able to crack Sherman's mind and figure out what was going on, he was just a man who'd been caught up in something out of his depth.

Watson did believe, to his core, that protecting innocent people would always be an important aspect of the work. He'd seen firsthand what happened to people who lost sight of that. When the work stopped being about people, when agents forgot civilians often paid the cost for their mistakes, that was when many lost their way. Deep down, Watson knew he'd been disconnected for too long and was starting to drift in that direction. If nothing else, this assignment had reminded him about the people behind the reports, the innocents whose lives were destroyed. It was possible that was what Gwendolyn had been hoping for all along, though Watson doubted it. Not even that lunatic would bet on someone forming a connection to Sherman.

After so many days crammed so full of the guy, it was hard to imagine what it would be like once he was safely dropped off. Peaceful, certainly, although the drives weren't so bad as long as Sherman stayed distracted. Easier to get around without that lumbering form and silly hat, even if Watson didn't entirely loathe having someone to chat with during the dull parts. If nothing else, conversation with Sherman was always interesting, since one never knew exactly what level of reality he was currently experiencing.

A more developed person might have taken all that to realize they would, in fact, miss Sherman as a whole. Watson simply kept on driving, scanning as they went for any potential threats. This was the job, hellos and goodbyes. Watson *was* the job, had been for a long time. He didn't let himself miss people, as a rule. Compartmentalization was how he stayed sane; that was the mantra he repeated when doubt crept in. Keeping things clean and separate was the only way he'd found to continue on, especially when times grew dire.

Rather than dwell on it, Watson resorted to his usual tactic when presented with uncomfortable thoughts. He doubled down on doing the work, checking every license plate and window for anything out of the ordinary, only to come up empty. It seemed that for the moment, they were having a nice, peaceful drive.

Didn't it figure, right when Watson wanted a distraction was the moment they dried up.

* * *

An ambush had many advantages over chasing prey. The element of surprise was more easily maintained, with a smaller window for discovery. It allowed one to scout and prep the site, laying groundwork for a home field advantage. Extraction was a simple matter of having necessary transportation stashed nearby.

For her money, Jenny preferred the benefit of not traveling most of all. Once they'd selected an ambush point, there was no need to dawdle; in fact, quite the opposite. They'd hurried along the highways, driving in shifts until arriving at their destination. Rumors said there was some sort of incident with a flaming car, but so far no one had captured the target. With the location scouted and Tom plying contacts for more information, Jenny was looking over some digitally-stolen building schematics, checking for rooms or routes that might be advantageous – or, failing that, structural weaknesses where they might make some shortcuts of their own. It wasn't terribly thrilling work, but she could do it from the comfort of a hotel room.

The door swung open and closed in brief succession; Tom never left a room vulnerable for longer than necessary. "Guess who brought home the goods?"

"Meeting went well, I take it." Jenny was more surprised than she let on. They'd been chasing more than a few dead ends in the past days, trying to pick up any tidbits they could get while lying in wait. Both knew that this would be their best, and probably last, chance. That was why Tom was out there swinging at wild pitches, hoping to hit a surprise home run.

"Better than well. Our bodyguard – Watson, as he's currently named – has quite a history. Getting anything from his secured files is past our reach; however, there turned out to be some useful information floating around out there. Seems a partner turned on him a few years back, double-crossed him during a job, shot our man in the leg, and fled. Still at large to this day; in fact, I suspect he's the one making this kind of intelligence available." Tom dropped a thin folder onto the hotel desk, which looked as if it might be overburdened already just with Jenny's laptop. "Very little love lost between those two."

Thumbing through the folder, Jenny quickly perused the few documents inside. Disciplinary reviews, recommendations for psych evals, even a few hand-scribbled and photocopied notes from those psych sessions. Not a tremendous amount, but between these and the side of conversation Tom had obviously picked up in the process, it began to paint a picture.

"Paranoid, prone to suspecting betrayal at every turn. Good for someone you need to stay alert, dangerous if anybody knows the right buttons to press."

"Yeah, that's where I landed too," Tom agreed. "Opens up some new possibilities. Good thing, because so far everyone who's tried the direct approach has either been arrested or blown to pieces. I much prefer a side-angle to start. Escalating to violence should always be the backup plan."

New ideas were unfolding in Jenny's head as she studied the documents. "We'll need some doctored logs and documents in case we get the chance to use props. Make the supply run, and don't skimp on quality. A guy like this is going to have an eye for the details."

"Text me what you need, and I shall provide." Tom paused long enough to take an energy drink from their tiny fridge and pound it down. Given that they were in a small town, across from a place that was as much eyesore as it was it was attraction, the fact that the local hotel had appliances at all was a victory. Tom's next stop once the job was done would be anywhere with good water pressure and clean sheets. He'd had enough of road trips for a while.

"Oh, I learned something else while I was out. Guess who got took a shot and missed last night? Cauldron."

Jenny's ears perked up. "That jerk who stole our target in Australia last year? He's pretty good."

"He was better than us, so I'd say at minimum that makes him exceptionally good," Tom countered. "And I'm not the only one who thinks so. Word is out that Cauldron failed, and it's making everyone else a little more cautious. Squashing randoms trying to make a name is one thing; getting a real player locked up sends a warning. Whatever else this

Watson might have going on, we can't take him lightly. Treat it like we're going against a full team."

While part of Jenny felt like that was overkill, the fact remained that being too prepared wouldn't come back to bite them the way walking in too casually might. Last stop, last chance, so it made sense to throw everything they had behind it. Whether it was the bodyguard, the target, or a combination of the two, so far that duo had slipped past every trap and attacker in their path. Tom had the right mindset: prepare like they were facing a bigger threat, overestimate what that team could do to ensure they wouldn't be caught off-guard. If an old pro could slip-up, so could they.

That wasn't going to happen. She hadn't traveled across most of the country's width to fail here and now. If the target didn't stop at the expected location, that was an acceptable failure. They'd been trying to predict the actions of someone with several states' worth of roads to choose from: assuming success was unrealistic. Predicting that correctly, and then failing on the capture, would be an entirely different beast.

"Expect a large list." Already, Jenny's hands were flying along the computer as she began breaking down potential plans into necessary components. "Also, dig into the local police response times. On the chance this goes bad, I have a hunch we'll be pretty hard to ignore."

29.

"Watson, by my calculations, our journey shall soon arrive at the ultimate destination."

It was the first thing Watson heard after emerging from the bathroom, one of the few times he and Sherman were apart. The commode and room as a whole were unexpectedly sanitary, more than he'd expected from the Ramshackle Hotel, Bistro, and Spa. For such a grand name, it was all one building, what looked like an older company's motel that had been gutted and renovated after acquisition. In their defense, Watson had seen both a restaurant and a door labeled "Spa" leading away from the lobby, so they appeared to be offering the advertised services. How luxurious they were was a mystery he'd have to live with, somehow.

Sherman was sprawled out on his bed, an array of books and maps spread across the comforter. When they had a room, this was his habit for selecting the next day's detour. In the car, the process was more cramped and agitating, but tonight Watson didn't mind at all. He was in a good mood, by force if needed, because there was nothing to be sad about. The job was nearly over, and once it was done, he could go back to the usual work. All of those things were positive, so there was no reason he should feel bothered, which was why Watson refused to let himself be.

"I was going to bring that up." Watson walked to the front of the room, checking through the peephole and windows. It was a habit he'd gotten into regularly the closer they drew to the goal. At the end, when victory was in sight: that was the time when jobs grew the most dangerous. "Assuming our last detour doesn't take too long, I could have you there by tomorrow night."

A rogue step sent a shot of pain through his leg. It was, for the most part, healed. There was a limit, though, to how far one could recover, and Watson's ceiling included living with the occasional twinges. He buried the expression of pain as he had so many others, continuing to do his work.

"We have been together for nearly a full week, Watson. Perhaps it is time you stopped bothering to hide your pain from me. I suspect the energy wasted on such pitiful attempts at deception could be put toward more productive endeavors."

It was odd to realize that not only did Sherman have a point, but Watson understood what he meant. At the start, he'd have only heard the words on the surface, not the intent behind them. Sherman was telling him there was no need to pretend. The secret was out, so he could grimace when the need demanded it without giving anything away.

"By now, it's on me for being surprised you caught that. When did you notice?"

"The first time I activated my cognition window after we met. In hindsight, your gait makes it blazingly apparent. After that, spotting the moments of pain held no challenge whatsoever. Based on what I gathered in that window, you suffered a bullet wound to your right leg approximately three years ago. One that has largely healed, with minor lingering issues. Given your excellent skills and assignment to a task theoretically requiring competence well below your level, I also deduced that to be the inciting event which caused your career to stall out, most likely connected to your deeply-rooted paranoia."

Watson nearly reached out to steady himself; he hadn't been prepared for that level of insight. It was easy to forget that there was more to Sherman than his odd habits. Under that hat, even if for only five minutes at a time, lived one of the most potentially powerful minds in the world. He was tempted to let the topic die there, but really, what was the point? The Incident wasn't much of a secret, not to those in the right circles, and Sherman was living with every detail of his life exposed, being constantly observed. The least Watson could offer up was one anecdote from the past.

"Byron Poole, formerly Agent 119. He wore many names during our jobs, but that was his favorite and the one he kept using after we split. That's the guy who shot me. We were in… a place I can't talk about, getting… a thing I also can't talk about. Let's just say there was a flash drive with information a lot of people wanted."

Taking a seat, Watson let himself relax slightly, mentally drifting back along the river of time. "Mind you, Poole wasn't just some other agent. We came up together, pulled in from other services thanks to the potential we showed. Did so many missions together I truly lost count. Major ones, too. We were garnering quite the reputation for effectiveness when dispatched as a team. So when this flash drive issue popped up, we had the right skills for the assignment. Just another job like any other, until the end."

It wasn't the crack of the gunshot, the smell of smoke, or even the pain in his leg that Watson remembered most from that day. No, that honor belonged to the expression on Poole's face: neutral, matter-of-fact, the same way he'd appeared in untold missions prior. That was what hurt the most. To Poole, it didn't even register as betrayal – just one more mark getting played.

"My partner shot me in the leg, escaped with the drive, and used the profits to start his own freelance company. Obviously, our government doesn't work with traitors, but those skills will always find a demand on the open market. Could have been worse; he missed all the major arteries and we pulled the bullet out clean. The doctors said I'm lucky to have mobility back."

"Preposterous. Ladling such a compliment on a mistress as fickle as fortune. You regained mobility because of your own efforts. That much should be plain to anyone of relative competence, regardless of whether they have my gifts."

"Thanks." Watson wasn't quite sure how to respond to that, so polite gratitude was a safe fallback. "But now I hope you can see why I don't take anyone at their word. In this business, treachery can come from any direction. Staying alert and ready is the only way not to be caught off-guard."

"You have cut off your arm to ensure no one will break your fingers," Sherman surmised. "I suspect your mind would present it as shedding the unnecessary to ensure survival. Adaptation is a fine technique, Watson, just be wary not to become stuck in one form."

Rising from the bed, Sherman dragged over a road map and set it next to Watson. This was his first time taking a good look at the physical highway layout since memorizing the initial route, as well as some backups. Sherman had been busy. The entire thing was covered in notes, drawings, half-formed musings, and what looked to be a recipe for gumbo. That one was especially confusing, as they hadn't eaten or talked about the dish at all yet, so Sherman shouldn't even know it existed, let alone how to make it.

The main feature of the map was not the idle writings or odd culinary instructions. No, that was a big red circle not much farther down the road from their current location. With good morning traffic, they'd be there before noon. It didn't escape Watson's notice that while all of their previous stops had been marked in some manner, this final one had by far the most pomp and circumstance. He could feel the circle's indentation through the paper; that was how hard Sherman had pressed down.

"Should any hope for you exist, that is where we shall locate it. A place where you can truly appreciate the weight and importance of your momentary role. There, we shall find an entire building of documents and mementos from my ancestor's favorite biographer. Perhaps appreciating the musings of one who stood so close to true greatness will inspire you to further heights."

It took some aggressive reading and a quick search on his phone, but Watson quickly figured out what the hell Sherman was talking about. "Someone made a museum dedicated to Sir Arthur Conan Doyle all the way out here?"

"Fine taste and dedication are not bound by geographic markers."

Normally, Watson would have vetoed the idea out of hand. This close to the end was not the time to take needless chances. Anyone who knew Sherman existed probably also knew his affinity for Sherlock Holmes. But it had been over a day since they encountered anyone else and their route was unlikely to be known, so it wasn't as if their pursuers would be sure the Doyle Museum was on the itinerary. Not to mention the attraction itself was so small there couldn't be much of a marketing budget.

The problem was, this had never been a *normal* mission: not from the way he was assigned it, to what it entailed, to how it played out. Things had gone so far sideways it was a miracle they were still chugging along, and some of that was thanks to Sherman. In the field with the car and the parking lot with the fire, he'd come through in the pinch. Knowing what likely waited for him at their final destination, Watson couldn't bring himself to deny one last stop, especially one this important.

"I'm sure I don't have to tell the world's greatest detective that a place like this is exactly where more kidnappers might lie in wait. If you really want to this, then we'll need to be careful. That means we go in one step at a time, letting me scout, and if I say we go, then we go, no arguments. Can you deal with that?"

"You are wildly correct. I did *not* need to be told any of that." Sherman reached over and... patted Watson on the head awkwardly, the way one might deal with a strange dog they suspected of having fleas. "Fear not, for I anticipated your concerns and devised a simple, yet ingenious, method of keeping our identities concealed even as we bask in the glory of history."

Part of him was afraid, part was curious, either way there was only path forward. "And what idea is tha—?"

"Disguises!" Sherman leapt, hurling his long legs over the side of the bed to the other side of the room, and began rummaging around in his bag. "I have put together some preliminary concept drawings that outline our best options. My only concern is the availability of some fashions and supplies in such a rural area. Tell me, do you have any experience that would lend itself to the construction of functional hoopskirts?"

When the hell had Sherman learned about hoopskirts? Watson quickly remembered that Sherman had been tearing his way through esoteric book after esoteric book, meaning there was really no way to tell what he had learned.

"My sister taught me some light sewing when we were younger, but nothing as intricate as hoopskirts."

"An anticipated failing. Very well then, we shall go with the next best plan: locate a distributor of cinema-grade prosthetics and makeup. The two of us will infiltrate as simple space aliens, our green skin and reptilian jaws keeping all observers too scared to draw close."

Slowly getting up from the bed, Watson made his way over to Sherman's steadily increasing stack of papers. "Let me give you a hand. I know this area a little better, and I don't think they'll be quite so space-friendly as you think. You still get some abduction stories out in this part of the country."

Together, the two of them began to sort through the drawings, choosing what disguises they would don come the morning.

30.

 Ethel Agneblot had lived a relatively modest life for the bulk of her days. Born to a farmhand and a cook, she grew up in a small town with no aspirations toward leaving. Life was simple, yet sturdy. She married shortly out of high school, raised four children before her husband's heart gave out, and took up working at a local diner once her children were grown. Ethel's only real indulgence in life was her penchant for mystery novels, kindled in childhood by her local library's selection of Sherlock Holmes books. She fostered a love for both the works and genre through her years, and when life got perhaps a bit too dark, she would often turn to those pages where ingenious solutions could always be found.
 Her personal hobby might have stayed just that, if not for the lottery ticket. After winning (at the time) a state record jackpot, Ethel had walked away with a couple hundred million once taxes were taken out. Although no one in town realized it, Ethel Agneblot was the reason that the local school districts had suddenly started operating with surpluses in the budget, nearby homeless shelters began bursting with food, and the town's modest church was suddenly being refurbished and expanded. Even after all that, and the remainder of her days spent on permanent vacation with her family, Ethel still had plenty left over to splurge on a museum dedicated to the author who'd ignited her love of mysteries in the first place.
 The Sir Arthur Conan Doyle Western Experience, originally without the "western" part until a similar attraction threated to sue, had once been some sort of retail business. From the outside, it seemed far too large to host such a simple exhibit. Watson's best guess was that it had been an early iteration of the big box stores before they expanded to become even more gargantuan. If the size shocked him, the people gathered in front of the building nearly made Watson stagger in surprise.
 There was a line for this place?
 Sliding into a parking spot, Watson took a moment to look over his outfit in the rearview mirror. Normally, dressing to blend in meant just that: picking an ensemble that sent a clear message he was no one of interest. One more face in the crowd, a minor detail to be looked over and ignored. Sherman's ideas about disguises were somewhat more theatrically

inclined, unfortunately. After quite a bit of back and forth, they had eventually settled on wearing suits to appear like traveling businessmen.

It was a far cry from what Watson wanted, which was to research local fashion and shopping options then drill down on the perfect ensemble, but they weren't dressed like a touring rock duo, so Sherman hadn't exactly gotten his way either. In the end, Watson was fairly happy with the compromise, if for no other reason than he doubted anyone chasing Sherman was expecting to see him wearing a suit.

The look might have been a little more appropriate if Sherman had ditched the hat. But even Watson had to admit this was probably the one place where donning a deerstalker made sense. Looking closer, Watson realized that Sherman wasn't even the only person wearing one; he could spot a few in the line waiting for entrance. It wasn't exactly snaking around the building, but there were a solid ten people making their way steadily inside. This place might be more entertaining than Watson had anticipated.

Getting into line, Sherman kept fiddling with his collar. Wearing one at all was a testament to the man's costume dedication, for from the instant it touched his skin, he'd recoiled. They'd planned on adding a tie, but that was a non-starter. It turned out Sherman wasn't fond of things too tight around his neck. A collar, unbuttoned down to his sternum, was the most Sherman could handle on that front. Fortunately, Watson had seen many normal people equally uncomfortable with the annoyance of a starched collar, so the fidgeting actually helped sell the cover. That was what Watson hoped, anyway.

As they drew nearer to the front of the line, Watson realized there was a man at the door whispering to each party. His skin tingled as adrenaline began to pump, readying him for the possibility that this whole thing was an ambush and every person in the line was about to pounce. He kept waiting for that to come, even as he could find no signs that an attack was imminent. This close to the end, anyone who wanted Sherman would be desperate. Anything was possible, and he had to be prepared.

Once they were nearly at the door attendant, Watson finally picked up enough conversation details to ease his pulse, slightly. It came only seconds before they had to step forward, leaving Watson still mentally shifting gears as the elderly man with a kind smile greeted them.

"Hello there, and welcome to The Sir Arthur Conan Doyle Western Experience. Admission is ten dollars a person, or you can answer a trivia question about the late author's life." His voice was slow and easy, the exact opposite of how Watson had felt seconds prior.

"Trivia, without question." Sherman snapped the answer out so fast Watson barely had time to register it before the question came.

"Oh, ho. Confident I see. The group before you had his birthday, so let's go a bit more advanced. When was Sir Arthur Conan Doyle knighted?" There was a twinkle in the old man's eye, something like a challenge and encouragement rolled together.

Without pause, Sherman replied. "October twenty-fourth, of the year nineteen hundred and two, conducted by King Edward the Seventh."

Whatever the old man was expecting, Sherman had surpassed. He blinked rapidly a few times, then motioned for them to go on through. "Spot on, my boy. Go ahead and enjoy yourself. And don't skip the cafeteria in the back, they make some mean lunch."

Stepping into the cool, dark entrance foyer, Watson was struck by the loving detail that had gone into each display. There were vintage copies of early Holmes books, as well as some of Doyle's other works, including a very worn yet still recognizable edition of *The Narrative of John Smith*. Worn but loved felt like a good descriptor of most of the trinkets Watson could see. Surprisingly, for such an out-of-the-way place, the museum was state-of-the-art, with audio tours, interactive exhibits, and detailed graphics by each display doling out loads of information. Information that Sherman was eagerly sucking down, reading every word he could find, despite the fact that this room was little more than an appetizer for the real displays to come.

"Not sure how much you'll learn from that, given how quickly you pulled up that date," Watson remarked.

"I must presume I will learn, or re-learn, quite a great deal. In truth, I have no idea where that information came from. Although I have endeavored to fill my mind since waking to find it empty, it never occurred to me that there was any need to research the subject of my ancestor. That information felt logged and assimilated. I suspect it was a subject I held passion toward before my change."

If not for well-honed self-control, Watson might have missed a step at that news. From what he'd read and witnessed, Sherman had displayed no capacity for recalling any specific information from before he'd been drugged. Language, motor-function, basic capacities stayed intact, but there hadn't been so much as a blip about who he was or why he'd been at the club that fateful night. Watson assumed the government had that information already. What was more relevant was if Sherman could retrieve it himself. Did that mean there was a way back for him? That one day, he could remember who he really was?

With some effort, Watson shoved those considerations out of his mind. It was certainly relevant, and would be relayed to Gregson, but the scientists would be the ones who figured out what to do with such information. They had the tools and knowledge to help Sherman get better, even if, technically speaking, he'd be easier to manage and test in this state. That thought Watson wasn't able to shove aside quite so simply.

Once the initial displays were devoured by Sherman, they moved on to the first real room, one detailing the birth and early life of Sir Arthur Conan Doyle. It quickly became clear that the structure would follow a standard path of plotting the life room by room, each focusing on major life events. What Watson found far more interesting, however, was that very few people seemed to be bothering with any exhibits. Most were going straight through, heading to the rear of the building, a few even casting curious glances at him and Sherman for lingering. Drawing attention, especially without knowing why, was an unacceptable risk. When Sherman started reading a long, very detailed display about the author's amateur boxing career, Watson quickly darted to the rear so he could see what was happening.

As it turned out, the answer was lunch. What had been described as a "cafeteria" by the doorman appeared more akin to a small restaurant. There were no waiters running the tables; instead, everyone proceeded though a long line at the front, selecting and paying for their meals. It fit the cafeteria bill in that regard, but the food looked and smelled a step beyond. Even across the room, Watson's mouth watered. Why did the lunch in a bizarre museum off the beaten path smell so good?

"First time?" An old couple had sidled up next to him, the man popping a heartburn pill while the woman questioned Watson. "It always surprises the tourists. The woman who built this place came from a long line of local cooks, and she used their recipes as the basis for the cafeteria. Trained the original staff too. Nice as the museum is, most of us come here because it's the best restaurant in the county. Try the chicken fried steak, it's amazing."

"I'll keep that in mind. Thank you, ma'am." Turning, Watson headed back to Sherman, who was already done with the last display and finishing up on a new one. Whatever else he lacked upstairs, the man could read like no one's business.

He approached casually, laying a hand carefully on Sherman's back. They'd worked out a simple communication system the night before. A slap to the shoulder meant run like hell. Pointing in a specific direction without obvious reason was an indicator to say nothing and follow. The hand on the back wasn't the direst of the options, but it was far from pleasant news. It meant that Sherman was to calmly and slowly walk with Watson to the exit, ready to bolt if needed.

This was the signal that enemies were there with them, and they had to flee. It meant they'd been outmaneuvered, someone had seen this coming, and with so little to go on, retreat was their only real option. It was with sincere relief that Watson realized Sherman had gotten the message and was playing along. Together, they made a rapid trek through the rooms they'd passed, until they arrived at the one just off the entrance, detailing the author's early life.

No sooner had they stepped through the door than the click of a gun's hammer being drawn back greeted them: the same obvious theatrics Watson had used himself, but in terms of a quick way to let everyone know the score, there was something to be said for such a gesture.

Watson began to turn, but behind him, another figure stepped into view. The old man, or so his makeup made him appear. That left the little old lady in front of them, gun drawn from her dainty purse.

"I knew this wouldn't work. Drug his food, slip out while he's asleep, that was supposed to be the plan, but your eyes are too sharp. Noticed the flaws in the makeup, I'm guessing. My apologies, Boss; we couldn't pull off the escape you wanted. Going to have to get messy with it."

On its own, the words held minimal importance, but the context of her gaze changed everything. Her eyes weren't looking to the man behind them, the presumable Boss in question. No, they were trained directly on Sherman.

A ruse, it had to be. Sherman wasn't capable of putting together anything like this on the fly.

Just like he wasn't capable of remembering anything from his life before. Or shouldn't be able to manage on his own, despite helping Watson multiple times on their trip. Helping him what, though, exactly? Survive? Or protecting Sherman from kidnappers until his own team was in place? Hadn't Watson himself been thinking about the dangers of underestimating this man?

He turned to Sherman, who was already meeting his eyes. "Do not cave in to your baser fears, Watson. They are attempting to play on your obvious weakness. Be more than they think of you."

It was a good speech, hindered by the fact that no sooner was Sherman talking than the supposed old man started forward, making an approach while Sherman kept him distracted. Was that coordinated, or was the attacker reading and reacting on the fly? No... No, Sherman was right. They were playing him. Or Sherman was playing him, using the foundation of trust they'd built to lure him into position.

"They were in line before us, wearing elaborate and needlessly complex costumes. They clearly *knew* we were going to be here." There was tension in his voice that Watson hadn't intended to put there. Not a good sign.

"Yes, Watson, under your constant watch I clearly coordinated an attempt on my own life, despite having neither the motive nor means to manage such a feat."

His heart was pounding, Watson could feel the blood rushing in his head, like he was being surrounded on all sides by an unceasing roar. The stink of gunpowder from the past suddenly invaded his nostrils. He could smell the shot, feel the pain, see the casual grin on Poole's face as he left Watson writhing on the ground. For no apparent reason, Watson's mouth had turned bone dry as he struggled to swallow, to breathe, to force himself through.

"You take a lot of showers on your own when we have a bathroom," Watson said, the pieces falling into place as he thought back through their journey. "Plenty of time for some quick texting. And as for motive, we both know you aren't as crazy or helpless as everyone thinks. Maybe you finally realized that they aren't going to let you play detective when we arrive; they'll put you back in a hole and spend the rest of your life keeping you just happy enough to survive long enough for more testing."

For however long he lived, Watson wasn't sure he'd be able to ever forget the look of unfiltered, absolute pain on Sherman's face at those words. Worse was that even seeing such an expression, he couldn't be sure it wasn't staged.

Somewhere, part of Watson was screaming about how crazy that was, how Sherman had yet to show even a modicum of suspicion or concern over his eventual fate. Sadly, it was drowned out under that endless roar in Watson's ears. A pity, too, because that was also the part of Watson reminding him not to get so focused on anything that he developed tunnel vision.

The sudden pain in his shoulder jerked Watson into motion, but it was already too late. He'd make a critical mistake: allowing himself to get distracted, making them both vulnerable. Whipping his head around, he could make out a dart protruding from his back. Crap. The old man didn't have a real gun raised, he'd fired a tranquilizer instead. Already, his brain was growing foggy as the drugs tore through his system, aided by his own elevated pulse.

In seconds, Watson had slumped to the floor.

In what had to be the very last thing Watson expected, Sherman planted those long legs atop his bodyguard's collapsed body, raising both arms in an old-fashioned pugilist's stance. The idiot should be running; instead he was trying to defend Watson in an obviously futile attempt. Sherman's mouth opened, no doubt to activate his window in hopes of finding a way out, but the dart hit him in the back before even a word slipped out.

Unlike with other drugging attempts, this one proved worryingly effective. No sooner had Sherman been hit than he froze up, tumbling over like a statue, caught by the old woman betraying her true age by dashing in at incredible speed.

"Sleep well, little prize. This drug targets your nervous system, so it should keep you out until delivery."

With all he had, Watson wanted to protest, wanted to fight, to struggle against the bonds of his own weakened body. Instead, he slipped further into unconsciousness, accompanied solely by the overwhelming sense of shame crushing down on him. This was his fault. He'd doubted Sherman, he'd let his paranoia get in the way just like Gwendolyn always warned it would. Instead of keeping his eyes on the threat, Watson had instead been too focused on a non-existent betrayal from his own charge. All he had needed to do was believe Sherman and they could have fought back together. They'd have had a *chance*. Such a simple task, yet he'd failed.

Watson was the one who had broken their trust. Watson was the betrayer. And now they were probably both going to die for it.

31.

The drop-off was simple enough. Whoever was paying (it didn't make good business to ask those sorts of questions) had rented out a facility less than half a day from where the target had been heading in the first place. Perhaps it was a way to thumb the nose at those they'd stolen from, keeping the prize so close, or maybe it was simple logistics. No matter who caught the pair, or when, they'd be moving steadily closer to the facility, so it would never be too far out of the way.

Whatever the purpose, Tom was thankful to be out of the makeup as they handed over the pair of tied-up bodies to a set of guards. For once on this trip, fortune was with them, and handoff went smoothly. Based on the small size of the building and the set of stairs leading down, Tom's money said most of the real operation was built out of the basement. With the prize delivered, Tom was more than ready to be done with this whole job... once *all* the loose ends were tied up.

Getting back into the car, Tom noticed that Jenny was nearly done scrubbing away the last specks of makeup from her neck. He'd been content with getting most of his removed; she was always the more fastidious one.

"Anything go wrong?"

"Nope. Turned them over without incident. I've been assured pay will come through secure channels in a few days. Guessing that won't happen once everything shakes out, though it would be nice to double dip."

"They've gotten what they want, so there's a chance they'll pay out happily. Even with the last-minute wake-up shots, those two are going to be bound and surrounded by armed guards. I know That Woman thinks this will help, I'm just not certain it will go the way she expects." Jenny dabbed at the lipstick refusing to part from the side of her mouth. "Regardless of what people say, no one is infallible."

"No, but word is *she* pays on time for good work and doesn't ask unnecessary questions, so I'd like to get more jobs from her. However it plays out, we did as instructed. Personally, I'm pulling for those two. Might shed some light on That Woman."

Jenny nodded. "I am kind of curious what she meant, about protecting her own kind. And how shoving that man into a room full of danger will accomplish that. Ah well, cash is better than answers, as my grandpa used to say."

Although Tom wasn't sure he entirely agreed with that sentiment, he still put the car in drive and headed toward the nearest highway. Whatever was going to happen, they'd be best served putting lots of distance between themselves and this place. One thing about taking the woman's jobs they'd learned from her reputation: the results were always explosive.

Sometimes quite literally.

* * *

The bag pulled away from Watson's face to reveal a room of people in nondescript clothing, most of whom were being driven out by a lanky fellow in a faded lab coat. He ushered all but two through the door, and even those he glared at while ordering them out of his way. Watson noted that the door sported several locks and rudimentary reinforcement but wasn't any sort of custom installation. That was the sort of information that would be relevant should he attempt an escape or manage to survive and report back. Not that such was likely to happen.

Getting captured was part of the job. Watson had been caught and bound many times, and these folks were clearly not amateurs. His arms were zip-tied to the chair's arms, as were his legs, with his torso tied by a carefully-woven knot and some durable rope. No wiggle-room; everything was just one iota of force away from cutting off circulation.

It pained him to do so, but Watson looked over to Sherman. He hadn't warranted such complex restraints. They'd merely cuffed his arms behind the chair, weaving the chain through holes in the back so he was bound to his seat. At least he wasn't suffering, which was minimal comfort to the man who'd gotten them in this situation to start with.

Much as Watson wanted to speak, to apologize, his body was still sluggish from the drugs. His tongue felt thick and slow, slapping against his teeth ineffectually as he struggled to recall the right muscle combination for speech. For others in the room, the act came much more naturally.

"*Finally*, we can get down to business." The man in the faded coat whirled around, stalking across the makeshift laboratory over to Sherman. Watson realized there was more to the room than he'd registered at first:

microscopes, beakers, machines, pages of paper, syringes, a mess of clutter and technology that painted a clear, unsettling picture.

Delicately, the man pulled away Sherman's hood, showing far more care that whatever goon had yanked off Watson's. Sherman was awake, insane eyes scrambling around the room like a wild animal on a cliff scrambling for purchase. Oh no. The hood. Sherman couldn't handle enclosed spaces; how would he have fared with no other stimulus for hours? Watson's only hope was that the drugs had kept him knocked out for most of the experience.

"A pleasure to meet you, my precious subject. I am called Doctor Dunaway, and it truly is an honor to meet one such as yourself. I must tell you, I've been on the project since not long after the serum's creation, and it is a wonder to see a human who has survived the effects. What brilliance lurks behind those eyes, unbound by the drugs in your system? Well, we shall see, won't we? Don't worry, I already did the worst of it while you were out."

Dr. Dunaway reach over and touched a small, shaved patch of hair near the back of Sherman's neck, turning the head so Watson could see. "I am not cruel, you see. I am a man of science, nothing more. I took what we needed from you already. Handy little extractor I invented. Punches in without the need for invasive surgery, though I'm told it does hurt like all living hell. Progress demands a toll, you understand."

He walked over to the largest section of lab equipment – also the messiest – where a beaker with clear liquid had just reached a gentle boil. From the desk, he produced a vial, its liquid tinged with dark purple. "The serum's creator is a true genius, you know. Quite possibly the only person in the world who doesn't need it. His generosity is why the rest of us even have this meager chance at greatness, a chance that so many of the mundanes reject just because of some paltry survival odds. Truly unforgivable, this worthless species called man. Not you, though; never you, Sherman. Because in your head resides one of the rarest, most powerful creations in existence. You have one of the only brains that has incorporated the serum and remained stable."

Dr. Dunaway held the vial closer to his face, getting lost in its lavender depths as his breathing deepened.

"We may not understand what factors are at play, but it doesn't matter. The creator knew what we would need to take, the cells and fluids we'd require. Funny how these things work, isn't it? You'd have spent all your life searching for a cure, and the most important material was in your skull all along." The vial was held out now, away from the doctor's leering face. "First, a cure: a way to save those who do not take to the serum well, yet still hold value. After that, once the creator gets your brain, it will only be a matter of time until a stable version of the serum is developed. Every human deemed worthy will be elevated to heights they could have never previously imagined. What a world we can build with such brilliance at our disposal."

The purple vial was set back down as Dr. Dunaway turned his attention to the boiling beaker. Waving to one of the goons, he made them fetch some tongs to remove the beaker from the heat. As there were only two such guards, Watson defaulted to thinking of them as Bald and Flattop, since the men's hair was their major differentiating feature. It was strange, the way his brain kept operating like there was a chance he'd manage to do something rather than struggle in vain.

"But as I told you before, progress demands a toll. As much faith as I have in the creator's methods, I cannot call myself a man of science if I omit something as essential as the testing phase."

Dunaway poured the beaker's contents into an odd device with what looked like frost on the coils. Hissing and smoke rose up as the concoction rapidly cooled, pouring the contents into a fresh beaker. Using extreme care, Dr. Dunaway filled an eyedropper with liquid, careful not to let so much as a drop touch his skin.

"Of course, to test a cure, one must first have a patient. We can't very well use Sherman. He's an unusual case. We will have to test what happens when a normal person's cells are infected and cured."

With all he had, Watson tried to struggle. Between the bonds and the drugs, he barely managed to strain the zip ties at all – and even that felt akin to victory, given how heavy his body was.

There was never a contest, though. Dunaway easily forced open Watson's mouth, squirting the eye dropper of liquid into his throat.

The effects were almost instantaneous.

No wonder the doctor avoided touching the serum; it must absorb on contact to be affecting Watson so soon. The first thing he noticed was his heart rate increasing, shaking off the lingering sedatives in his system as everything began to dial up. Lights grew brighter, smells sharper. He could feel the air on his skin and taste the sandwich he'd eaten last night. It was like being peeled raw. Every ounce of selective attention or focus was shredded under the sensory onslaught. Worst of all, this feeling was a cakewalk compared to the storm brewing in Watson's brain.

So many thoughts were bubbling up from deep down. Lost memories, forgotten songs, stray sentences started and left unfinished, everything. Watson remembered *everything*. That might have been useful if he could control and sort through it, but Watson was remembering it all at the same time. It was like being trapped in an impossibly huge theatre, playing endless movies of one's own life, all blasting at maximum volume. It quickly turned into noise, an impossible amount of screaming information kicking at his sanity, intent on breaking it down.

This was what it felt like to be Sherman? How did the man find the strength to breathe, let alone keep walking and talking and moving through the world?

The experience was so intense, he might not have noticed the sharp pain in the back of his head, save for his skin's heightened sensitivity. What came next, the feeling of something punching into his skull, would have broken through regardless. Turns out the doctor was right: that device *did* hurt like hell. He tried to glare at Dr. Dunaway, who had pulled back with what looked like a hydraulic syringe invented in a world without safety regulations. The vision began to waver, turning intermittently blurry as Watson's eyes started twitching at irregular intervals.

"One minute should be long enough. The serum integrates quite rapidly, and it usually takes between five and ten for the brain to self-destruct. We can do this a few times if needed." With no regard for Watson, Dr. Dunaway took the device back over to his table, where he removed a small container of something from Watson's skull. Ordinarily, Watson would be probing, trying to find out what exactly was being used. Unfortunately, at that moment, even paying attention took everything he had.

Using a fresh eye dropper, Dr. Dunaway put a small amount from the vial into a glass dish and set it in a microscope. Once he had that prepared, he took a dropper full of the purple liquid. Leaning in close, he licked his lips. "Cure Test Number One, used on sample at the one-minute mark." A squeeze, the purple landed, and for a moment there was nothing.

Then: a fist shot into the air, followed by a joyous yelp. "It worked! The creator was right!" Forgetting himself, the doctor slapped the nearest goon, Bald, on the back. "Everyone in this room, you have just been witnesses to history in the making. We now have the ability to de-integrate the serum after exposure. From here, it's just a short path to the final goal, and when history looks back, we will be among the few who helped take one of the many small steps that led to a leap in evolution."

Normally, Watson loved a talker since they gave away so much information, but with every passing moment it was harder to keep his mind in the room. One stray thought had him back in third grade getting kicked in the stomach by his old gang of bullies; another jolted him to the first time he tried hummus; then it was off to a memory of a three-hour delay in a crappy small-town airport. There was no rhyme or reason. Every thought opened countless doors, screens – even that metaphor was too complex to keep in place anymore. Watson was barely hanging on, and the "barely" was starting to fade.

"Now, the next question is how the cure will work at the five-minute mark, and the ten, if he makes it that long. We'll also do a test on the posthumous cells. We need to find out at what point, if any, the cure no longer becomes effective."

Dr. Dunaway reloaded his syringe and walked back over to Watson.

"I'm sure this is all quite distressing, but take hope. Soon, you won't even be sane enough to feel pain or fear. The last few minutes before your death should be quite peaceful."

32.

Awareness was a tricky thing for Sherman. He didn't really experience states of awake and sleep like the rest of the world. Fitful sleep often gave way to fitful waking, then back and forth. When one had trouble discerning reality from imagination in either state, the difference between them grew less relevant. That said, the specialized knock-out drug had certainly left him in a state closer to true unconsciousness, which kept him from going mad inside the hood. It also demanded a few minutes, upon returning to himself, to fully understand the situation.

They'd been captured, the contents of his brain pillaged with the intent of improving the serum. It was, perhaps, forgivable by some that he did not immediately realize the peril Watson was in, but not to Sherman. Those seconds of ignorance meant less time to work, and there was so very much to do. He needed to get out of these cuffs now, or Watson would be killed twice. First his brain, as it devoured itself, then his body when his autonomic systems failed.

There was only one chance. Even as Sherman watched Dr. Dunaway use the high-tech syringe on Watson, he was gathering his focus, shaking off the last of the sedatives – which were actually clearing quite easily, now that he thought about it. Already he could see Watson feeling the effects of the serum, his brain forcibly entering a state human minds were not designed for.

Only one person that Sherman knew of had been able to endure the transformation. Only him, only his mind. Fat lot of good that actually did, given how much of it he could use, but the enhanced cognition window was all he had left. The only chance they had was his brain.

"A case..." The words slurred out softly, too gentle for the celebrating doctor or his guards to notice. Sherman was trying to call forth his window, but the last of the sedative was making the process slower, one final annoyance before the effects fully faded.

At the end of the day, no one really knew what this ability was. Even the name, enhanced cognition window, was invented by Gregson and the other scientists to describe the perceived effects. Reactive, by nature. Sherman could feel the shifts in his brain as he concentrated, much the same as any competitor or athlete would bring themselves into a state of focus prior to an event. He could feel the world growing still as the information stopped assaulting his senses. Now it pressed gently against him, that endless ocean of information he'd still not learned to navigate. The silence, the stillness, this was the only time he got away from his own warped brain. This was his last true bastion of peace.

Staring across the room, Sherman could see the changes manifesting over Watson's expression. Tightening of muscles, shifts in breathing, erratic pulse; he was going down the same path as nearly every other person who'd taken the drug. Soon, he'd either be past curing, or dead, which was *well* past curing. No one was coming to help; it was just the two of them. Scratch that: with Watson incapacitated, everything fell onto Sherman. And even with his ability nearly activated, no fresh ideas were popping up.

There was one option left. One route Sherman had never taken. He could release all control, let the information flood him in his enhanced state. There was no way of telling what would come of it. True, it might help, but it could just as easily destroy Sherman. His entire existence was an anomaly; there were no precedents to pull from. Whatever he did, whatever choices he made, the potential results would be a mystery.

Well, he was hardly the world's greatest detective if he backed down from a mystery, especially when his assistant was in need.

With one more look to Watson, Sherman gritted his jaw and narrowed his focus even more. Sherman saw only the oceans of information that had previously been assaulting him and were now pressed tightly against his awareness, eager yet barely restrained. Fully aware this might be his last moment of even semi-sanity, he tore away the restraints.

Sherman opened his mind and attempted to swallow the sea.

* * *

It had taken more than a little dirty work, but Gwendolyn finally felt like she'd purged all the major leaks from their information chain. There had been fewer than she expected, and as of this afternoon, everyone she even suspected to be compromised was under full review. That was supposed to be good news, especially since Watson should be getting near the destination. In theory, they might have used a more circuitous route, but Gwendolyn knew her agents. Watson preferred the direct approach whenever possible. He would definitely try to push through and make it. So why hadn't Gwendolyn heard anything?

Not just from Watson himself: no spottings, no contacts, not so much as a blip. The man was escorting one of the most valuable targets in the country, with multiple pursuers, and Gwendolyn hadn't gotten so much as a whisper. It didn't sit right. One didn't reach a position like hers without learning to trust their instincts, so if this felt off, then it probably was.

Unfortunately, that didn't leave Gwendolyn many options. They had no way to track Sherman or Watson, and without knowing their route, it was impossible to be certain what direction they were coming from. Still, Gwendolyn could play the odds.

Orders would go out to have teams along all major highway routes, ready for contact. If Watson did end up needing help, the very least she could do was make sure it was nearby. Outside of that, her hands were tied. It was one of the hardest parts of moving from the field to a desk, being stuck inside while others put their lives on the line. She wanted to grab a gun and go kicking down doors, but those days were behind her.

Despite his issues, Watson was one of the most capable people under Gwendolyn's management. All she could do was believe in her agent and make preparations in case they recovered a body. Hope for the best, be ready for the worst: that was the way to survive this job.

Today, Gwendolyn just happened to be leaning on the hope side a little harder than normal.

* * *

For a stretch of time impossible to measure, both in actual seconds passed and how long it felt, Sherman's greatest fear came true: he ceased to exist. There was no more Sherman as an impossible amount of information flooded into his brain at once. Facts, observations, memories, instincts, everything, *everything* was tearing its way through his mind. Amidst that tsunami of information, there was no room for personality or desires... not even a sense of self.

All he could do was endure until, without even realizing it had happened, Sherman began to return. It wasn't like getting his head above the waves, though. The feeling was more akin to learning that one could breathe under water. He was still being flooded – only now, Sherman had the clarity to understand what that meant. The reason he was limited when he'd kept that ocean of knowledge distinct from himself was that it was inefficient. Having to reach out and pull every bit of information he needed took too long, not to mention it risked missing important details. No, this was better. Sherman didn't have to ask or inquire. It was just all there, in him, around him. Sherman hadn't been drowned by the torrent; he'd bonded with it.

"The case is afoot."

He heard the words fall softly from his mouth as the final shifts occurred, a sense of certainty slipping over him. For the first time since waking up in that corpse-filled club, Sherman Holmes was completely in control of himself and his faculties.

Snapping his eyes open, he automatically clocked the time on one of the goon's watches. Based on previous attempts at using his enhanced cognition window, Sherman had approximately five minutes before the stress of his elevated state forced his brain to partially shut down and recover. Not long to work with, but manageable for one who used those moments wisely.

First, he had to determine the situation and devise an optimal plan of attack. That part took a mere smattering of heartbeats to complete. Based on the voices he'd heard, sounds of prior movement, and the lingering scents in the air, there were nine people in the building. One was Dr. Dunaway; the rest should be presumed guards to account for a worst-case scenario. Two were in the room with them, both armed, but neither was paying any attention to Sherman.

All focus was on Watson. His eyes were bulging, along with the veins in his neck, as he struggled to hang on. The guards were watching impassively, while Dr. Dunaway appeared to be soaking in every detail. Next to him was the purple vial, the only cure they had. That single container of chemicals represented the entirety of Sherman's hope. Securing it was top priority.

It seemed Sherman would have to resort to fisticuffs, but to do that, he'd need to free his hands first. At the mere thought, his brain tapped into videos and books of magicians, even pulling from ones in his prior life. Strange that he could recall something so innocuous, yet even in this state his personal memories remained tattered. A contemplation for a day with lower stakes, to be sure.

Seemingly before he'd even decided to escape the cuffs, Sherman had a deep understanding of how to manipulate his digits and force a dislocation in order to slip free. Had they bound him more carefully, the endeavor might have drawn attention; however, there was some advantage to being seen as little more than living cargo. They mistakenly thought Watson to be the greater threat. While that was admittedly true ninety-nine percent of the time, for these five-minute bursts, Sherman was more than a victim, a botched experiment, a guinea pig whose only value was what lived in his brain.

Right now, he was a force unlike nearly anything else on the planet. Silently, he rose from the seat, laying the cuffs carefully down on the chair. With one glance, he calculated the optimum angle of approach, as well as what the ten most likely scenarios to play out would be. In this state, it was so simple, so obvious and evident, he marveled that he'd ever felt confused. But he had, and he would again soon. Worst of all, seeing from that many angles showed him just how dire their straits were. The chances of him being able to subdue all the threats before time ran out were ludicrously low. Of course, standing around debating wouldn't make the situation any better. Best to at least try.

It was time for to show these criminals the dangers of messing with the world's greatest detective.

33.

Only Watson saw Sherman rise. Everyone else was facing the man losing his mind. At first, he took it for a hallucination, one of many that were filling his vision. There was something off about him, though. Even as Watson's mind was melting down, he couldn't tune out the details it kept forcibly dragging to his attention. That, in fact, was part of what was causing the meltdown to begin with. Watson could see the careful, quiet first steps Sherman took, sneaking up behind the nearest guard. If he'd been able to form coherent words, Watson would have called out and warned him not to. None of these guards was exactly a top dollar mercenary, but they'd make short work on someone like Sherman.

To his absolute shock, Watson didn't have to witness his asset being brutally knocked around. Instead, Sherman casually picked up a microscope with a heavy base from a nearby table, took aim, and slammed it down into the side of the guard's neck. There was a sound of something breaking, along with a brief scream from the guard, who fell hard to the ground. Nearly anyone delivering that blow would have accidentally crushed the windpipe, but judging from the gasping on the ground, Sherman must have simply broken the neck. A small kindness, although more than Watson would have shown in their situation.

At least that settled it. If he was watching Sherman behave competently, let alone easily dispatch a guard, Watson was definitely hallucinating. He still tried to watch, even as keeping his vision focused became difficult. This was probably going to be the last thing he ever saw.

Fake or real, his final show might as well be a good one.

* * *

The first guard was easy. Caught unaware, a simple blow with a heavy object shattered the vertebrae in the neck, causing temporary-to-permanent paralysis, depending on various biological factors and treatment received. Sadly, the achievement cost Sherman his element of surprise. Taking everyone out covertly had been considered; unfortunately, the time he had didn't permit for such endeavors. Too much to do, and now less than four minutes to go. His only hope was the direct approach.

As both the remaining guard, a bald man with a shocked expression, and Dr. Dunaway turned around, Sherman moved. As tempting a target as the gun made, digging through the disabled goon's holster to get it would leave him too open for counterattack. Best to catch them while they were still on their back feet. Before the bald guard could draw his gun, Sherman had already closed the gap between them.

Just by seeing the guard's muscles tighten, Sherman could tell the man was trained. After watching him slightly adjust his stance, Sherman knew he'd fake some punches in a boxing stance then transition into his real skill: locks and holds. Before the guard had his fist raised, Sherman knew precisely where the punch would be, and took special care not to remain there.

As the guard wasted a punch, Sherman utilized the opening to drive the heel of his palm into the man's momentarily exposed throat. Baldy tried to recover, but he instinctively moved to cover his throat, and in the seconds before he righted the error Sherman struck once more, this time kicking him directly in the genitals. The strike was so hard that the guard leaned over, with a grunt of pain. His head was instantly grabbed by Sherman, slamming his face into the detective's knee.

The broken nose and jaw turned out to be enough, dropping the guard at last. Sherman heard the rustle of cloth but didn't run. Instead, he reached down and grabbed the bloody-nosed henchman's gun. Coming to his feet, he found Dr. Dunaway already standing, the other gun in hand. This was a risk he'd known about when devising his strategy, and there was a reason Sherman had prioritized taking the guards out first. *They might have actually shot.*

"A poor bluff, Doctor." Sherman raised his own pistol, meeting Dr. Dunaway's eyes. "You will not fire upon me. I am, by your own words, a valuable treasure. The feeling is not mutual, so I would advise you to lower that weapon before my limited patience runs out."

Three minutes left. He had to get this wrapped up before he passed out, or there'd never be such an opportunity again. They wouldn't underestimate him twice, not after this display.

"You'd really shoot me? Come on now, Sherman, I'm the only person you've met who can actually offer a cure. Isn't that what you've been hoping for?" Dr. Dunaway nodded over to the purple vial. "Just enough for one dose, so if you want to save both of you, then you need me alive and cooperative."

"An even worse bluff," Sherman replied. "We both know you would never truly cooperate."

"You raise a reasonable point." Dr. Dunaway pointed the gun up in the air and fired off the entire clip, filling the room with a distinct, annoying ringing. On the plus side, the bullets were clearly subsonic, since neither man started bleeding from the ear. Unfortunately, that still left them plenty loud enough to be heard. That done, he grinned as he dropped the pistol to the ground. "That should get the rest of the team running this way, and you've only got one clip left. Once you're out of bullets, subduing you will be a trivial matter."

The door was locked, secured by multiple deadbolts, but a dedicated team would break through relatively quickly. One more element to keep track of, so it was time to clear the plate. Motioning to the chair, Sherman gave a simple order.

"Cuff yourself."

"Thanks, but I'm not playing along," Dr. Dunaway replied. "Do whatever you want, I know where my orders come from."

"You raise a reasonable point," Sherman echoed back. Without another moment's pause, he shot Dr. Dunaway in the left knee, drawing a sharp hiss of pain from the man, but not a scream.

Much as Sherman had to do, this was necessary as well. He'd seen the bodies piled up in that club. One club, one test batch out of who knew how many? So many lives lost without meaning, and this man was part of it. Not the top, clearly, yet certainly a complicit cog in the machine. Tucking the gun into a pocket on his jacket, Sherman walked quickly over to Dr. Dunaway's station and lifted the beaker filled with serum, as the doctor had called it.

"You have murdered innocent civilians and left untold families to mourn their loss, all for what? One experiment, the idea that genius is more valuable than life. A ridiculous notion, yet one you were willing to gamble so many people's futures on. Very well then, Doctor. If that's really what you want, the least I can do is provide it."

With one foot, Sherman pressed on the fallen doctor's neck, a gentle, constant pressure that didn't relent. Dr. Dunaway tried to hold back, struggling in vain to breathe through his nose. At last, after wasting precious time, he broke, opening his mouth for a deep gasp of air.

"Let the punishment fit the crime." Sherman poured the entire beaker into Dr. Dunaway's mouth. Some was spit out, a fair portion didn't hit the mouth at all, but plenty made it in. Seconds later, the doctor began to twitch and spasm as the fate he'd visited on so many moved to claim him.

Tossing the beaker over his shoulder, Sherman turned back to the table. There, sitting idly by a Bunsen burner like it was any other innocuous liquid, was the cure. With it, the damage could be undone. No more pain, no more fits, no more muddling through a world he could barely process enough of to properly understand. Sherman lifted the vial, examining it carefully lest some last-minute trickery had been laid. From what he could tell, which was a tremendous amount at this point, it appeared to be exactly what Dr. Dunaway had mixed together. A treatment, made from something in Sherman's own brain.

With a hurried spin, Sherman darted over to Watson and grabbed him by the jaw. "Listen to me, Watson, push past the noise and hear these words. I do not know how much is needed for a cure to be effective, so you must swallow every last drop. No matter the taste, or what you're experiencing, choke it down. This may very well be the only batch of cure in the world. Treat it as such."

At a nearly imperceptible pace, Watson's jaw opened, his hands clenched in visible effort. This far in, he'd be more madness than man; even this single act probably demanded incredible discipline. Sherman wasn't quite sure how he could remember so much *about* the experience without recalling the experience itself; one more mystery to add to the pile. All that mattered in the moment was that Watson's mouth finally parted wide enough for Sherman to pour in the purple liquid.

Shouting from the door reminded Sherman that, no, Watson wasn't all that mattered, not in terms of variables to track. They had a little time left, based on some rudimentary calculations about the door's integrity. Whether it would be long enough or not remained to be seen.

As the last of the liquid vanished down Watson's throat, his shaking lessened. That thundering pulse slowed slightly, and Watson's eyes actually managed to focus on Sherman, if only for fleeting intervals. With jerking, unnatural shifts, Watson's jaw moved as he forced his tongue to form rough words.

"The cure... you had... the cure..."

"An effortless deduction. While it might have returned me to normal, without the cure you would have died, and quite soon at that." Sherman smiled with a joy he didn't feel, working to ease Watson's mind. Losing that vial had in fact hurt quite a bit, but it was his choice to make and his burden to bear. Watson would need clarity for what came next. "Any detective who cannot handle so simple a task as taking care of his Watson has no right to claim the title of Holmes."

More slamming from the door. Less than a minute now – they were down to the wire. Grabbing a small but sharp knife from Dr. Dunaway's area, Sherman went to work on Watson's restraints, cutting through the zip ties.

"Focus on me, Watson, hear these words well. In roughly thirty seconds, I am going to collapse. Not long after, that door will give way and six guards will be coming through. That model of pistol holds eight bullets to a clip, and I used one on Doctor Dunaway. Seven bullets to deal with six enemies seems like an impossible task, but it won't be."

Why had they been so cursedly thorough with Watson's restraints? Every tie he cut was costing Sherman time, and he had to get it done before unconsciousness took him. This was an essentially hopeless situation to begin with. With Watson restrained, their thin chance of escape would vanish, assuming he could even talk his bodyguard into playing along.

"I know you, Watson. I know that a man of your training will attempt to go for cover, picking them off one-by-one. But you will not have enough time. The stress on your brain is going to force you to pass out soon. There's only one chance."

Sherman finished with everything but Watson's hands, the point he'd saved for last so the spasms would have time to die down. By virtue of positioning, it also enabled Sherman to look him in the eye for the last part of the instructions, something that was not at all an accident. Asking a man like Watson to go against his gut was like asking the sun to go dim for a day. Still, he had to try.

"By my estimations, there is a strong chance that as the cure purges the serum from your body, you should reach a point of equilibrium.

A small window similar to mine, where you will be operating at a level high enough to make those shots."

"Estimations?" Watson's tongue didn't sound so stilted this time, and he was already flexing his freed right hand.

Finishing on the left arm, Sherman grabbed the gun from his jacket. "Yes, estimations. My data for this drug is limited to my own experiences and the speed at which Doctor Dunaway saw a reaction in the Petri dish. I could be wrong, Watson, however my plan is the only one which offers even a chance at survival."

The door was splintering, Sherman could hear it despite the buzzing that had begun to fill his ears. He'd held on too long, pushed the limit, and his brain wanted nothing more than to take a nice rest. Not yet. Not this close.

"I cannot convince you of this, Watson. I don't have the words or the time. All I can say is that in these, our final moments, why not try just once doing the primary job of a Watson?"

Sherman pressed the gun into Watson's hand as he leaned in and locked eyes, mere inches between them.

"Have some damn *faith* in me."

34.

Without another word, Sherman collapsed, spared from hitting the ground only by the speedy reaction of his bodyguard, who gently laid him down on the cold concrete floor. Watson was far from back to normal, but he'd regained basic control of his motor functions, which were very useful in the given situation.

Based on the dents the door was showing, it wouldn't be much longer before the whole thing gave way. There was enough time to flip one of the lab tables for makeshift cover. Probably not enough to deflect bullets, but it would provide a hidden spot to strike from. On any other mission that would have been his course of action, regardless of what some asset said to him.

Except Sherman was no longer just some asset. Watson had doubted him, got them both into this situation, and yet Sherman had still traded away his own chance at recovery to save Watson's life.

At a certain point doing this kind of work, everyone had to square themselves with death. It came with the territory, and no amount of careful planning or professional courtesy could keep it away forever. Different people found different ways to make their peace. For Watson, he found his center by focusing not on how long he lived, but rather on the kind of person he was during that time. Was he helping people who needed it? Was he using his dangerous talents to make the world a better place? Was he the kind of man who could look his reflection in the eye every morning?

In that moment, Watson didn't really care whether Sherman was right or not. What mattered was that someone Watson had failed, betrayed in his own way, had turned around and trusted him with their very life. Watson was either the kind of person who could return that level of faith, or he wasn't.

As the door began to break, Watson planted his feet and raised the pistol. Better to die as the man he wanted to be than to survive as someone he couldn't respect. The road here had been long and strange, with dark patches and turns he'd have never imagined coming. Yet, here – at what appeared to be the final mission – Watson had found one last surprise.

He'd have never imagined that, in the end, he'd go down protecting a friend. Truly, Watson didn't think he was capable of forming that bond anymore, but apparently that was one more limitation that Sherman chose to ignore. Bad as things were, that simple realization brought a smile to Watson's face as the door gave way and the first face began to burst into view.

Through all of this, Watson had been feeling a steady sensation of relaxation trickle out from his brain, his body resetting after the ordeal that had been the serum. It was a comforting feeling, one that helped him keep a clear mind to make the decision. Yet as the door finally broke, the feeling changed. It was no longer just relaxation he was feeling: Watson found himself overwhelmed by an unnatural sense of peace.

Although the world appeared to slow, Watson recognized that, in reality, he was thinking faster. Perceiving faster, really. With a single glance, he could see so much. The entering guard's plan of attack based on his hand and foot position, the angle where a bullet would strike based on how Watson held his gun – he could even make out the reinforcements coming behind the first guard. All that information that tormented him before suddenly became his ally.

This was the other side of the coin: a state of mind only those who'd survived indescribable torment were capable of reaching. Watson waited an extra three seconds, allowing the next guards to move into a better grouping position. In that time, the first guard had gotten his gun nearly up and pointed. His finger never made it to the trigger, though, as Watson took aim between his eyes.

Between the sound of the shot and the spray, Watson's second target, the larger guard on the heels of the first, hesitated for a brief moment. It was a mistake he'd never have time to regret, as an identical shot took him above the brow.

No matter how many times he'd done it, no matter how essential it was to survival, Watson never liked killing. By his reckoning, it represented a failure in resourcefulness, believing if he'd been a better agent then things could have ended differently. But sometimes it was either him or them, and in those moments, Watson knew who he wanted to survive.

As he fired a third time, taking down the guard who'd been moving for cover, Watson realized that this time, it *was* easy. Seeing the world so analytically made it simple to boil down what was happening to factors and variables, nothing more than angles to calculate. Somewhere deep down, the truest part of who he was realized just how dangerous that made this drug. Turning normal people into capable killers was bad enough; suppressing their humanity was on an entirely new level. Watson could only imagine what might happen if someone with nuclear access got their minds in such a state.

The fourth guard was slightly further back, working to cover the fifth. Smart; he'd clocked the three near-impossible shots and realized something was amiss. Protecting his ally was a good instinct. Unfortunately it meant little when all Watson needed was a nanosecond of opportunity. Both guards went down in quick succession, even falling down entangled together.

That left only Watson and one remaining guard, a shorter fellow with his gun drawn, but not raised. If he ran, Watson wasn't sure what he would do. No one could escape, not with everything they knew. But he loathed firing into someone's back. Worse, he knew he'd do it without hesitation right now. When things were so cut and dry, there was no other choice. If possible, Watson could try to wound with the first shot, but even that would depend on the angles.

As it turned out, the internal debate proved moot, as the final guard attempted to dive and fire on Watson in a shockingly acrobatic display. Watson felt the waste as he shot; the man clearly had talent. One day, he might have made something great of himself.

Instead, the final guard's body landed and stayed put. The entire exchange had taken mere seconds, despite how long it felt from Watson's perspective. It had all happened so quickly; Watson was the only one to even get off a shot. Looking around the room at the carnage, one thing became abundantly clear.

They couldn't let *anyone* have this drug.

Seeing what it had made Sherman capable of was scary; feeling what it could offer a man with Watson's talents terrified him to his very bones. This was a taste of what Sherman had, a fraction of it, and the power had turned Watson into an unparalleled Grim Reaper. If he could reach Sherman's level, what manner of monster would he become?

A pair of twitching legs drew Watson's attention past Sherman's unconscious body. Dr. Dunaway was spasming badly; his condition easily could have been mistaken for an epileptic fit. He was sweating and shaking. His eyes, already unstable, were wild and bulging. It was strange, Watson thought, to see this state from the outside, after having so recently been in it.

"I wonder, if you die from this, does that make you Sherman's first kill? Seems likely since he was clearly a civilian before, but life can throw us all kinds of surprises. Still, were that the case, it would be a shame for blood like yours to be the first on Sherman's hands."

The last bullet put an end to Dr. Dunaway's twitching, as well as the substantial count of dead bodies that could be laid at his feet.

"Guess that's a mystery we'll never solve." Sherman didn't need to go down that road. It was one more thing Watson could guard him from, now that he was finally doing the job right.

As he rifled through Dr. Dunaway's pockets, Watson noticed that his body was slowing down. Strike that, *everything* was slowing down. This was the price of operating his brain on a level it was never intended for. Thoughts grew harder to form, actions demanded focus to accomplish. Sherman was right; if he'd gone for cover, Watson would have been a sitting duck once the serum wore off.

There was still enough discipline left in him to see things through. Finally, he located what he'd known would be on the doctor's body: a phone. The ones in charge always had the phones. Punching in a specific set of numbers, Watson walked back over to Sherman, pausing to take a fresh gun off one of the dead guards.

"Direct line to Gwendolyn. Message relay: Asset recovered. Location temporarily secured. Trace this device's GPS for a location. Requesting extraction." Watson set the phone down on a nearby table, turning on the speaker function, then positioned himself to wait.

When the team arrived, they found Watson sitting in front of Sherman at the far back of the room, both men passed out. Yet every team member on the scene never forgot the way that, even unconscious, Watson's firearm remained trained on the door.

35.

Gray was replaced with white.

When he'd closed his eyes, intending no more than a blink, Watson had been staring at the blank gray walls of a concrete basement. Now he was seeing a bleached white, which meant he was somewhere far worse than an enemy's base surrounded by hostiles.

He was in a hospital.

A test of his appendages resulted in all fingers and toes wiggling as expected, so no major paralysis or broken bones. Stirring more substantially, Watson shifted his entire body, checking for noticeable injuries. Lots of soreness, a few bits that hurt more, and a headache that could slay a dragon, but nowhere near the worst condition he'd woken up in.

"Glad to see you're awake. Apparently, your brain needed longer to recover. Must not be accustomed to getting used."

Gwendolyn was sitting there, punching in orders for some sort of work on her tablet, but still waiting in a chair for Watson to wake up.

"Where's Sherman?"

That drew a momentary look of curiosity from Gwendolyn, one that vanished like a trick of the light. "Being checked over in a highly secure location. He's a little more... tenacious than I'd been led to believe?"

Although he could make some educated guesses, Watson asked anyway. "What did he do?"

"It's what he wouldn't do, which was leave your side. Not until we had Gregson come down and explain that you needed rest to recover was he willing to go. Had some unpleasant things to say for anyone who tried to make him leave before then. Agent 386 broke down in tears."

"I've seen 386 headbutt a tractor without missing a step. Sherman must be in top form." To his own surprise, Watson chuckled slightly, earning some minor protests from his ribs. "But he's okay, right? No last-minute surprises from Doctor Dunaway and his crew?"

Gwendolyn tapped a few more times, then rose to her feet and set the tablet down in the chair.

"Sherman is fine. Your mission, despite more hurdles than we expected, is an unqualified success. Not only did you keep the asset safe, you recovered a lab's worth of equipment and notes about the drug that created him, not to mention a pair of living guards for us to question. Once our people crack the code they were using, we'll hopefully have entire new avenues to research and explore, all thanks to you. This was a big win, Agent 221. Your critics have no room to maneuver for now. Next assignment, we'll get you something appropriate for your skills."

The moment should have been a harder choice, but it wasn't even close. Down the road of his old life, Watson knew what was waiting for him: more jobs, more betrayals, more turning into a person he didn't want to be. For a time, that had been the optimal use of his talents, the way he could best help the world. But times, like everything else, were always destined to change.

"I'm glad to hear that, because I have a specific assignment in mind. There's an asset the government has that they don't understand. He needs helps, protection, guidance. He needs a friend as much as a bodyguard. It's been a long time since I kept a name for longer than one mission. Joel Watson has a nice ring to it."

This time, there was nothing fleeting about the curiosity in Gwendolyn's eyes. "You want permanent bodyguard duty for an asset who is going to be contained in a secure facility? I'm sure I don't have to explain how that might be a hard sell. We do still have a budget, and that's a sizable redundancy."

"Well, no," Watson admitted. "I'm going to guard him as he goes about his life. Your team will handle perimeters, secure lodging, have a response team in play should they be needed, all of that. At his side, I'll handle any unexpected complications that might arise."

A long stare from Gwendolyn was the only reply for a full minute. Finally, the senior agent let out a minor grunt. "Guessing you've got some kind of card to play that will explain why on Earth we would change our entire plan for securing and studying the asset."

"See, that right there, you're already doing it wrong," Watson said, pulling himself up straighter. "You won't make progress by putting him under glass. Sherman has been with the scientists for three months, me for a week. Only one of us got to see him fully activate that cognition window."

Not many things could get a true surprise out of Gwendolyn, but for a moment Watson saw the telltale eyebrow waggle only the most perceptive agents knew to watch for. She walked over to the door, whispered something inaudible to whoever was outside, then locked it securely before returning to Watson's side.

"Tell me *everything*."

Like any well-trained operative, Watson heard the order and complied, detailing all of the major events in the course of his trip with Sherman. It took some time, and required occasional breaks for water, but he managed to relay the last week of adventure with relative efficiency.

After Watson stopped talking, Gwendolyn spent some time on her tablet, allowing his voice to recover. It was nearly a full hour later when Gwendolyn set the glowing screen aside, once more pinching her nose as she tried to shake off the ocular strain.

"Nobody likes what you're trying to sell."

"Tough. Despite everything that's happened, I still have a few friends who owe me favors; call them in if needed. You know I'm right. Sherman needs some level of stimulation to survive, so you'll already have to cope with him being out of the lab sometimes. Hell, that was part of why we did this move in the first place. I'm just asking them to extend the slack a bit more. If they bury Sherman in some underground lab, they'll spend the next decade making no progress while whoever actually made the drug gets closer to perfecting it. We're in a race, Gwendolyn. Unless we have some way to neutralize those threats when they arrive, we're going to be annihilated. Sherman can barely tell a muffin from a muppet half the time, but with that drug's help, he was able to effortlessly take down trained operatives. I've tasted a drop of what that power can do. If someone finds a way to perfect it, they'll be running the world before the rest of us even know there's a threat."

"And you want to pin the entirety of our hopes, our one lead in this mystery, on the brain-damaged man who calls himself Sherman Holmes?"

Watson shrugged. "If you've got a different person with access to unimaginable levels of intellect once per day, who is also willing to help us, feel free to make a pitch. Otherwise, yeah, you're going to have to work with Sherman. One week in the world, he's grown leaps and bounds more than he ever did in the lab. Thanks to him, we even got some actual leads. Like it or not, whoever wants this drug isn't stopping anytime soon, and they're proving to be dangerously competent. Sherman might be the one ally we've got who can play on their level, unless you'd rather have him as a test subject."

"Make no mistake: even if you get your way, he will continue to be both," Gwendolyn said. "That man's brain contains secrets that could change the course of history. We're not letting that go. However, I can also admit that there is some value in having a super-genius, limited or not, on our side. It's possible I could set up something a *little* bit looser."

Despite seeming to be good news, Watson noticed there was a serious tone as Gwendolyn continued. "Keep in mind, this only applies if he has a top-tier resource as his personal protection. You do this, and you're stuck. The deal only lasts so long as you're willing to be responsible for him. Is that something you're sure you want to take on?"

Doing this job meant that deception, half-truths, manipulation, and countless other forms of obfuscation all became second nature. Interestingly, Watson had also discovered that sometimes, when played at the right moment, an unexpected infusion of truth could be the most effective tactic of all.

"In the years since Poole shot me, I've eroded basically every relationship in my life besides you and my sister. Maybe it's because he's too crazy too lie, maybe it's because he had my back even after I stabbed him in his, but whatever the reason, Sherman is the first new person I've trusted since that day. I'm pretty sure if there is a way back for me, he's part of it. And if he's going to survive, he needs someone who gives a crap about him as more than an asset."

Watson paused, looking far ahead, considering his future from all the angles he could. There wasn't any need, though. His gut told him what to do, and on this point, his instincts were in agreement.

"You asked me before if I'd bet everything on Sherman. No. I wouldn't. But on the two of us, working together, I'll stake all I've got. Give me the position and let Sherman into the world. I think it needs him more than you realize."

Despite her somber expression, Watson couldn't help noticing there was a touch of lightness in Gwendolyn's voice. "I suppose if I have to lose one of my best people, letting him spend the rest of his life as a bodyguard beats out having to cut him loose entirely."

"Agreed on all but the title," Watson replied. "I'm not a bodyguard anymore."

"Then what are you?"

There was something almost Sherman-like in the satisfied smirk that stretched across Watson's face.

"Assistant to the World's Greatest Detective, obviously."

Epilogue

Slowly, as the wheels of government often turned, the upside to working for an agency that technically existed only as a subsection on a Top-Secret spreadsheet was that they had fewer oversights and hoops to jump through. At least, they did when Gwendolyn was dragging in a batch of traitors to lay at the DOJ's feet. Driving out the rats, along with "finding" Dr. Dunaway's lab, had earned them some substantial goodwill, every ounce of which was burned up to make Watson's idea a reality.

It took only a week, which had Watson wondering just how surprised Gwendolyn had really been by the idea, because it sure *felt* like some groundwork must have been laid. He opted not to push it, since he was getting his way, and the week of recovery was a nice break. Some real food and sleep weren't hurting either, in between the calls. Strangely, even without the pills or a job to focus on, Watson found his rest largely nightmare-free.

So far, Sherman had video-chatted him several times a day, every day, without fail. Often, he didn't even seem to be talking to Watson. The call would click on with Sherman midway into a rant about the dangers of combining necromancy and gummy animals. However, he did inquire about Watson's health at least once per call.

Watson used that week to handle all the details of his transfer. Agent 221 had a few loose ends, most of which he was able to put on the plates of others. Some weren't so easily passed on, unfortunately, but that was the nature of the game. Nobody retired with a perfect batting average; striking out was part of playing. Still, looking back on his career, Watson felt a strong swell of pride in his chest. Agent 221 had done a good job for many years. It was time for him to rest.

On the day before Sherman would move in, Watson checked out of the hospital and went to look over their new lodging. As he punched in the address, he suppressed a groan. Was Gwendolyn being cute, or had it really worked out like this? Ordinarily, Watson would have assumed the former, but life seemed to work strangely around Sherman Holmes.

Arriving at North Baker Street, Watson exited his nondescript rental sedan and examined his new home. A brown brick building stared back at him, nestled in between a store selling novelty-themed lunch boxes and what appeared to be a gym except for the large pool of pudding on the sidewalk. Their building went up several floors, where Watson knew there would be apartments filled with other residents – mostly normal, with perhaps a few staff members on hand, just in case there was an emergency.

Stepping up to the building, Watson paused to let two women, one wearing a flight suit and the other street clothes, walk past on their way to the lunch box store. They'd wanted a place where Sherman could, in theory, blend in when permitted to mix with normal society, and Portland certainly fit the bill. This might be one of the few places in the world where a wild-eyed oddball in a deerstalker hat would fail to raise so much as a single eyebrow.

In the foyer, Watson found Gwendolyn waiting for him. Together, they headed upstairs to the third-floor apartment. Originally, it had been four different units, but some eccentric owner had smashed them all together to create a luxury suite. Sadly, Portland's housing boom didn't quite reach this far, not for the prices such square footage demanded, which left it lacking a suitable tenant.

Now, Apartment 3B had been refitted and fortified, complete with multiple escape routes leading out of the building. It could be a fortress or a trap, depending on what was required in the moment. Bullet-resistant glass in the windows, steel reinforcing every door and exterior wall, Watson wasn't sure if he was more amazed they'd done this so fast, or gotten the permits at all.

On the one hand, it was encouraging; someone was putting real resources into this. On the other hand, this kind of investment demanded a return. It appeared Watson wasn't the only person scared about the dangers that serum posed. Somebody higher up was funding this on the promise it would make Sherman more useful. If they didn't deliver results, there was no guarantee the gravy train might not suddenly go off the tracks.

Just one more ball to juggle, along with Sherman's condition and the people hunting him. For the moment, all that mattered was inspecting the facilities. Between the apartment's unusual size and the four small balconies they could access, it should be roomy enough to suit Sherman. And the fortifications, along with the tactical plans he and Gwendolyn were developing, made Watson feel more at home. Things went smoothly all the way until they were back downstairs. Passing a small directory by the mailboxes, Watson suddenly stopped short.

"Gwendolyn, give this person a different code name. I know you're having fun with the Holmes thing, but I'm tell you now it will definitely set Sherman off."

The older agent's annoyed sigh could be heard across lobby. "Not one of ours. I dug in, and everything checks out. Guy is just a retired detective; the name is pure coincidence. Thought it might be a problem, then I also thought about how few spots like this exist in such a crowded town. Help him deal with it; that's what you're here for."

While it was hard to disagree with Gwendolyn's point, Watson did wish they were starting off with something simpler than an upstairs neighbor who had the surname Moriarty. "I'll figure something out. Should we move on to the perimeter?"

"Oh no, we're not done with the inside yet," Gwendolyn replied. It could have been Watson's imagination, but he thought there was a touch of malicious glee in the woman's voice. "I still need to show you to your office."

Gwendolyn pulled open a door Watson had overlooked, revealing a relatively spacious office with two desks facing one another. Light streamed in through a small part of the window, the rest covered by a brown sheet. That must look out onto the street, when in use. Watson stepped inside, giving it a thorough scan. Coffee pot, desks, a sink, a mini-fridge, and an enormous leather chair. That last one gave him pause, and looking it over, the pieces quickly fell into place.

"Sherman made some demands too, didn't he?"

"Can't be much of a private investigator without an office, especially since we aren't letting strangers into the apartment." Gwendolyn looked over the handiwork proudly. "Have to say, given the time frame, I think we got good work done. It will be fully ready tomorrow when you bring him over. We took care of licenses and all that as well, so the two of you can hit the ground running. Just have to put a name on the window."

"There is no fathomable way Sherman didn't already have a suggestion for that."

"He did indeed," Gwendolyn confirmed. "But seeing as you work here too, I thought you might want to weigh in before we locked it down."

It was a kind gesture, and an unnecessary one. "I'll pass. Whatever he picked, I'm sure it's bad, as much as I'm sure it will be very *him*. If I'm going to do this, there's no sense in half-measures. Use the name Sherman picked out. We want people to know upfront the kind of detective they'll be getting."

Watson felt very good about that decision, and his willingness to trust Sherman, even if it was on a fairly inconsequential matter. That feeling, sadly, wasn't quite as strong after Gwendolyn told him the actual name, but Watson still didn't regret it.

Sure, it would be a little embarrassing, but that was life with Sherman Holmes.

* * *

She moved through the shadows with ease, never appearing for more than a few moments, and only when no one was looking. Her dark outfit and hair aided her flight down the shadowy cobblestone streets until she turned down a near-invisible alley. From there, she slipped through a secret door, into a hidden corridor, and down to a basement they'd sealed off from normal entry. When one was constantly hunted, such measures became second nature.

Arriving at the door, she tapped in a careful rhythm. Only once the code was completed did a series of locks begin to turn. The last one unbolted just before the door inched open. From the gap peered a flash of copper hair and a pair of eyes that made most people uncomfortable. There was something about them – too-focused, too intense – that set people's teeth on edge. Today, they were also eager, hopeful, waiting for the tidings this messenger brought.

"I won't be done until this evening, but I wanted to let you know the news. The other survived, and there are rumors he might stay out in the world, to a degree. We can't reach out yet; the man is nuclear hot. But perhaps you could use Tom and Jenny to send some sort of message. They handled this job surprisingly well."

The wild-eyed woman merely shook her head. "No messages. Give him time; he's only just scratched the surface. Let's wait until he's a proper adversary before we challenge him to a game."

Without another word, the door slid shut and the locks were reengaged, one after the other. The dark-haired messenger headed back for the surface: more errands to run. Even if her employer wouldn't admit to it, she'd seen the joy in that overly intense gaze.

At long last, her boss was no longer the only one of her kind.

* * *

"World's Greatest Detective Agency."

Seeing it emblazoned across the front of the window in big, tacky gold lettering didn't make the name any less ridiculous. Nor did reading it aloud. Watson stood across the street, examining the sign, looking for a silver lining to point out. Sherman, on the other hand, was having no such issues.

"Brilliant work, just as I drew it! The style, the confidence, the cosmic vibration, the appropriate evaluation of my skill level, all of it executed satisfactorily. Give your keeper my regards, Watson. She kept her end of the bargain."

"She sure did."

Silly name or not, it was hard to say it didn't fit Sherman. Anyone so desperate they were willing to roll the dice on a name like that probably wouldn't object if the help they got was… non-traditional. And seeing the guy so clearly, enthusiastically happy, Watson found he didn't really care about the name. It was the job that mattered: both Sherman's to help people, and Watson's to help Sherman. Sooner or later, whoever invented that serum was bound to have created another survivor. If they were on the side of evil, Sherman could very well be the lone person capable of fighting back. When that time came, he had to be ready.

The drizzle coming down on them forced Watson to wipe some moisture from his face. It didn't escape his notice that the location that was selected for Sherman's new base also happened to have an unusually high amount of rainfall yearly. He wondered if that was coincidence, or if Gregson had pulled some strings to get his subject an optimal environment. Either way, Sherman was enjoying it, periodically tilting his head skyward.

"By the way, Watson, this makes one of three."

"One of three what?"

"On the day we first met, I told you my predictions would catch up eventually. As of now, you are officially a resident of Oregon, are you not?" The satisfied smile Sherman was sporting said more than his words ever could.

As much as Watson wanted to laugh it off, he also made a mental note to research how one would go about fist-fighting a gorilla. It certainly wasn't on his list of future plans; however, one could never be entirely sure where life with Sherman Holmes would lead.

For today, Watson was content to watch Sherman scramble up to the front of the building, looking at every facet and feature before he bolted in ahead of Watson. Realizing too late he should have stayed close, Watson hustled to catch up. Moments later, the door whipped back open to reveal Sherman, gesticulating wildly upward.

"Nemesis! Watson, our true nemesis lives in this building, on the floor above our own! Ready yourself for battle, his attack will come in moments!"

"No! He's just an old man…" Watson trailed off as the door slammed shut once more. No doubt about it, he definitely should have gotten ahead of the Moriarty situation. Dearly as Watson wished he could call someone to handle this, *he* was the one people would end up turning to when these situations arose. That was what it meant to care for someone difficult, someone like Sherman. It wasn't the perfect job, but no matter how he turned the situation around in his head, there was nowhere else he'd rather be using his talents.

Watson was the assistant to an utter madman who might just save the world.

It was time to get to work.

Case #1: Closed.

About the Author

Drew Hayes is an author from Texas who has now found time and gumption to publish several books. He graduated from Texas Tech with a B.A. in English, because evidently he's not familiar with what the term "employable" means. Drew has been called one of the most profound, prolific, and talented authors of his generation, but a table full of drunks will say almost anything when offered a round of free shots. Drew feels kind of like a D-bag writing about himself in the third person like this. He does appreciate that you're still reading, though.

Drew would like to sit down and have a beer with you. Or a cocktail. He's not here to judge your preferences. Drew is terrible at being serious, and has no real idea what a snippet biography is meant to convey anyway. Drew thinks you are awesome just the way you are. That part, he meant. You can reach Drew with questions or movie offers at NovelistDrew@gmail.com Drew is off to go high-five random people, because who doesn't love a good high-five? No one, that's who.

Read or purchase more of his work at his site: DrewHayesNovels.com

Printed in Poland
by Amazon Fulfillment
Poland Sp. z o.o., Wrocław